THIS
BODY
WON'T
BREAK

THIS BODY WON'T BREAK

LEA MCKEE

PART ONE

"Beware that, when fighting monsters, you yourself do not become a monster... for when you gaze long into the abyss. The abyss gazes also into you."

-Friedrich Nietzche

ONE

THE CLOCK ABOVE my door has traded in its hands for knives. They cut and slice, shatter the minutes and seconds from existence. Countless days have led me to this point, *this* day.

I'm supposed to feel prepared, ready to take the next step. I don't. I know nothing about life outside these four concrete walls, and now I'm expected to live it.

Another minute is cut away, falls to the floor to join its assassinated cousins. Ten more and the light beside my door will turn green, I will make my last exit.

One thing left to do.

Pulling my books from their hiding place between the mattress and wall, I lay them out next to me. I take a minute to feel the weight of their hardcover bindings, admire the artwork and illustrations, and commit it all to memory. A small sigh tumbles from my lips as I choose the first victim. I tear the stiff cover from the pages, force myself to move onto the others until they're all naked. Three neat stacks of pages cower before me, held together only with a mesh-like glue, lighter, more easily concealed.

Taking the covers, I shove them into the laundry chute, listen to them plummet into the bowels of the Institute. They won't turn up until I'm long gone.

A double beep from the PA sends a light tremor down my spine, disconnecting every vertebra from the whole. A wave of static drips out before the automated voice. "Five minutes to initial departure."

I set to wrapping the pages in my uniform. The black, white, and dull shade of green marks us as inhabitants of Zone Three. Forcing the covered tomes into my travel pack, I pull the strings tight. A small smile tugs at the corners of my mouth, a sort of satisfaction. There is no indication of the pack's contraband contents.

"One minute to initial departure."

The light above my door flashes, a countdown. Sixty seconds. The surge of adrenaline is a wild animal chasing the anxiety from my veins. I smooth out the unflattering green pleats of my dress and pull my unruly hair back, twist it into a tight bun. The tattoo on my wrist peeks out from my sleeve. I yank the material down to cover it. A small O needled into my skin sometime before short term memory made its way into long term in my mind, will forever label me as an orphan.

My eyes trace the half-circle of wood that make my desk, my fingers trail across its rough surface. There's a small impression in the center of my mattress from too many years of use, I wonder if they'll replace it. "Well I guess that's it," I whisper to myself, or maybe to the room, unwilling to believe my entire life weighs less than a waterlogged mop. I haven't forgotten anything. This room is a clone of all the others in the Phase Two Institute, and now it's empty, ready for the next orphan to take my place.

It is the beginning of a new month, August. The name representing my birth month has never held as much meaning as it does on this day. All the orphans born in August of the same year leave today. We are adults now. Ready to take the first step for reintegration into what remains of society.

When the world went to hell the New Terra Alliance sprang up like a hand raised in a classroom. Ready to answer all the hard questions and offer solutions to the catastrophes we created. If it weren't for the NTA we might all be dead.

The light turns green. The metallic clicking of the lock disengaging resonates in my bones. A groan as the steel door rolls away. I step out, looking back as the door closes, catching a last glimpse of the only home I've known for nearly fifteen years. The others stand with me in the hallway, their cheeks stained with tears, jaws taut with nerves. I try to stand a little taller. Though I recognize their faces, I don't *know* any of them. Orphans from the same birth month rarely have classes together. The NTA doesn't support non-academic friendships.

"This way please," a voice calls from the end of the hallway. It's her. Of course, it is. We lock eyes, but there's no happiness there. Her deadpan stare bores into me and a sudden weight settles in my stomach. Dianna, the closest I've had to family or even a true friend if I'm honest. Burning fingers claw up my throat.

I may never see her again.

I was thirteen when she arrived. She was different from the other staff. She went out of her way to talk to me, offered for me to sit with her in the kitchen during meal times instead of sitting alone. She's a woman driven by nerves. Always tense, always cautious. She'd often say nasty things about the NTA and then make me swear not to tell, her eyes jerking all around to make sure no one else heard. I never truly understood her, but she was always there, giving me a new book to read, telling me to keep each one hidden. Books that don't aid in the advancement of knowledge are forbidden. Religious beliefs are strongly discouraged, as is any opinion that doesn't directly support the NTA. It makes sense, there aren't many of us left. We can't afford to stand divided.

"Dianna," I whisper when I am close enough for her to hear. Her shoulders tense, but she doesn't respond. Her fists clench at her sides, the knuckles stark white against the dim olive of her slender hands. A splinter lodges itself in my stomach.

The silence is heavy with unsaid words, the tapping of our shoes on the tile is the only sound. We've delved deep into the labyrinth of the institute now. I barely recognize the route we're taking through the lonely halls. We only leave once a year, each time to a different place, though usually to visit the different work sectors. To see what we could become when we leave Phase Three. The observatory where they watch us on small screens, the laboratories where they look for a cure, water purification plants, the government building where aged men sit in large chairs, fingers clicking keys on their letter boards. We've seen the inside of many buildings. I often wonder if there is a job where you can work outside. Where there aren't walls two feet thick keeping out the warmth of the sun and the soft sounds of the wind.

Some people look at us like we're diseased, others as if we don't even exist. It's because we're wards of our Zone. Some people will always think little of us. Some will always pity us. Though I believe some also envy us. As orphans, we are taken in by the NTA, offered shelter, safety, schooling, and hot meals three times a day. It's more than many have nowadays. At least our government cares enough not to leave us behind. They've given us a chance.

A heavily enforced metal door is ahead. GATE D is marked above it in black letters. Dianna swipes a card over the reader and presses a small button on the wall.

"East wing for departure," she says, looking into a surveillance camera above her head. She turns her head further. No one else would recognize what she's doing, but I do. She's checking for other cameras. They've always made her uncomfortable. She doesn't like to be watched, doesn't like to think there's someone listening to every conversation she's had for the last five years. I don't understand why she doesn't quit, train for a different placement. Maybe she will when I'm gone.

"Dianna," I say again, more insistent this time.

She turns to look at me, her pale green eyes shining under the fluorescent lights. "Everyone line up, the travel team will take you the rest of the way."

As everyone else reforms the line, pressing close to the door, a hand closes around my wrist and pulls me out from the crowd. Dianna tugs me into an alcove to the right of the others, her usually calm expression marred by worry, jaw tight.

"Where were you?" I can't help myself, I haven't seen her in almost a week, the staff doesn't get days off. I was starting to think she'd been infected. "I didn't think I was even going to get to say goodb—"

"Joanna, listen, we only have a minute." Her fingers dig into my wrist, nails biting down. She scans the ceiling above us. My eyes reflexively follow hers, finding the nearest camera is over ten feet away. Not close enough to pick up our voices.

I pull my arm away. "What—Dianna, what're you doing?"

She shakes her head, web-like veins flair beneath her parchment skin. Every inch of her is hard and on-edge. "Jo, shut up. Listen to me. Phase Three isn't what you think it is. None of this is. What we've been doing here, the classes, the lessons, physical training, none of it matters. It was all a waste of time."

My mind attempts to plod through the mud of what she is saying, but I can't seem to find traction. There's unadulterated fear seeping through her skin, twisting her words into terrifying sounds.

"They aren't raising you to become valuable members of society, you are nothing but livestock to them. They are raising you like farmers raise pigs-"

"Get moving, we have a schedule to keep." The last of the others have gone through and the door guard moves towards us, agitation furrowing his thick brows. I ignore him.

"What are you talking about?" I demand, my voice taking on a tone unrecognizable as my own.

The guard places a firm hand on my shoulder and I want to smack it away but I don't. "What are you talking about?" I demand from her again, but she is altogether composed, not the frantic woman of a moment ago.

"It's time for you to go Joanna. He's waiting for you," she says, sounding like a teacher chastising a student, not the only friend I have in the world. But there's a warning in her eyes, as legible as the print in one of my books. *Don't,* she tells me, as she has hundreds of times before. *Don't draw attention to yourself. Pay attention, but never ask questions. Questions don't lead to answers here.*

My lips part but no words fall out. My hands ball into fists, but there is no suitable outlet for my frustration. I'm not sure whether to scream or cry. I want to tell her I'll miss her. I want to give her a hug so she knows how much it's true.

I can't do any of that. The gate guard is hovering behind me. We aren't allowed to be friends, never were.

I leave her standing in the hallway, unable to even say goodbye. My face is hot, skin crawling as though a thousand ants are milling just under the surface. Stepping through the door, it's as though I can already feel the chill of early morning raising the small hairs on the back of my neck.

TWO

THE VAN SLOWS for the hundredth time and I brace myself for the bumps of choppy pavement. There are ten of us seated on the unforgiving wooden benches in the back of the van. There are no windows, only a small, dim ceiling light to see by. We're all shifting in our seats, our joints creaking, and our muscles stiff. With each passing minute, I've felt more and more sick to my stomach. I hate tight spaces. The air is hot and thick, I'm having trouble breathing it in. If it wasn't for the soothing movement of the tires chewing pavement, I wouldn't have lasted more than a mile.

I can't bring myself to take part in the idle chitchat of the others sharing this van, my mind focused on Dianna's last words to me. Each syllable she spoke was the swing of a bat, bruising my bones and disfiguring my world.

I try to focus on something else, *anything* else.

"...we're only at Phase Three for a month, then they

send us away for training…" the girl next to me says.

"…why a month though? Any test I've ever taken didn't take more than an hour…" A boy across from me laughs, a hint of sarcasm in his voice.

"…guess they want to make sure we make the best choice, right?" the girl again.

Another girl across from me pipes up, I know her. We had a few classes together when we first got to Phase Two. "Greg came here three months ago. He promised he'd write me when he got out, but he–he never did." I don't understand how her comment is relevant to the conversation, but then again, I don't understand a whole lot right now. My mind is being ransacked, all the filing cabinets containing the collective knowledge I've obtained in my life are being dumped out, the papers shredded. I can't even remember her name.

"Hate to break it to you, but maybe he just wasn't *interested* anymore. If you know what I mean." A blond-haired boy waggles his eyebrows at her.

She narrows her brown eyes at him, "That isn't true. He would've written if he could. He promised me. You don't know him. You don't know *me* either. Something— something must have happened to him."

We all look away from her then. It's possible something could've happened to him. It's called TEN. The virus borne of nuclear fallout. It makes any other terminal sickness seem like the common cold. Her Greg was likely infected. *Or maybe he wasn't,* my mind whispers. The expression I last saw on Dianna's face reflects back to me on the inside of my eyelids. It will be burned into my memory forever.

A chuckle from somewhere down at the other end of the van forces the hairs on the back of my neck to stand on end.

"You guys are cute. Am I the only one who's figured it out? Thirty days kids, that's what you got. Make the most of it."

Moving forward, I can just make him out in the far corner. His name is Cash. I recognize him from his height, taller than most, his head almost touching the roof of the van, with hair wild and dark like the feathers of a crow. He has attempted a perimeter breach twice now, once more and he might have finally gotten what he seemed to crave; exile and a slow, painful death. No one can survive prolonged exposure.

The others laugh nervously, dismissing his words as if they weren't even spoken. But I am paying attention. When his steely grey eyes meet mine, I don't look away. I hold his steady gaze because I see something there, a likeness. He knows something, perhaps something more than what Dianna told me. I make it my business to find out what that is.

Two loud thuds on the side of the van send me snapping to attention. We're here. A ball forms in the back of my throat and I choke it down.

"Respirators!" I hear a voice call from outside and we all pull the air purifiers over our heads, fasten the buckles on the back.

The doors open and I squint into the blinding light of the setting sun to see the darkened silhouette of a guard standing outside. "Please exit in an orderly fashion," the shadow says, his voice muffled.

Standing, I duck my head to keep from hitting the roof and pull my pack from the floor between my feet. I am the last one to exit and nearly stumble headlong into the guard, legs unsteady. The stinging in my eyes subsides with each impatient blink, my sight returning in fragmented pictures painted with spots of orange and blue. The sun is warm on my face and the silent breeze pulls at the fabric of my dress, lifts the sweat-dampened auburn hairs that have liberated themselves from my bun. We're in a gated area, tall black metal fences surround us, sharp silver wire looping the whole way around the top. A river of foul looking water borders to our left, a wide metal tube pumps a greyish fluid into its depths.

All the other vans are lined up next to ours, their passengers disembarking. There are many I don't recognize. They must be the August born orphans from our sister institutions. I am in awe of how many of us there are. One hundred and twenty aspirants for the four institutes in our zone.

"Follow me and stay together," the man says, no longer a simple silhouette against the light. Now I can see he carries a long piece of metal slung over his right shoulder. I've never seen a gun like that before, but as I scan the guards manning the gate, I notice they too are carrying guns. Once, I may not have noticed or even questioned the need for such firepower, but with the whisper of Dianna's words still ringing in my ears, I am unwittingly paying more attention. This is a testing facility for wards of the NTA, not a military compound.

We march around the line of vans and I see it. Phase Three. A monstrosity of stone, grey brick and steel, it stands towering above the foliage surrounding it. The heart of the building may once have been magnificent, a castle in its time, but now concrete fills in what used to be tall windows. A double door stands in the center of the stone and the encompassing structure is more metal, an addition of concrete and shining steel to make the building as wide as it is tall.

A great cloud of soot looms above, choking the sky. It tumbles out from a cylindrical stack on the northern side of the building, turning everything beyond into a hazy shade of grey. The beauty of the red sunset is marred, a dirty thumbprint on the face of a stunning photograph. The air smells of sulphur and something else, something like leather and molten leaves even though it's the height of summer. My feet are heavy as I leave the crunch of gravel to ascend the smooth stone staircase and step into the shadows.

Through the threshold, there is another door entering a glass box structure with a white roof. I can see through it to the other groups who have already passed through.

Claustrophobia, that's what my analyst called it. When the older girls locked me in with the brooms and towels. The air was thick with dust, and the acrid taste of chemical bleach was a thick coating on my tongue. Apparently, tight spaces and I don't much get along.

We pack into the box like a bunch of sardines and someone calls, "Arms up!" *The walls are glass, I can see everything, everyone, it's alright here.* I lift my arms.

A roaring hiss proceeds the release of a glacial vapor forced out from some unseen ventilation above us. It billows out until my skin is covered in icy condensation and I'm blinded as if trapped inside a wall of white stone. Impulsively, I reach for my respirator, fingers clawing at the rigid plastic. I bring my arms down hard and hit someone with my elbow, she cries out. My heartbeat is a raucous of thunder in my chest, my lungs feel constricted as if caged.

I need to get out.

The door on the other side of the room opens and I am already there, pushing and tripping and sprinting through. I step out, hunched over, gasping for unrestricted breath, a dull ache forming on the precipice of my skull.

A warm touch on the back of my arm, a calm voice tells me I may remove the respirator. I don't even wait for her to finish before I reach back, fingers fumbling to undo the buckle. The mask clatters to the floor and I'm painfully aware of the silence that follows.

Forcing myself to straighten, I whisper an apology to the woman and step back with the others. Their eyes steal pieces of my dignity with each sideways glance. It's as I begin to wonder how much longer the silence can possibly stretch on that the lady picks up my respirator and tells the others to dispose of theirs in the bins to our right. She beckons for us to follow her to the main atrium and I allow myself to look up.

Plain. Not unlike the home I left, white tile, white walls, fluorescent lights. We stand in a wide hallway, the glass box to our backs and a wide-open space bathed in orange light ahead.

"Hey, Joanna, you ok?" A girl beside me asks. It's the one from the van, the girl I used to know.

"Yeah," I say, clearing my throat. "Thanks."

"Mhmm." She brushes her short black hair back from her face. Feint red impression marks make a circle around her small mouth and nose from the respirator. "It's Danny, *remember?*" She laughs a quiet laugh, "Don't worry about what happened back there, they should have warned us about the death chamber. I bet the other institutes have them, I heard ours was the smallest in our zone."

"Yeah, a little heads up would've been nice."

We're guided in and asked to stand quietly as we await our dorm assignments. The entire roof is glass, the pieces angled, allowing the remnants of sunset to soak the room in a glow of fragmented amber light. Like being underwater if the water was on fire.

The tapping chatter of heels echoes from the hallway opposite us on the parquet floor, a woman enters. I can tell without knowing for certain she is a person of authority. A stiff blue blouse buttons up to her chin and is tucked tightly into a pair of pressed trousers. Confidence is evident in the set of her shoulders and the way her eyes command attention from the crowd.

THREE

"MY NAME IS Susan Dunne. I am the assistant director of this branch." She weaves her fingers together at her front and forces a pained looking smile to her lips. "Welcome to Phase Three." She seems to be making an effort to meet each set of eyes staring at her. "You have all had long journeys and likely need to use the lavatories and have a rest, so we will get on with room assignments. There will be a more formal welcoming ceremony tomorrow. Males and females will have separate rooms, but share the common areas. There will be four to each room."

A guard standing to her right hands her a clipboard, his eyes scanning the crowd.

"As I call your name, I would like you to raise your hand and remember your corresponding wing and room number." She begins in alphabetical order and I find myself tuning her out, her voice fading to a distant drone in the background.

The guard is much more interesting. His eyes dart from face to face, looking but not finding. His hands are fists at his sides, readied but not aimed. Where all the other guards in this compound must be in their mid to late thirties, he doesn't look a day over twenty-five. There is something in the line of his square jaw, the shape of his mouth that makes me think I've seen him before. Even from this distance, I can see the pale green of his eyes shining in the dying light. The color—it's unnatural looking, almost ethereal, so out of place among his otherwise strong features.

An elbow to the ribs breaks my stare and empties the air from my head. Danny's eyes are wide as she nods toward Ms. Dunne.

"Joanna of Zone Three," she says, a note of impatience in her voice.

I hastily raise a hand.

"Thank you. You are in the North Wing, room five."

His eyes blaze into mine. An electric current runs through me, I am a live wire, shooting sparks from every nerve.

I know him.

I can't possibly know him.

I busy myself inspecting a chip in the tile by my feet, skin bristling, burning.

"You know him or something?" Danny asks in a low whisper, her voice dripping in sarcasm.

"Is he looking at me?"

"Sure is."

My teeth clench.

"Room five? Guess we're roomies."

Ms. Dunne finishes off her list of names and the excitement in the room grows with anticipation of a good rest and the use of a toilet. I don't dare look up, the pressure of his stare is one-hundred pounds on my shoulders. *Why is he staring?*

"North wing is the hallway behind me, East is to your right and West to the left. You will be escorted to the showers at nineteen hundred hours, for now, you are dismissed." Sentries appear at the entrances to each of the hallways, waiting to escort us to our living quarters.

"North, follow me." *Him.* His voice is deep; the monotone vibrations boom in the cavernous room, making all the other voices seem as though they've been sucked up by the shadows. One more glance my way before he turns on his heel to lead all of us who are northbound to our living quarters.

I pull my pack tighter onto my back, praying that no one has cause to inspect its contents. My movements are careful, mechanical as we come to a door that has a window filled with little boxes of wire. He swipes us through. We begin to pass the rooms and everyone is rushing into their assigned number. The man enters a room about halfway down and I get a sinking feeling it's mine.

"Did he go in our room?" Danny asks, speeding up.

Suspicion confirmed.

Over Danny's shoulder, I see the room is simply furnished, a long desk and four locker-like shelving units cover the wall to our right. Two identical metal framed bunk beds are against the far wall. Cash lounges on the bottom bunk of one of the beds, the guard standing over him. A thick vein pokes out from the collar of his uniform.

"You have the wrong dorm. Odd numbered rooms are female dorms."

Cash sits up, hands high in false apology. "North wing, room five. That's what the boss lady said."

The guard grabs him under his arm to help him stand. "Wait in the hallway while I check your *proper* assignment." He escorts Cash out with him, not a glance, not a word in our direction. I exhale. He isn't looking for me.

"Ladies," Cash says, nodding to us as he leans against the wall to wait.

Danny ventures inside, clearly amused by the situation. I follow her in, eager to put distance between me and Cash, between me and the soldier who sparks a distant flame in my memory. "I call top!" Danny shrieks, tossing her backpack on the top bunk, rushing to a door in the corner of the room that can only be a bathroom.

A mouse of a girl with nervous eyes hovers in the doorway. "I'm Joanna." I try to smile. She looks so fragile she might shatter under the pressure of her own discomfort. She wears a burgundy dress that hangs limp on her slight frame, marking her as an inhabitant of one of our sister institutions. "Top or bottom?"

"Umm, bottom," she mumbles, head down as she crosses the room to sit on the bunk under Danny's.

"I'm sorry girls, there seems to have been an error with our paperwork." Ms. Dunne announces as she enters the room with Cash in tow. "Normally we have a few empty bunks, but this group has filled all our spaces. If any of you are uncomfortable with having this young man in the same room, I can see if any of the other girls would be willing to switch places with you." She's all business, the apology is a formality. Her true feeling of annoyance is transparent in the slight roll of her eyes.

Danny is the first to speak. "I'm ok with it."

"Me too," I say, though I'm not sure I am. Under normal circumstances I wouldn't want the notorious Cash anywhere near me. These aren't normal circumstances. I need to know what he knows. This is almost too convenient.

The other girl gives a small nod but says nothing.

"It's settled then. This will only be a temporary situation until we can make other arrangements. If you have any problems, there is always a guard stationed here in the hallway." Not another word, she pivots on her heel to leave. Danny follows her to the door.

"Excuse me. Sorry. I uh—I have a question."

Ms. Dunne arches a brow at Danny, doesn't answer.

I can sense the discomfort in her voice, I busy myself with the strings tying my pack together, trying not to eavesdrop.

"I had a friend who came here a few months ago. He uh, he said he would write to me and he never did. I was wondering if you could tell me which sector he went to train in. I just—I wanted to try to—"

Dunne's jaw tightens. She looks anywhere that isn't at Danny. "That information is confidential," is all she says in reply, clicks her heels out of the room. My instincts tell me she's hiding something. If Greg succumbed to the virus, why not tell her?

Cash takes up residence in the bed under mine. I shudder to think I'll have to sleep not four feet above him.

The itch of anxiety is scratching down my back, filling my head with bricks. *How do I get him alone?*

Danny goes back into the bathroom. I know enough about her to gather she doesn't want to be bothered.

I clear my throat. "I didn't catch your name," I say to the mousey girl who is sitting on the edge of her bed, looking dangerously close to tears.

"Cash," he says, winking in my direction.

"I know who you are. I wasn't talking to you," I snap, shocked at the hostility in my tone. I'm about to apologize but he's laughing. He is *laughing at me* and I am suddenly fuming.

"Right, and you're Joanna, right? You used to eat with Dianna in the kitchen."

At the mention of her name, a thick cloud forms in my mind. *Did he know her too?* Surely not how I knew her.

"Sophie." The new girl pushes the dirty blond curtain of her hair back, she's got a pale complexion, the shade alarming close to looking green.

"Nice to meet you," I say, grateful for the opportunity to cut off pleasantries with Cash.

We sit in silence for a time, all of us organizing our things into our respective lockers. It's Cash who breaks the silence, "Anybody else notice all the *guns* in this place?"

Danny and Sophie remain quiet and shake their heads. "I did," I say, placing the naked books I brought with me in the top of my locker under a sweater. Dianna gave them to me from her own hidden collection. Fiction isn't part of our learning curriculum. It isn't even allowed within the walls of the Institute. *Pride and Prejudice, Lord of the Flies* and *Into the Wild* are the ones she told me I could keep.

Absently, I trail a fingertip over their bare spines, I've read each at least three times and can't help but feel like they are all set in alternate universes. It's baffling to imagine the world was once as the authors describe it. So beautifully magnificent, majestic, filled with mystery and intrigue and *freedom*.

"I don't think you're supposed to have those," Cash whispers, far too close to me. I turn to see the look on his face is approval. So, he thought he was the only one who didn't follow all the rules? I still think he's insane. Who would willingly expose themselves? Without a respirator outside these walls, anyone is as good as dead.

"You stay out of my business and I'll stay out of yours, ok?"

His eyes widen, the grey-blue of his iris' so dark they're almost black. "I think we're going to get along."

FOUR

THE SHOWER ROOM is at the end of our hallway and is nothing more than walls lined with semi-private stalls, thin off-white plastic curtains dangling in their entryways. The entire floor is cool cement and slopes to the center where a large drain waits to suck up all our sloughed off grime. The guys got to go first, so the floor is already wet and the air humid and smelling of soap. There is a tall shelf piled with uniformly folded white towels and I grab one as I walk in, the fibers rough to the touch from too much bleaching.

"Here's hoping for hot water," I say as Danny enters a stall near the back.

I go into the stall next to Danny's and hang my towel over the curtain rod.

"It's hot!" someone calls out, spurring me to undress faster. I crank the water tap hard to the left. It takes a minute, but before long steaming water is rushing from the spout and I have to inch my body into it to keep from scalding my skin. The water at our institute was never actually cold, but hovered at a luke-warm temperature that was bearable but never enjoyable. This, I could get used to.

"Hey, what were you and that kitchen lady talking about before we left?" Danny asks as we towel dry our hair. "She looked really upset."

I turn away from her, dropping my towel into the wash basket, not sure if I want to answer, not sure I want a friend right now.

"Nothing," I say. "She just wanted to say goodbye," I lie, afraid of what she might think if I told her the truth.

Danny's face screws up into a pucker. "Fine, don't tell me."

I was always a terrible liar. I don't try to reassure her, instead changing the subject, "I'm going to get some sleep, I'm exhausted."

That's not a lie, my head feels like it's full of cotton, my limbs heavy. I gather my things and leave her there with the other girls who are still toweling off or chatting as they brush the knots out of their hair.

He's still in the hallway, standing right across from my door. At first, I think he must be waiting for me and my breath catches, but then I realize that the door to our room is in the center of the hallway. It makes the most sense for a guard to stand there, he's not there for me. He doesn't even know me.

He leaves his post as I reach for the knob and I instinctively back away. A million thoughts are racing through my mind, I am a statue, frozen in time as he moves toward me. He pulls a card from a clip on his waist, waving it in front of the reader, unlocking the door. I tell myself to calm down.

"Thanks," I mumble, pulling my body from its concrete encasement. His hand closes gently around my wrist. Every bit of heat leeches away. I'm left shaking against the chill. The pressure on my wrist is making me hyper-aware of just how fast my heart is beating. I don't know him. I can't know him.

I study the pale green of his irises for a second too long. "You dropped this." His warm breath is a soft whisper on my neck. He presses a small piece of paper into my hand and I fight the urge to drop it and run away.

"No—I think you—" I start, eyes looking from the paper crumpled in my hand back to him. He shakes his head, almost imperceptibly, as he peers up at the camera watching us from the end of the hall, its red light blinking. He releases me so fast it's as if he was never touching me at all. The rest of the girls start to exit the showers, a plume of steam trailing behind them. I stumble back as Danny enters the room, her hair still dripping.

Crumpling the paper into my fist, I push past her into the bathroom, ignoring Cash's raised eyebrows as I slam the door and shove the lock into place.

I'm taking in lungful's of air as if there isn't enough in this room, in this world to sustain me. It feels like I'm inhaling acid instead and I don't know why. I don't know why he looks so familiar. I don't know why Dianna told me everything I know is a lie, and I don't know why I feel so damned frustrated. I look into the mirror above the sink, trying to tune out the muffled conversations on the other side of the door.

What is happening? I want to scream.

"Jo, you ok?" Danny.

"Fine, I'll be out in a minute."

I let down the lid of the toilet seat and sit down hard, batting the damp hair away from my face. That's when I remember there's something in my hand. It could be nothing, or it could be a hive of bees waiting for me to open my hand and let them out, to let them free so their words can sting every inch of me. I peel back my fingers, the motion strained and robotic. The faint outline of words scribbled in black ink are visible on the other side. Before I can think any more about it, I've unfolded the paper, smoothing the crumples with my palm. A single sentence is on the page, written in an almost illegible scrawl.

If you want answers, slip this note under your door at exactly 1am, my mother sends her regards.

-Knox

All the air rushes from my lungs in one great gust. Dianna. Dianna is his mother. The realization slams into me like a fist to the stomach. The shape of his mouth, the slope of his nose, the jade green of his eyes, they are all features he shares with his mother. Sitting back against the cold porcelain of the toilet back, the shaking of my hands stops and my pulse slows, skips, slows some more.

"Hey Jo, I gotta get in there." *Cash.* I drop the note and fumble to pick it back up. Dianna never said she had a son. Or did she? She said something once, something about how her little boy always liked to read too. I think. I'm not sure.

"Joanna?"

I'm on my feet. I lift the lid of the toilet and drop the note into the water, watching as the ink smears into an indecipherable blur. My stomach turns. Dianna, who was like a mother to me, had a son. She had a beautiful son, and she never told me. How could she not tell me? Maybe I don't want to know what they have to say, maybe I want everyone to stop trying to help me and leave me the hell alone. I hit the button on the top of the toilet and all the knots of tension in my body slosh and swirl away, right down the drain. I have a choice. I will always have a choice. I can't force myself to believe that I am livestock, that my life is a waste. I *can't*.

There is a clock on the other side of the room, above the desk. As I lay on my side in bed listening to the shallow breathing and soft snores of the others sleeping, I watch as the minutes tick by. It's 12:55am now, and even knowing I'll have to get up in six hours, I can't seem to force my eyes to close.

Who will I become if I find out my whole life was a lie? What does that even mean? Where would I go? It's not as though I can leave. The questions leap and twirl around vulgarly in my mind like some demented circus parade that's about to open its gates.

"Raising you like farmers raise pigs.." Like farmers raise pigs to slaughter. I finish the sentence in a whisper, needing to test the phrase on my tongue. It tastes like doubt, feels like a dirty knife wedged in my side. Why can't I think of another ending that would fit? It doesn't make sense. Unless she meant it as a metaphor. When we finish our training, we'll be on our own, living on rations

and relying on respirators. We'll become more susceptible to the virus without the NTA's protection. But we always knew that day would come, and I've welcomed it. No, that can't be it.

It's 1:00am. I cup a hand around my mouth in an attempt to stop my rabid breathing. Nearly every fiber of my being wants to jump down from my bunk and run to the door before it's too late. I imagine it, I imagine the words falling from his mouth. What if the sentences he clips together change everything? What if his words chew me up and spit me out? What if they're both insane? Maybe they're conspiracy theorists, the ones they taught about in class. The ones who spread lies to the public to cause mass chaos among the population.

The more important question at the forefront of my mind is, what if not knowing eats me alive? *Like farmers raise pigs to slaughter.* It's an echo inside of me, a carousel of tormented secrets, round and round it goes until I think I might upturn what little dinner I managed to ingest.

So many questions, so little time. I hear nothing but the incessant throbbing of my own heartbeat in my ears as identical shadows appear in the small slit between the door and the floor. He's waiting for me.

That's when it hits me. Its Dianna. *My* Dianna. Even if I can't trust the guard waiting outside my door, I know I can trust her. I start to sit up, shimmy the covers off my body with stiff movements.

But then the clock strikes 1:01am and he moves away. It's too late. He's gone. Maybe it's better this way. Or maybe I just made the biggest mistake of my life.

My head is spinning, spinning until eventually I

collapse under the weight of a million invisible hands suffocating me into sleep.

I'M CLIMBING. I pull myself from branch to branch, pine needles scraping at my bare arms. I'm at home here, this tree is an old friend, a mother welcoming me into her strong embrace. There is an insistent chill in the air trying to pull the warmth from my bones. I move faster, higher, beating out the chill with my effort. I haul the spicy scent of the molting leaves of autumn through my nostrils. I'm catching up. The dark figure above me is only a few branches away now and it's as if I've swallowed a chunk of the sun and it's a boomerang in my chest. I'm laughing, I'm going to win this time.

The next branch is too high up, my fingers can brush it, but can't grab hold. I search for another way but it seems there is none. I stand on my toes, cursing my height, keeping my balance with a hand pressed to the rough trunk of the old pine. I'm thinking about jumping, sure I can make it. But then there's a hand reaching between the dense branches above me. I glance down, feeling dizzy at the sight of the ground. It's so far down, too far, must be thirty feet. Though somehow, I know I can trust the hand reaching out to help me, all I need to do is grab hold.

Moving in tighter to the trunk, I thrust my hand up. As his strong, calloused fingers close around my hand I see his face. Smiling eyes, the color of fresh spring grass hold my gaze. Knox. I lose my footing, Knox didn't see it, and he can't hold on, my hand slips free of his. I fall, the ground rushes up to meet me. Somewhere in the distance, there is a woman screaming.

FIVE

THE SCREAMING FADES to an insistent buzzing from the PA system as I open my eyes. I reach up with shaking hands to feel the scar on the side of my head. I finger the silky horseshoe shape, where no hair will grow, and am reminded of how I came to be here. I had an accident, I was in a coma. By the time I woke up the virus had taken my parents. Just like that. Gone. Three years old, that's how old I was when the NTA took me in as an orphan.

I don't even remember what they looked like, my parents. Where the majority of the orphans were here before they were even out of diapers, some as newborns, I am of the minority. Three whole years I spent outside of the institution, and because of my head injury, it's all a blank. No one can even tell me what happened to me. All my file says is that I was dropped off at an emergency health unit with a cracked skull, hemorrhaging blood. I'm lucky to be alive, is what they tell me. This isn't really living, is what I want to tell them.

I guess we have our ancestors to thank for that. It was a war, the war to end all wars. Nuclear blasts so enormous they wiped out entire cities, and eventually entire continents. Our small piece of this land is the only inhabitable chunk left. Some people speculate TEN is some kind of chemical aftereffect which evolved from the exposure to nuclear radiation. I think it's mother nature trying to destroy what's left of the savages who destroyed her. She takes her punches in other ways too. A tsunami took out what used to be Japan, and a series of earthquakes and tornadoes devastated the what used to be known as the United States of America. I'd like to see a tornado. I'd settle for knowing what rain feels like.

"Breakfast will commence at 0730 hours in the communal dining hall," the garbled voice says. It's 7am. Straightening my hair back down to cover the scar, I kick off my blankets. I've been having that dream for years. The analyst back at Phase Two said it's brought on by anxiety, symbolizing a loss of control, but I always felt it was a memory. But this time was different. Last night was the first time my subconscious mind put a face to the climber above me.

If it truly was a memory, it wouldn't make sense for the other climber to be him, but nonetheless, in my dream, I knew him. I knew him well enough to trust him with my life, and he let me fall. *I shouldn't trust him*, that's what it must mean.

"Trouble sleeping?" Cash asks me as I climb down from my bunk. He's still lying in bed, blankets piled near his feet, arms folded in a knot of slender muscle behind his head, nothing but a pair of boxer shorts to cover him.

"Excuse me?" I say, averting my eyes as he sits up.

"I thought a bomb went off at one point, you were moving around so much."

"Light sleeper?" I ask him, dodging the question.

"Insomniac is more like it. Something about this place seems off." He stands up, locking eyes with me as he passes. "Wouldn't you agree?"

"I'm starving!" Danny exclaims, jumping off her bunk, her short hair matted on one side and bushy on the other.

"Me too," I say, stifling a laugh at her appearance.

After pulling my hair into a loose bun and dressing into some clean slacks and a blouse, I go to join Danny at the desk on the far side of the room. She's reading one of four small files that were on the desk.

"What are those?"

"Schedules," she says, curt.

I pick one up and begin to read. After breakfast, there's a space marked down for 'Welcoming Assembly,' and then, 'Health Examinations,' and an hour marked out for, 'Lunch IR,' which I understand to mean lunch-in-room, followed by something called, 'Green Room.'

"What do you think *green room* is?" Danny asks.

"Not sure. What about you, Sophie?" I ask as she folds herself neatly into the chair next to Danny. "Any idea?"

She shrugs. Red stains ring her eyes. She looks like she's been crying and she's doing her best to hide it. I sit down next to her. "Are you alright?"

"What? Oh—Oh yeah, I'm fine. It's allergies or something."

I put a hand on her shoulder, feel a bit weird about it.

I'm not very good at comforting people. "Allergies?" We both know that's not true.

She turns to me, not bothering to hide how her eyes are welling up again, "It's just–I don't understand it. I'm worried something happened to Greg, like, maybe he got sick."

I don't really know how to respond to that, I think she sees the discomfort in my face because she quickly wipes the back of her hand over her eyes and tries on a smile. "It's fine. I-I'm fine. I miss him. You know?"

"Yeah, I do. I didn't mean to be rude yesterday. Dianna, the woman who worked in the kitchens, she was a good friend of mine."

She's looking at me incredulously. We aren't supposed to speak to the staff any more than what's necessary, and she knows that as well as I do. What she doesn't know is there aren't any cameras in the kitchens and there's a blind spot near the entrance on the left side of the serving line. It amazes me how many things I would never have paid attention to, would never have known or learned if I hadn't met her.

The clock reads 7:28am and my stomach muscles tighten, hoping Knox isn't waiting when they unlock the doors. I should've kept the note. I should have slipped it under the door. I am an idiot and a coward. The buzzer sounds and the red light next to the metal door turns green.

I stride out with Danny on my heels, with a look I hope comes across like confidence. I'm ready to try to give some sort of signal to Knox, mouth an apology at least. A guard stands in the same spot Knox did yesterday. When I see his thin face and blank stare, I can't help feeling a sinking in my gut.

Breakfast goes by in a blur of clattering cutlery and muffled conversations. I take a single bite, but can barely taste the powdered eggs. The texture alone is enough to upset my stomach right now.

The welcoming ceremony that follows is a formality I can't seem to focus on, my mind numb and limbs heavy with exhaustion. Lazily, I scan the guards on either end of the large gymnasium, but don't find the face I'm seeking. Once the formalities are through, the lights dim and a white screen lowers behind where the director is standing on the dais. He's a large man, rotund, with greying yellow hair and red cheeks. I sit up a little straighter, it's not too often we watch moving pictures. The director has begun to speak in a low monotone, his voice easy to tune out. The images come to the screen all at once, the colors so vivid I find myself squinting. It shows a world I do not recognize as my own, but understand to be how this world was prior to the war and the spread of the virus.

Next is a clip of war, shown in black and white. There is no sound, but I can imagine the loud banging and the popping of gunfire as soldiers are thrown into the air from the blasts and shot down dead.

"That's morbid," Danny says beside me.

"I don't see the point in showing this to us," I retort, catching a glare from one of the guards.

The following clip is a close-up of a man, shoulders up. Sound begins to float through the speakers in the front. He is a doctor or a chemist, I surmise from his white uniform. His eyes are sad, all his possibly once attractive features dragged downward. He explains the situation as if to a colleague or a superior and I get the feeling this film was made for someone important, captured shortly after the virus became airborne.

"The virus has evolved. We are finding cases now that didn't involve direct contact, which can only suggest that what we have all feared has finally come to fruition. The virus is airborne. Our team has been working day and night to find a cure, something, anything at all, but we are at a loss. There seems to be nothing that will kill the virus without killing the host. I would advise that you inform the population of our situation. A curfew may be necessary. Masks should be worn and no one should overexpose themselves to high traffic areas." He sits taller, his expression darkening, "As I've said, there is no cure, bu—" The picture cuts out, though it didn't seem to me as though the doctor was done speaking.

Danny squints at me, eyebrows furrowed, I'm not the only one who noticed the messy cut off.

The last thing the doctor said is still running through my mind. *No cure*. The virus, once contracted, will run through you, over you, and break your body down. Ten days. That's the longest the human body can survive once its been contracted. So that's what they decided to call it, TEN. I'm sure there's a more scientific name, but that's what everyone else knows it as. At least in the walls of our small institutions, we're safe. Safe from the contaminated air, I'm not so sure about anything else anymore.

The screen stays black for a moment and I look back to see someone fiddling with the tape, switching it out for another. This next sequence is a little less grim. It shows the world as it is now. It's a map showing the remaining populated areas of our planet in small blue dots. I can point out where we are. I've seen this map before, though not with a headcount. We're in the eastern section of what was once known as Canada. There are only five other areas containing blue lights, all NTA controlled, while the rest of the earth remains in darkness. The image grows closer until it's focused on our cluster of zones, showing all four of them.

The map fades into another video. We stare into the icy blue eyes of Commander Tobin Rivers. The face of the NTA. It's because of him we're safe. Since he came into power almost ten years ago, there's been a reduction in loss of life both from the virus and other threats. Within the borders of each zone the people are generally safe because he has made it that way.

"Welcome to Phase Three." The Commander says, "Your future starts today. Each one of you will play an integral role in our endeavor to right the wrongs of the past and move forward into a brighter tomorrow." He grins, showing two rows of perfectly straight teeth in a square jaw, "A tomorrow without illness, crime, or war. In thirty days, you will join those who came here before you and re-enter society. I want to personally thank you for the contributions you will all someday make and wish you all the best during your testing."

There are a few shouts of assent from the crowd, someone yells "We are the future!" And several voices repeat the chant.

The screen goes black, and the director steps back up onto the dais, raising his hands to quiet the crowd. "This institution is known by some as the 'sorting facility,' as many of you know, you will only be with us for thirty days. By the end of that term and after extensive testing, it will be decided to which area of society you will be best suited for. Some of you will go on to be scientists, helping to find a cure for the virus that has plagued our nation for generations. Others will become farmers, growing the food that we consume every day. There are many options, all are essential and each are in high demand."

He folds his hands behind his back, considering the blank space above all our heads instead of the faces of the people listening to his well-rehearsed speech. "When you leave here, you will be going to a role specific training facility where you will spend a period of six months to three years training. During your time with us, you will be tested, mentally, physically, and medically to ensure optimal placement. Speaking of which, the first round of testing begins now, so I would like to thank you for your time and wish you all the best of luck."

Short and sweet. Bittersweet, something doesn't feel right and I'm kicking myself for not heeding Dianna's warning, worried I may not get another chance. That Knox will leave me to fend for myself. He steps off the dais and Ms. Dunne takes his place to a round of half-hearted applause I can't bring myself to participate in.

"Will those staying in the East wing please rise and follow the escort at the doors back to your quarters, you will be called in alphabetical order for testing." The others have already started to filter out. They are a current of energy, a river, restless as it breaks over the stones of uncertainty. I itch to join them in their ignorant bliss. I wish I could pretend. I wish I didn't care to know the truth, but I do, I *need* to. They say curiosity killed the cat, but satisfaction brought it back.

SIX

CASH IS THE first one to walk in the door from testing. He goes straight to his bunk where he sits down hard and lets his head hang down. Sophie and I are sitting at the desk, reading over the schedules left for us. Danny enters next and I am about to ask her how it went but she is already in the bathroom. The door is slightly ajar and the sound of her retching into the toilet makes my skin go cold. My legs are numb as I stand to see if she's alright. I catch a look from Cash as I pass, he shakes his head at me.

"What hap—"

"Will all those with names beginning F to J please exit the dormitories and follow your nurse to testing." A tremor rushes through me, I take hold of the chair back to steady myself.

"Hope you don't mind the sight of blood," Cash whispers, the syllables clipped, his eyes betraying nothing.

I hesitate, my feet are cinderblocks and I can't seem to

lift them, there is a rushing of unidentified sound in my ears.

"You better go, Joanna," Danny says coming out of the bathroom to climb up into her bunk, "It's not that bad, I'm a wimp. Don't really get what they're testing for though, if we don't got TEN, we should be fine right?" She gives me a half an eye roll, brushing off the fact that she was throwing up not fifteen seconds ago. Her blasé demeanor allots me enough courage to walk out the door. The few others in my wing with names beginning F-J have already started to follow the nurse down the hall and I rush to catch up.

We pass through a few doors on our way to the testing labs, which seem to be closer to the back of the building.

"The testing administrators will be with you shortly, please choose a room and have a seat to wait," the nurse tells us as she moves into an office down the hall. There is a long horizontal hallway where about fifteen doors stand open on the opposite wall all the way down to the left and right of where we stand.

I go into the room closest to me and immediately my stomach drop to my toes. The walls are covered with all sorts of medical paraphernalia. Some I recognize, some I don't. A yellow bin fixed on the wall next to me has a vibrant candy cane bordered sticker which reads 'hazardous waste.' I can see a haystack of used syringes through the plastic. There is no chair in the room, only a metal slab covered with a thin white sheet. Before I can even consider sitting down the door closes behind me.

"Hello, my name is Anette, I will be administering your testing today." She is a tall woman, with hair held up in a tight ponytail, a few of the blueish black strands too short to be confined by the elastic.

When I don't say anything in response, she continues, "Great, let me input a few things here before I get started."

She starts to click some keys on a glass tablet in her hand. I can see she's entering my name and zone and watch as a plethora of files materializes on the screen. "Have a seat on the table," she says, placing the tablet down on a desk to pull on a pair of transparent latex gloves.

I lean back and pull myself up onto the cold metal. The room becomes smaller somehow and I tell myself it's all in my head. This is regular testing. Everyone has to go through this.

"If you could lay down please."

I lay down, shivering against the steel.

"What are you testing for?" I regret the words as soon as they leave my mouth. Her eyebrows pull together and she won't meet my eyes.

"This is standard testing," she says dismissively as she pulls what appears to be a heavy looking thin rectangular pillow from a shelf on the wall.

Dianna's voice whispers in my ear, *questions don't lead to answers here, Joanna.*

I set my jaw, unconvinced, not ready to be so easily dismissed. "I understand that but you didn't answer the question. So, what exactly are you testing for?" the words come out rough, borderline hostile. *Why can't I shut up?*

"If you are experiencing feelings of anxiety, I can administer a sedative." She lays the heavy pillow across my hips and presses a few buttons on her tablet, decidedly ignoring the question.

"No, that won't be necessary," I say, trying to sound calmer than I feel.

A small vibration emanates from the device, at first, it's surprising, and then it's soothing. After about ten seconds the vibrations leave me nauseous and weak, and I'm gritting my teeth against the feeling. I'm about to pull the thing off me when the vibrations stop and she is asking me to sit up.

"I'm going to take a few blood samples now and that will be all for today, we will finish the medical examinations at the end of the month."

I am not afraid of needles, we've been required to give blood every month since the age of twelve, but for whatever reason when I see her gather up her syringe and sample tubes a lightness forms in my head like it's been hollowed out and filled with helium.

She has wrapped a rubber band around the upper part of my arm, cleaned the soft skin in the crease of my elbow and now is ready to insert the needle. I look away, feeling the hard bite of the tip as it forces itself into the vein, pushing deeper under the surface of my skin. I close my eyes and force myself to breathe as she pushes tube after tube into the IV.

"Done," she says, and the elastic band comes off and the syringe slides out, leaving a trail of hot blood to flow down my arm. "Sorry for any discomfort," she says mechanically, pressing a cotton ball to the blood, fixing it there with a piece of flesh colored tape. "Don't worry, many people get nauseous at the sight of blood."

"I'm fine," I say, though it's far from the truth.

"You can wait outside with the others. You'll be

escorted back to your dorms soon."

I nod and stand up. The instant my feet touch the floor I'm disoriented. I try to hide it, try to pretend there isn't a swarm of black spots crowding my vision. *I'm fine.* I'm hot. I'm burning up. I'm surprised I haven't caught fire and I think the only thing keeping the flames at bay is the sweat that's covering me from my neck down. I reach for the knob, but it's a blur of silver on a white background, and force my feet to propel me out the door. I overstep and launch myself into the wall on the other side of the hallway.

"Joanna?" A familiar voice says, but I can't see. I'm blind against the blackness seeping in from the edges of my vision and I feel embarrassed and weak and confused. I am too many things, and then suddenly I am nothing. I am drifting away on a black cloud in a sky of unshed tears.

THE SWAYING, IT'S so comfortable, so rhythmic. Warm. But the light, the light is blinding behind my eyelids and I wish someone would turn it off. The voices float through my foggy mind, garbled and distant.

"Is she ok?"

"What happened?"

Cash. Danny.

"She's fine, but she'll need to rest."

"Put her in my bunk, she's usually up top." Cash. I want to groan. *No, I do not want to lie in your bed!*

"Give her some space." That's when recognition flickers in my mind and the nerve endings in my body decide to come back to life all at once. Knox. He carried me back to my room. Wait, why was he carrying me? I fainted. *No.* This is not happening.

"Joanna," he whispers as he lays my body down onto the bed, I can feel the movement as he sits down next to me.

I think I could open my eyes, but I don't want to. The embarrassment is too much to bear. He sighs and brushes his hand against mine. I tense, his knuckles freezing in response. "I'm only trying to help you. *Please*. Please let me help you." he says it so quietly I'm sure the others can't hear.

I give a small nod, it's all I can manage and I'm not ready to open my eyes yet, the room is still spinning.

"Get her something to drink when she comes to, she'll be fine," he says to the others, and the warmth leaves with him as he stands. "I'll be in the hall if there are any problems." The solemn click of the door closing might as well be a gunshot.

SEVEN

ONE.

TWO.

THREE.

The minutes saunter past like gun-toting soldiers off to battle, off to never return. I'm wide awake but immobile, I'm lying in the same awkward position Knox left me in. The strength has returned to my body along with an oppressive weight that has settled into the marrow of my bones. I need to get up. I need to face the rest of the day.

"Jo, you ok?" Just the sound of his voice is somehow irritating me.

I groan, contracting the tight muscles of my stomach to heave myself up. Four eyes stare back at me when I open mine.

"Hey buttercup, thought we'd lost you for a minute there."

I hold up a hand in warning, hoping the look in my

eyes is enough to shut him up. "Don't."

"I got you some water." Danny holds out a glass for me, "What happened?"

As soon as the cool liquid touches my tongue I find I'm far too thirsty. My throat is full of sand and the water seems to stick there, turning it to mud.

"I d-don't know," I mumble. "Probably should've eaten breakfast."

Danny laughs, Cash smiles, and I feel a little lighter. "Look at you, you're about the size of my little finger. I'm surprised you didn't dry up like a prune with all those samples they took." He winks at me and I'm so glad they aren't making a big deal out of this that I playfully punch him in the arm. He falls back, nursing his imaginary injury. "Oww! Watch out for this one, she's feisty!"

Even though it's forced and I know it's not fully wholehearted, I'm laughing too, because it's easy. It's easier than thinking about the truth, it's easier to pretend that in this moment my life is normal.

Misconceptions are a funny thing. I can't help the stab of guilt when I meet Cash's laughing eyes. I know what I have to do now. I can't go on hiding from truths I'd rather not hear, content to believe in what someone has written down in a book and taught me to be fact. I've spent my whole life conforming to an ideal, to becoming a member of a society I know so little about, without question. Well. Now I want answers.

Lunch arrives shortly after Sophie comes back from her testing, looking drained, but much better than I'm sure I did. Within minutes I've cleared my plate of the soup and bread and Danny is offering me the rest of hers. I accept, feeling full for the first time in a long time.

There's only Cash and I now. Danny is in the bathroom and Sophie seems to have fallen asleep in her bunk. "Where do you put it all?" he asks.

"What do you mean?"

"I'm pretty sure you ate a whole loaf of bread." His eyes are smiling again and it's as if my skin doesn't fit properly anymore. No one has ever looked at me like he is. No one except Dianna. Like a friend, an equal. I try not to let him see the smirk on my face, concealing it with a poorly manufactured scowl.

The flippancy of a moment ago has drowned in the abrupt severity constricting his voice. "Can I ask you something?"

I stiffen. "Depends."

He lowers his voice a few octaves. "I know that you know something isn't right here. This *place*. It's all wrong. I know because I feel it too. I've seen things Joanna, which is why I tried to get out. I'm not some idiot with a death wish."

My eyes widen. I shift uncomfortably in my seat. I'm unsure what to say except; "That wasn't a question."

He leans forward until our faces are only inches apart, whispers, "What was on that piece of paper that guard slipped you last night?" the words are acid flowing into my ears, dripping down my ear canal, branding my insides. I pull myself away from him as Danny swings the bathroom door open, her sharp intake of breath is mildly exaggerated. "Umm.. If you guys are having a moment I can go back into the bathroom."

Later, I mouth to Cash.

EIGHT

GREEN ROOM IS not what I expected it to be. The instant Knox opens the double doors for us to enter, my mouth detaches itself from my jaw and falls to the floor. I try to ignore him staring at me. I can't believe what my eyes are seeing. It's as though someone has dropped a white veil over me and my eyes are projectors, throwing impossible images against the white backdrop.

Before me lies a room double the size of the gymnasium. The walls are glass, allowing the afternoon sunlight to bathe the entire space in warm light. And inside the glass dome, everything as far as the eye can see is green. Trees reach for the ceiling. Small bushes cluster in patches separated by wooden beams, and flowers of all kinds speckle small gardens with lustrous reds and soft shades of purple and blue. The air is humid and hazy. I can taste the soil and tartness of bitter leaves on my tongue. There is a soft shushing sound coming from little nozzles strategically placed around the room to mist the vegetation with water.

I've decided I never want to leave this room.

I am the last one in our group to step inside and Knox closes the door behind me.

"What is this place?" I hear myself ask aloud, though the question was mostly for myself.

"This is where they grow a lot of the food for this zone, they bring all the newbies here to get their minds off the testing."

I spare him a cursory glance and find his jaw is set. The rest of our group has joined the others wandering through the maze of foliage. There's a guide somewhere up ahead explaining to them what this place is and why it's here. I move to follow, knowing it would be considered strange for me to be speaking with a guard, but Knox stops me with a whisper. "Wait."

I scan the ceiling and walls for cameras, but don't see any in immediate sight. It's too humid, I realize. They wouldn't work in here.

I almost don't turn around. Almost, but then I do. I don't like what my stomach does when our eyes meet. I don't like the way I feel like I know him. And I really don't like how his eyes hold me hostage, making it impossible to move.

"I need to talk to you," he says. "Just stay a few steps ahead of me."

I nod, not knowing what else to do. I can hear the crunch of his boots on my heels, feel the vibrations running through the ground and into the soles of my feet.

"Left."

I turn into a grove of blooming lemon trees, the heady citrus smell awakening all my senses.

"Right."

Onto another trail surrounded by dense, low-hanging pear trees, my palms growing sweaty. *Where are we going?* My heart is beating so fast it's becoming an unnoticeable flutter in my ribcage.

"Step off the trail into the trees. Left. Breathe, Joanna, I can see you shaking. I'm not going to hurt you."

I step into the trees, my legs fighting the movement as if they're wading through water. A light touch on my hip and I've whirled around, remembering how to breathe.

"Didn't mean to scare you," he whispers.

I take in his somber expression, the way his hair looks like liquid amber in the sunlight, and a jolt runs through me as he reaches out his hands and runs them lightly down my arms. The sensation isn't unwelcome, but it's enough to set my nerves on edge. I pull away, move half a step backward. "What is it you want?"

"You don't recognize me at all, do you?"

My lips part and fragments of forgotten memories catapult into my mind. The touch of a hand, the laughter of a small boy as I chase him through fields of knee-deep grass, and the smell of campfire.

"It doesn't matter if you do or not, I just want to—"

"I do know you, but I don't know how."

There's a light in his eyes now and someone has pinned the corners of his mouth up so high I'm afraid he'll never be able to frown again. His arms are around me so fast I don't even have time to blink. My face is buried in his chest, my arms are wrought iron rods at my sides. I want to push him away but I don't. The smell of campfire that's barely a whisper in his clothes is soothing me into submission.

"I'm sorry," he says. "I get that you're confused and we don't have time for me to explain everything right now."

I'm sure my cheekbones are filled with all kinds of pink and red right now, and there's a cork in my throat that won't let me speak so I just stand there, as still as the trees surrounding us.

"I'll come for you tomorrow night. I'll show you everything Jo, and then we have to leave."

My head is buzzing. There are so many questions that need answering. "What's actually happening here? We can't leave, I mean, where would we go?"

He looks sad when he says, "We don't have time now for me to explain, but we're going somewhere safe, where no one can hurt you. Your mom has been waiting almost fifteen years for this."

NINE

MY WORLD HAS been shattered. I have a mother. She isn't dead. They lied to me. I am a daughter and I have a mother who wants me back. I'm lying in my bunk, it's long past lights out and I can't help the tears silently dropping down the sides of my face. At first, it was shock, then disbelief, now the only word to describe it is frustration. It tightens my muscles and curls a fist around my heart. It's a cluster of storm clouds in my head, the warm rain pooling behind my eyelids.

After Knox told me, I had ten thousand questions, but his radio blared to life, calling him away. He left me with a dumbfounded look on my face and a stutter in my steps as I found my way back to the group.

Hope is a cruel emotion. It makes you cling to it, even though the logical part of your brain rebels against it, tells you it isn't possible. My mom died fifteen years ago–that was a fact. I had accepted it. And now a few words from a stranger have me questioning it. Because if there's even a small chance my mother lives, I will do what it takes to get to her, to meet her. Or I guess, to *reunite* with her, even though I hardly remember her at all. Because that's what hope does. It takes logical people and makes them do crazy things, stupid things, and in the end there's a solid chance it'll let you down.

Tomorrow night. Tomorrow he will tell me the truth of everything and I'm finally ready to hear it.

"Joanna." A whisper. Close, too close. Cash.

I close my eyes and feign sleep, hoping he'll leave me be, but I can feel him moving around and the next time he speaks his words are a silent plea right next to my ear, "I need to talk to you."

I move to turn over, hoping he hasn't seen the stain of tears on my skin.

A sigh and then he's pulled himself up onto my bunk and I have no choice but to sit up and make room or be crushed. I put a couple feet of mattress between us and pull my knees up into my chest. I've never been this close to a boy other than Knox and the feeling isn't getting any more comfortable. I toss a glance over at Danny and Sophie, find them to be already fast asleep.

"I heard you and that guy talking in the Green Room."

My fingers twitch, curling into a fist. "You have no respect for privacy, do you?"

He smirks, waiting for me to fess up. I won't do it.

"Fine, don't talk to me," he practically snarls, "Go it alone."

He's moving to climb back down and I stop him. I rub the chill from my arms, pulling the blanket up higher to cover myself. I need answers and Cash may have exactly what I'm after. "What is it you think you know?"

He positions himself across from me and in the dim blue glow of the emergency lighting I can see the earnestness in his eyes. "When I tried to get out the first time, it was purely curiosity, and I'll admit a bit of stubbornness. The second time was because of something I saw."

"And what exactly was it that you saw?"

He looks away and runs a hand through his dark hair, grabbing it at the base as if he wants to rip it out. "A folder. When I was caught and brought to the director's office, he wasn't there yet and—and there was this folder on his desk that said February Harvest on the label. Being me, I opened it."

A connection is forming in my mind, but I can't seem to tie the pieces together.

"Inside was a list of all the orphans from that birth month, a page for each one. And right on top was a letter from Susan Dunne, that director lady who gave us our room assignments here. I only read a part of it before the director walked in, but I got the gist. She was insisting that the February Harvest be delivered ahead of schedule because there was a shortage of product. And one consistent in all those pages of names was a red stamp on the bottom right corner. O-Negative. I'm not sure what it means exactly, but I know it's a blood type. It can't be a coincidence that every orphan is the same blood type, can it?"

"Product?" I spit the word out, not wanting to believe what I think he's trying to tell me. The word *livestock* is echoing in my mind.

He takes my hand in his and instead of pulling away, I hold tighter, wishing he wouldn't say what I'm damn near certain he will. "You know… I never paid much attention in science class, but I do remember that O-Negative is the universal blood donor type." he pauses and looks away. I wish he would get on with it. Peeling a band-aid off slowly has never helped anyone. "So, think about it, what does the virus attack?"

"Blood cells."

A hint of a smile is playing on his lips. I think he's glad I'm keeping up with him.

I wish I wasn't.

"So, it would stand to reason that since there's no cure, regular healthy blood transfusions or organ transplants could stabilize a patient."

"I don't know Cash. I'm not a doctor."

He trails a finger over my hand, still entwined with his, "You're smarter than that Joanna. There's a reason we weren't taught more about the disease. There's a reason no one in this building will look us in the eyes. And there's a reason Dianna told me to stop looking, to keep quiet."

"You knew her?"

He shakes his head, "No, not well anyway. But when I asked her what it all meant, she said she couldn't say. But she told me to keep my eyes open and my mouth shut. She told me if I tried to get out again, I better make sure I don't get caught."

Questions don't lead to answers here…

He traces the O needled into my wrist over and over again. I pull my arm away from him, wishing I could rip the ink from my skin. If he's right—if *we're* right—it never stood for *orphan* at all. "She didn't tell me Jo, but I figured it out. Have you?"

He's right, and I have figured it out, so, I finish off his train of thought, spitting the words out as if they taste foul, "We are the product."

TEN

WITH MORE QUESTIONS than answers, my sleep was restless, leaving me feeling like a bag of smashed apples when I hauled myself out of bed this morning. I was the last one to breakfast and the last one into the locker room. I had to run to catch up with the other girls and got the last of the gym clothing, a size too small, for my tardiness. I might as well be naked. It's a second skin, thin, concealing nothing and emphasizing everything.

"Come on, let's go! I want to see you moving!" Andrews. The fitness instructor at this institute is a psycho. Tall, lanky, with a glimmer of excitement in his eyes and a malicious smirk I want to smack off his face.

My legs are burning. The flames lick up my body, the effort necessary to keep moving is constricting my lungs.

Shuttle runs, the bane of my existence.

I try to adjust the tank top so that it covers my breasts and lower stomach at the same time as I run, but the effort is useless. I wouldn't call myself curvy, in fact I'm more the opposite. With my small breasts on my even smaller frame I'm more like a wooden plank than a woman.

Cash is training next to me and slows to match my pace as I touch the ground on the white line and turn to sprint in the other direction.

A whistle blows, signaling the end of the first phase and I slow to a brisk walk.

"Walk it off people! Two minutes of rest and we start again."

The long ponytail I threw my hair into brushes the middle of my back, I grab a towel from the stage and blot the sweat off my neck, Cash following my lead.

"You look good sweaty," he whispers.

I startle, laugh, unsure what sort of response that warrants.

"So," he says, drawing out the word. "How are you holding up?"

I haven't told him anything about Knox, or his plans to take me away from this place. Though if he was listening in close enough yesterday, he may already know. I feel guilty somehow just talking to Cash, as if the things Knox tells me are intimately private, dangerous to speak of out loud to anyone but him. Like Dianna, I scan the immediate area for cameras, find four right away.

"I honestly don't know."

He takes a step closer to me. His eyes scan the bodies milling around us and then he whispers, "One way or another I am getting out of here. I don't care what I have to do."

"Keep your voice down, you—"

"Joanna." The physical training instructor calls me with a lazy wave of his arm and I give Cash a sidelong glance I hope communicates to him that we will talk later and jog over. "Ms. Dunne has asked to see you. Carl will take you to her office. You are dismissed."

I meet Cash's eyes. They seem to say *be strong.* I shed my distress as a snake sheds its dead skin and leave it behind me to desiccate on the gymnasium floor. I'm not sure what Ms. Dunne wants or has found out. It could be nothing, or it could be any number of the things I've done in the last forty-eight hours or so. I've recently stopped believing in coincidence, so it's likely the latter. I try not to pay attention to the way the rest of the group stares at me as I follow the guard out of the gymnasium. Great, now I'm *that* girl. The one who got reprimanded for whatever their naïve minds make up in place of the truth.

I don't need any more eyes on me than I already have.

The guard knocks twice on a door near the front atrium where we first arrived and six seconds later it opens and I walk inside. Ms. Dunne is sitting at a large wooden desk; neat piles of paperwork make small towers along the left side. A file lays open in front of her.

"Please, have a seat."

I sit in the cushioned chair across from her and force a neutral expression to my face.

She flips through the file in front of her, considering its contents. I sit quietly and try not to squirm. I focus on the spot just above her head and notice a small fishbowl sits atop a filing cabinet behind her. The little red fish inside it attacks the surface of the water, gobbling up bits of some sort of food. And I feel sorry for it. That fish is just like me.

She feeds it, makes sure it has a clean home to live in, but it will never leave that bowl. Not until its dead.

"So, Joanna, I hear you're having some trouble adjusting, is that true?"

Making a face I hope looks both surprised and honest, I say, "No ma'am, not at all."

She nods and pulls a bottle of smooth white tablets from a drawer in her desk. "I'm glad to hear that Joanna. If, however, you do begin to feel overwhelmed, these should help with that." She plops them down with a rattle in front of me.

I take the bottle and search it for a label, but there is none. "What are these?"

"It's something to help you with any anxiety, standard procedure. And be sure to eat at meal times, we don't want another episode like yesterday, your health is of our utmost concern."

There's no way in hell I'll be taking any of these pills, but she doesn't need to know that, "Thank you."

I stand to leave, but it seems she isn't finished, "Oh and Joanna, I was hoping you could speak to your whereabouts during Green Room yesterday? The guide said you were unaccounted for."

There is a sharp double tap on the door and I'm thinking I may get out of here without having to answer that, but Ms. Dunne's face is set in a hard line and she makes no move to allow entry to whoever is on the other side.

She searches my eyes, looking for some clue perhaps? I betray nothing and look away as I tell her, "I'm sorry about that, I was there, I just wandered a little too far into the trees. It won't happen again."

"See that it doesn't." A sigh as she checks the hand position on the slender gold watch circling her wrist. "It's nearing lunch time. Carl will escort you back to your room."

She presses a button on her desk and the door opens. It's Knox, and he is escorting a man into the room. Our eyes meet for an instant. Knox's eyes register surprise before his expression returns to one of professional neutrality.

"Glad to see your family had no bearing on your decision. Sometimes the blood of the covenant is thicker than the water of the womb," the other man says to Knox, winking. He's tall, taller even than Knox who must be close to six feet in height. The man has eyes the color of faded denim, complimented by the deep brown of his hair and the navy blue of his uniform. A gold tag reads RIVERS in black block letters. Little pins of yellow and red and purple decorate his left breast pocket, under his name tag.

I stumble in my haste to stand, unsure how to proceed because standing right in front of me is Commander Tobin Rivers. The NTA incarnate. Should I bow, or shake his hand, or say nothing at all and scuttle out of the room?

"Commander, you honor us with your visit." Ms. Dunne stands, offers the Commander a slight bow of her head. "Please come in," she says, then seems to notice I'm still standing just to the left of her desk. Her smile falters, "Joanna, you may go."

Her words knock me out of my stupor and send me staggering towards to the door.

As I cross paths with the Commander, I notice his easy

smile is gone. It's replaced by a taut jawline, the tension paling his skin, pulling his shoulders back and closing his hands into white knuckled balls. He looks at me as if I'm a ghost, or some phantom come back from the dead to torment him. And then just as quickly, he has looked away, and I'm out the door. Feeling foolish and insecure, I shove the bottle of pills in my pocket and don't dare look back as I follow Carl away from the office. There's a sour taste in my mouth, and I'm left wondering why in the world Commander Tobin Rivers is making house calls to a Phase Three institution.

ELEVEN

IT'S ALMOST TIME now. The others are asleep. Our afternoon was filled with written testing I couldn't concentrate on, a meal I couldn't taste, and a shower that did little to subdue my nerves. I haven't had a chance to talk to Cash alone again, and I found myself wondering why he isn't telling everyone what he knows if he's so sure. If it's true, then we all have a right to know. In fact, I'm shocked no one else has figured it out.

I climb down from my bunk as quietly as I can. It's three minutes to 1:00am. Knox will be here soon.

"Where are you going?"

"I should've known you'd still be awake."

Cash props himself up on his elbow, tosses his black hair back from his face. "No one goes to sleep in their clothes unless they aren't planning on sleeping, Jo. Your ninja skills are for shit."

There's no time to explain in detail, but he deserves to

know what's happening. "Knox, the guard I was talking to yesterday, is going to help. He says he can get us out." It's a small lie, Knox never said anything about taking anyone else with us, but if it's not safe, how can we leave anyone behind?

"Are you sure it isn't a trick? He could be luring you into a trap, they're already watching you more closely than everyone else."

"I trust him." I'm surprised at the conviction in my voice at saying those three words. Maybe I shouldn't trust Knox, but I do. I feel like I've known him my whole life.

Cash purses his lips, lays back down. "So, where are you going?"

"I don't know. He just wants to talk."

"You can't leave me here, Jo. If you're getting out, I'm coming with you," he says to the bottom of my bunk, a hardness in his tone.

"If there's any truth to anything we've found out, we can't leave anyone here." Looking at Sophie and Danny sleeping soundly in their bunks, I know it's true. If they're in danger here, how could we possibly leave them? Or any of the other so-called orphans for that matter... I could never live with myself.

Cash turns away from me at the same time the light beside our door flares green and I turn the handle down and step out.

Knox is waiting, a grimace tainting his features. The anticipation of this moment is like a buzzing in my blood.

Closing the door smoothly behind me, I turn to him, awkwardly biting my bottom lip. *What now?*

I catch sight of the security cam near the end of the

hallway, wondering if whoever is on the other end can see us from this angle.

"Dwight is on cams tonight, he's with us, no one else will see."

"Okay." I hear myself whisper, "What now?"

"We have twenty minutes and I want to show you something. I need you to stay close to me. There shouldn't be anyone patrolling the route I'm taking you, but if we're seen, I am taking you to the infirmary because you're ill. Understand?"

"Yes."

"Then let's get moving." On leaden legs, I follow Knox through a door at the end of the hall, making sure to stay right on his heels. We walk in silence, his steps are measured, sure, mine are sloppy and sleep deprived.

He opens a door leading down a long, dimly lit corridor, vaguely reminiscent of what I would imagine to be a tunnel. My lungs constrict. The air inside is chilly, but my skin is suddenly burning. I follow him through the tunnel, keeping my eyes downcast, watching his feet move one in front of the other. Try to mimic the action. The silence here at night is eerie, miasmal. I'm waiting for someone to catch us, waiting for a boogeyman to appear around the next corner, firearm raised, finger poised over the trigger. Every nerve of my being is screaming at me. *Hide! No, don't hide, run! No, no, go back! GO BACK!* I tell my cowardice to take a hike and focus on what I have to do. It's easy. This is all so, so easy, a ten-year-old could do this.

See? I could be a good liar.

The tile is different here, it's a peach color, and the

walls are concrete. The tunnel connected us to another building. Up a flight of stairs, down one last hallway and we stop.

"When I open this door, I need you to be quiet. Stay to the right side of the hallway."

I nod once, sharp.

Now I know why he said to stay to the right. When we enter, the lights in the hallway are out, concealing the right side in shadow. The left side is a wall of windows, large panes of glass looking down into a wide space below.

My first instinct is to turn around and leave, but I am drawn to it, drawn to the white room filled with too many things for my tired mind to process. There are at least one hundred people sleeping on little beds, red tubes sticking out from their too pale flesh. They look uncomfortable, the way the lower half of the bed is raised up, I could never sleep like that. They're all so similar, so young. *Wait.* I know her. And him, and that girl over there. They left last month, they were the orphans from July.

"They're sedated. It's like this for a few weeks while they harvest the blood, and then they keep some of them for breeding and testing." He's talking very slowly, calmly as if trying to negotiate a hostage situation with a madman. I realize he's trying to be gentle, but the words falling from his lips are pure poison. I don't notice I've started to shake until he turns me away from the window, "After that, they harvest the organs and burn the bodies."

Realization hits me like a fist to the gut. I can't breathe, someone has ripped out my lungs and burned them. There's liquid leaking down my face and it won't stop. "What are they doing to them?" The question squeaks past my trembling lips, but I'm afraid I may already have the answer.

Knox isn't answering the question and all at once there's a fire igniting down my spine. It's anger, it's hatred, and it's betrayal. It's all those terrible, ugly things that make you feel like ripping the universe to shreds. This must be someone else's life, their story because this can't be right. *What are... How could they... I don't...* I can't even form a coherent thought.

"What is happening down there? Tell me!" I'm yelling and I can't help it, my skin is prickling and my head is throbbing. I need him to explain this to me *now*.

Knox takes me by the arm and drags me back out the way we came. Back down the hallway. Into the stairwell. I pull away from him, fuming. "Start talking, I-I need you to tell me."

He stops. Sits on the steps. Puts a fist to his mouth. There's a profound sadness in his eyes when he finally looks at me.

"The only way to treat someone with the virus is through transfusions of healthy blood and organ transplants."

"O-Negative." I hiss, the words skating past my clenched teeth.

He nods. "It's the universal donor type. Every child born an O-Negative is government property. You are the insurance policy. You are what keeps the remaining population from extinction."

All my blood is rushing to my toes. The anger of a moment ago seeps away, draining me of what energy I had left. I slump down to sit next to Knox and he places a warm hand on my knee. I have more questions but I can't find the right words to ask them.

So, this is my fate, I think. My life is forfeit.

As if he's read my mind and made sense of all the random chatter inside, Knox tells me what I need to know. He tells me, "They wait until you turn eighteen because you are at your full growth potential, that way they can harvest the most blood." He tells me, "They impregnate many of the girls under sedation in vitro to procure more O-Negative blood for future generations." And he tells me, "Organs too, once the blood is almost depleted, they take the organs for transplant. Some of them are used for testing, to help find a cure, and then that's it. The bodies go into the incinerator."

He tells me more things, but I've stopped trying to make sense of the words he's saying because I've seen it with my own eyes. It doesn't matter why or how or when. I find I'm crying again, helpless, completely useless. There are over one hundred people down there and I can't do anything to save them, to stop this massacre.

"There has to be another way," I say between sobs. Knox pulls me close to him and I rest my head on his shoulder. He rubs soothing circles into my back.

"Your mom found another way, but no one would listen to her. When the NTA found out she falsified your real blood type and you were taken away, she ran. She didn't have a choice. They would have executed her or exiled her, and all her research, all her life's work would have been for nothing."

"She's a scientist?"

"A pathologist, and a brilliant one."

"Why would she go to all this trouble to get me back? I don't understand, it's been fifteen years. She doesn't even *know* me. How could I help you? I'm nobody."

His chest rises and falls. I look up to see a distance in his eyes. "You're still her daughter Jo. You were three when they took you. I can see the pain in her eyes every time she looks at me. Every time she has to see that her best friend's son is alive and well while her daughter is rotting in a facility, waiting to die."

The green in his eyes seems to visibly darken.

"When?" I say, changing the subject. Shifting away from him. "And what about the others? We can't leave them here."

His head shoots up as if he's remembered something. He checks the watch under the cuff of his uniform.

"*Shit.*" He stands, rakes a hand through his hair. His eyes are wide. "We have to go. We have three minutes."

He takes my hand in his and hauls me to my feet, taking the stairs two at a time. I trip after him.

I'm breathing heavy now, the extra exertion too much for my weathered body and mind. "When?" I breathe.

"Soon," he says, tugging me around a corner after he's checked to make sure the path is safe. "Dunne has been asking too many questions about you. It's becoming more and more dangerous to wait. If she senses something is off, she'll have you in the Harvest Ward before the week is over."

I gasp and a sharp pain stabs me in the side.

"Tomorrow," he says, decided. "I can have everything set up for tomorrow night."

"And the others?"

We're coming around to the door that will take us into the dormitories. He checks his watch, sets his jaw in a hard line. "We're making plans to try to get more people out Jo, but right now, this only works for one person and I made a promise to your mother. I intend to keep it."

We are almost at my door. "But—"

"Knox, is there a problem? Why is this one out of her room?"

It's the guard, the one with the gaunt face who seems to be the other guard who rotates shifts with Knox, and he's standing right in the hallway, directly adjacent to my door.

Knox lets go of my hand as if he's been shocked, clears his throat, "She was feeling ill. I was taking her to the infirmary."

The guard squints his eyes at me and if I look anything like how I feel then me being ill isn't far off from the truth.

"The infirmary is that way," he says, jerking a thumb back in the direction we came from.

I see Knox's shoulders tense. He doesn't answer.

Say something!

"I-I forgot my medication. I mean, he uh—he said that the nurse would ask to see it, to make sure I'm taking the proper dose."

That seems to placate him enough. "Well, your shift is over," he says to Knox, and steps up to my door, waves his key in front of the reader, "Go on and get your meds, I'll take you from here."

He gives the other guard a tight nod. I can tell he's actively trying not to look at me, not to turn around as he walks briskly out of the dormitory. I take a step over the threshold of my doorway. Cash's eyes are open; he's been waiting for me. When he sees the other guard behind me, he rushes to close his eyes again.

"You know," I say to the guard, "I'm feeling a bit better now, maybe—I mean, uh, I should probably just go back to bed."

He shakes his head. "Can't have you getting anyone else sick, grab your medication. I'll wait here."

"Ok, give me a second."

I fish the pill bottle out of my locker. Run over to the bathroom and empty two of the little square pills into the toilet. They have to think I've been taking them.

"YOUR BLOOD PRESSURE is high," the nurse tells me. She's a younger woman, with kind eyes and slender fingers, glasses perched on the tip of her nose. I wonder how she ended up in a place like this. "Are you feverish at all?"

She's already pricked my finger and done the spot test that shows if I've contracted TEN. I haven't.

"No. I-I had a nightmare." *I'm living in one.* "When I woke up, I felt really sick."

"Nauseous?"

I nod.

"Have you been taking your medication?" She asks, eyeing the pill bottle I gave her.

"Yes."

She checks my temperature and listens to my lungs. I'm surprised when she tells me they sound good. They don't feel good.

She's writing some notes on her clipboard.

"Do you like working here?"

70

She seems surprised by the question, hesitant to answer. This is against the rules. We don't talk to staff. We definitely don't ask them personal questions.

She offers me a closed lip smile. "It's a good job." A lie, I can tell by the barely concealed grimace creeping over her delicate features.

"It's ok. I wouldn't like to work here either."

"Why's that?"

I'm being reckless. I shouldn't be asking her anything. "I just—well it's just so—I don't know. Never mind."

She writes something else on her notepad. The way she's pursing her lips makes me nervous. I try to see what she's writing and she notices. "You know," she says, setting the clipboard face down on her worktable. She sits down beside me. "I think you would benefit from seeing one of our counselors. They can help you adjust."

What's the point?

"I'm sorry, I didn't catch that?"

Did I say that out loud? I need to get out of here. "If you think it would help."

"I do." She stands back up. "You don't seem to have a fever or any other sign of illness. It's likely you're just anxious. Go get some rest, I bet you'll be good as new tomorrow."

"Thank you," I say, getting up, overly eager to leave.

"One more thing… It's human nature to be curious, but I wouldn't get in the habit of asking too many questions."

"I understand."

"Do you?" She looks at me earnestly, challenging me to say something more, but I've already said too much and she doesn't expect an answer.

I catch her name tag as she turns to go back to reading her book. The cover doesn't quite fit the pages. It slips back enough for me to catch a glimpse of the true spine underneath. *Catcher in the Rye*. It's banned. She shouldn't have that. The control shifts in my favor and I don't hesitate to use it. I can't afford any more questions, "Kate," I say and she startles. "I don't think I'll be needing to speak to that counselor."

Her eyebrows scrunch up in confusion, "I think—"

"Enjoy your book," I tell her, watch as her eyes widen and her fingers struggle to put the fake cover back in place. "It's one of my favorites."

TWELVE

THIS IS DISGUSTING. I stare at the words on the paper in front of me. We were each given a questionnaire to fill out. Under the line where I am to put my name, it reads: *This questionnaire was designed to aid in the recommendation of training courses to meet your specific personal attributes. Please complete this form by answering all questions honestly and to the best of your ability.* It has questions like; *What are your strengths? Do you enjoy working with others? Where do you see yourself in five years?* The fact that they would go to such lengths to reassure us, to create this pointless questionnaire to waste some time is revolting.

Danny and Sophie are dutifully scribbling out their answers, looking hopeful and determined. Cash is lounging in his chair, twirling his pencil between his thumb and index finger. He knows as well as I do that these pieces of paper are going nowhere but the shredder.

We haven't had any time to talk today, between Phys-Ed and some leisure time in the crowded art room we haven't been able to get a minute alone. The only words I could give him were, "You were right. I saw it all," while we walked side by side from dinner. Now he's all hard edges. He can't sit still. He needs more information. More importantly, he wants to know the plan. He keeps mouthing "when," to me when the others aren't looking and I don't know what to tell him. Knox's plan only works for one person. I'll have to tell him. I'll have to tell him that there are plans to get more people out, that I'll come back for him, and for everyone else.

The speaker in our room comes to life, "Joanna of Zone Three, please come to the office."

Danny and Cash are staring at me. Sophie pretends she didn't hear anything.

"What's going on? That's the second time in two days. Is everything ok?" Danny asks, her pencil hovering over an unanswered question on her form.

"Yeah, everything's fine," I lie, catching the way Cash is gripping his pencil like a lifeline, the way his eyes beg me for more information. "I'll uh—I'll be right back."

This is not good.

"IT HAS COME to my attention that you are still having some trouble adjusting. It's been recommended for you see a counselor and I'm inclined to agree," Ms. Dunne tells me, her hands clasped together on top of her desk.

"Oh–If, I mean, if you think that's best."

"I do."

She opens a drawer on her left and pulls some things

out, sets them down across the desk.

My books. Spineless, coverless stacks of paper. My lips part and my stomach drops to my toes.

"Do you recognize these?"

"You went in my locker?"

I swallow, trying to look like my insides aren't tangled in knots, like my palms aren't suddenly slick with sweat.

"I need to know," she says simply, "where you got these."

I can't tell the truth. I'm also not quick enough to come up with a good lie.

"I see," she says, taking my silence as an unwillingness to answer her question. "Then you give me no choice."

"What?"

She stands, pressing the button on her desk that opens her door. "Tomorrow you will be moved to another room. We can't have you disrupting the others."

I want to yell at her, scream at the top of my lungs. I also want to laugh, because if everything goes as planned, I won't even be here tomorrow. Then I remember something she said before.

"I thought you said there weren't any other rooms available..."

She doesn't try to hide the surprise in her expression, or the annoyance in her tone when she tells me another space has opened. "You'll have a medical exam in the morning before we transfer you to your new room."

"Another one? That isn't on our schedule."

"Yes. It's quick and quite painless. It'll be over before you know it."

THIRTEEN

THEY'RE ASLEEP. It's 11:00pm and I can feel the elasticity in the atmosphere, as if there is a rubber band around the room waiting for its chance to snap. It's time. I need to talk to Cash. I don't wait for him to come to me this time, instead, I climb down from my bunk and sit on the edge of his mattress. He stares up at me, waiting. Impatience in the tight line of his lips.

"So?" He pushes when I can't find the words right away.

"It's all true, Cash. They're farming us…" I go on to tell him the extent of it all, even though a voice in the back of my head is whispering to me it'd have been better to keep my mouth shut.

I divulge to him every piece of information Knox gave to me and do my best to describe what I saw. I am surprisingly calm reiterating the information, as if I'm telling a story that is not mine. As if the weight of what I am saying has no bearing on me. I'm walking through a fog and my head is filled with smoke. Is this what 'being in shock' feels like? Or am I losing my mind?

"It's happening tonight, isn't it?"

"Yes, but Cash—"

"No Joanna, you can't leave me here. I *am* coming with you. Your friend will have to change his plans. I can't stay here, not anymore." He's inches from my face now, daring me to say he can't come.

All the air rushes from my lungs as I think about what Knox will say, what he will do, but then I say, "Ok."

"Ok?" He shakes his head; his hands open as if to say *that's it?*

I drop my shoulders, the knots in my back muscles shifting with the movement. "I don't want to leave anyone here, you know that. If our situations were reversed, I wouldn't want you to leave me either. It's different for everyone else, they don't know the truth, and there's still time to fix this, to get everyone else out before it's too late." At least that's what I keep telling myself.

"Do you really believe that? That this Knox person and whoever he's working with can get them out. This whole place is crawling with guards. Guards with *guns,* big guns."

I shake my head, "What choice do we have? We can't do anything from inside this building. I have to believe he's telling me the truth."

He looks unconvinced, but there's a determination in him now, he's ready for action, "So what do we do now?"

"We wait. He'll be at that door in thirty minutes."

Cash is immediately moving. He's pulling his pants back on over his boxer shorts. Tugging a sweater over his shirt. Lacing his shoes. I realize I should be doing the same thing. I take some black pants and a sweater from my locker and tiptoe into the bathroom. I'm wondering how we're going to leave. It's not as though we can walk out smiling and waving. An icy frost creeps up my arms and I try to rub out the chill, but my hands are no warmer.

I scrutinize my reflection in the mirror, trying to find the strength I will need to go through with this. All I see is a little girl, scared and alone. My auburn hair falls limp around my chalk-white face. Dark circles claim my eyes. My lips are red, angry and chapped. I look like I'm dead already.

When I go back in the room Cash is pacing the floor. He's not helping my nerves.

"Sit down," I whisper to him as I pass by. "You're freaking me out."

He obeys. Sits down hard, head in his hands.

I shove my pajamas back into my locker, see my notepad and pen on the bottom shelf. *I shouldn't.* But then I do anyway, I can't leave without saying anything. I take the pen and paper and scratch out a quick note, slip it under Danny's pillow. She needs to know I'll be back, that she shouldn't ask questions about where I've gone. It'll only get her in trouble.

"Jo."

I jump back from her bed, turn to find Cash standing by the door. I look at the clock. 12:58am. It's happening. It doesn't seem real. My heart is beating so hard against my rib cage I'm afraid it might be swollen and doesn't fit there anymore.

We stand side by side, both of us look back towards

the girls. Does he feel as guilty as I do?

Green light. Door opens.

Knox smiles when he sees me. That smile quickly fades when he sees Cash standing next to me.

"Wha—," he starts, suspicion in his green eyes.

"He knows," is all I say at first. Knox remains silent, his expression unchanged. "He knew before I did. He's my friend. We can't just—"

"No." Knox is standing in front of us, blocking the doorway with his broad shoulders and sturdy frame.

"What do you mean 'no'?"

"This plan doesn't work for three, Joanna. If I had been prepared, maybe, but I'm not."

Cash takes an authoritative step out the door, forcing Knox backward. "Look, man, I'm not staying here. Either you take me with you or none of us leave."

My jaw unhinges.

Knox's arms flex. A thick vein protrudes from his neck. "Is that a threat?"

Cash straightens to his full height, putting him an inch or two above Knox. Though his lanky frame is anything but intimidating when put next to Knox. Cash eyes the fire alarm to the left of the door. *He wouldn't,* I think, but then I realize I don't really know him at all. He might.

"Cash!" I speak the word as a warning.

"You sure know how to pick 'em, Jo," Knox says, a strain in his voice, and then, "We don't have time for this shit."

He's moving. He walks down the hall, his stride heavy-footed, his head shaking. We follow him. My eyes throw daggers at Cash, but he is pointedly ignoring me.

"Stay close to me," Knox calls back in a harsh whisper.

We come to the Green Room a few minutes later and Knox swipes us in. It's dark inside. Small pod lights give off enough glow to see by. Leaves and branches scrape my bare arms as we traipse through the foliage towards the very back of the room. We stop. Everything is still. The air is thick, compressed with the smell of damp greenery and warm soil.

"What are we doing here?" Cash is first to break the tepid silence.

Knox spins on his heel and I have enough time to see the menace in his eyes, the recoil of his arm before his fist connects with Cash's jaw.

Cash is staggering back, dazed. Knox is moving in for another shot. Then I'm standing in front of him. I don't know how I got here but before I know what I'm doing, I've got both hands on Knox's chest and I'm shoving him away with all the strength I have, "What the hell are you doing?"

Hurt. That's what I see in Knox's eyes. He's appraising me, every inch of me. I'm naked, exposed. Suspicion. Betrayal. Anger. The emotions are plain on his face. They couldn't have been clearer if he had painted a picture for me. He's breathing fast, low. Throws a fist through his hair.

I'm hot, so suddenly hot that sweat is beading at my hairline and the air is cold against my skin.

He's not looking at me anymore, he's unbuttoning his uniform, eyes piercing Cash as he tries to soothe the ache in his jaw. "Don't *ever* threaten me," he says, his voice cold, disconnected. "That was a warning. Next time you won't get back up."

He tosses Cash his shirt, starts to unbuckle his belt. I turn around, a blush clawing up my neck.

A wad of something hits me in the back and I whirl around to see a similar uniform lays in a crumpled heap at my feet. "Put that on," Knox says to me, not meeting my eyes. "And you, give me your pants." To Cash.

I gather up the clothing, trying and failing not to look at Knox. Trying not to see the solid lines of his chest through the thin white tank, or the muscle wrapped in dense cords around his arms.

Moving into the shadows cast down from some orange trees, I start to peel off my clothing, trading them for the starchy, stiff material of the guard uniforms. I pull on a hat that was folded in with the clothes, vaguely remembering that the guards outside had worn them.

When I return Knox and Cash are ready, Knox wearing his tank and Cash's pants, and Cash wearing Knox's uniform, two sizes too big for his slender frame.

"There is going to be a diversion. On my signal, we are going through that door." He points to a concealed glass door a few yards to our right. You'd never find it unless you knew it was there. "It's going to be chaos out there so stay close. If anyone says anything to you, ignore them and keep moving, I'll take care of it."

"So that's it, we're just going to walk out of here?" I say.

He still won't look at me. "Everyone will be heading for the gates. We're going in the opposite direction. I'm not saying it won't be messy. I can't promise that you won't get hurt." He finally looks at me. "But I can promise I will do everything in my power to get you out safe. I made a promise Joanna." A pause, "If anything... happens, get to the road on the other side of the river, follow it north until it ends. There's a trail there, it's hard to see in the dark but you'll find it. Follow it in and find a place to hide. Wait for me there, if I don't come, someone from our safe house will be patrolling and they'll help you."

I'm nodding, but the very idea of anything happening to Knox twists my stomach and sends my heart beating out of its proper rhythm. The boy from my past, my childhood friend. I may not remember, but I can feel it, a connection I can't deny ties us together.

"Tuck your hair into the hat," Knox commands and I obey, twisting it up into a bun and shoving any loose strands into the sides.

Something clicks about what he's told us and a swift fear grips me. "The other side of the river?" My hands start to tremble and I clasp them together, hiding my jitters. There was a small pool in our institution, but swimming was never part of the mandatory curriculum for Phys-Ed. Even with my head above water I felt suffocated, as if the pressure alone could collapse my lungs. "I can't swim."

Nothing is said for what seems like too long. Each second of silence with their stares boring into me is a pickaxe hollowing out my insides.

"Let's hope it doesn't come to that. I'm a strong swimmer, I can get you across." Knox says, "And you, can you swim?" To Cash.

"Yes." He spits, the word wreaking of bitterness.

I try not to think about getting into the water, try not to

imagine its invisible hands dragging me down into the dark. I shift my focus, "What are we waiting for? When is this diversion happening?"

Knox checks his watch and pulls two respirators out of the bushes near his feet, hands one to each of us. "Any second now. Put those on."

I pull mine on. "What about you?"

"I'll be fine. I've already had the virus, the chances of me being infected again are low."

Cash and I are gaping at him. There is no cure. There *can't* be a cure. "That can't b—"

An ear-splitting *crack!* in the distance. A blow to the earth so strong the reverberations rattle my teeth. The glass roof quivers under the pressure of the explosion. A siren blares to life. An ache forms deep in my ear canal. I've never heard anything so loud. The sprinkler system activates and a downpour of cool water drenches me in an instant.

"Now!" Knox yells through the commotion. A warm hand closes around mine and I hold tight as he drags me out of the Green Room, Cash on our heels.

FOURTEEN

THE NIGHT IS dark and filled with the echo of chaos. Men are running, yelling at each other, yelling into their radios. There's a rushing in my ears and a wrecking ball inside my brain. I'm *outside*. That alone is enough to shock my system. The breeze is cool, and the air smells of asphalt and something musty. The stars. I can't remember the last time I saw the stars. Have I ever seen the stars before?

Knox tugs my hand and we run. *Focus Joanna.* He was right, everyone is running towards the gate. We're the only ones heading in the opposite direction. We stick to the shadows, away from the spotlights. I can see the river over the embankment, a slit of undulating silver in the moonlight. So close.

Gunfire sounds behind us and I duck my head. Move faster. Push ahead of Knox. My shoes slap and crunch the gravel, my clothes are wet and clinging to my body, adding pounds to my frame. My muscles are screaming, straining as if I'm wading in water already. We step off the gravel and onto the grass. The river is below us, not more than twenty feet down the hill.

"Knox!" A brutish voice shouts from behind us. I freeze mid motion. I keep my head down, hoping the brim of my hat covers my feminine features, praying none of my long hair has fallen out. "The Commander is looking for you, get your ass out front!"

A quick glance around us tells me we're alone. There isn't another body in sight, everyone has collected at the gate. Everyone but this guy.

Knox looks at us, he jabs his chin in the direction of the river. "You two search the riverbank!" He hollers at us for effect, then speaks in a whisper, meant only for our ears, "There's a cut in the chain link fence beside the river. Go. Now."

"Where's your respirator?" The guard calls out.

Knox is already jogging over to where he stands and Cash is dragging me down towards the river.

"I didn't have time." Knox replies, "I wasn't on shift tonight. Just came from the barracks. Do we know what's happened…?" Their voices trail off as we go our separate directions and I'm praying the other guy believes what Knox is telling him.

Cash is already at the fence, feeling around for the severed metal. "Here!" He calls to me, holding it open. I crouch down to go through. He races ahead of me. He's already in the water. I can tell he's still touching the ground, but the water level is at his chest. Fear curls its unrelenting fist into my chest, pushes me back, kicks my legs out from under me and renders me immobile.

Fear is a bitch who gets a sick satisfaction at watching you squirm.

I force myself into the water, easing my body into it from the edge of the embankment.

"Come on!" Cash whispers.

I let go and find the water is up to my neck. It's cool hands already trying to crush my windpipe.

"It's ok," he says, "I'm right here. Put your arms around my neck."

So, I do. He leans forward and I position myself behind him. Circling my arms around his neck, I clasp my fingers together. He starts to move and we sink a little more. Cash's head is just above the water. His legs are kicking under us. His arms create wide half-circles to our sides.

The current is pulling us downstream, closer to the gate. Cash is fighting it, swimming in a diagonal path to keep us as far away from NTA eyes as possible. If I close my eyes it's easier, try to imagine this is all a bad dream and soon I'll wake up. You can't die in dreams.

We aren't even halfway across when his labored breathing cuts through my false sense of security. We're slowing, drifting, and the way Cash is trying to spit water out of his respirator makes me want to scream. There's still thirty feet of river to cross. I don't know whether to laugh or cry. We're not going to make it. We're both going to drown.

I let go. Try to mimic his actions.

The water is alive. Its grip drags me down the second I've separated from him. I'm kicking my legs and trying to push against the water with my arms. I plunge under for an instant. That's all it takes. It's in the chamber of my respirator and it's not leaking out of the mesh as fast as I need it to so I can breathe. I panic. There's a throbbing in my head and a burning in my lungs.

I do the one thing I can think to do and unbuckle the respirator. I'm under again, but the respirator is off and I'm fighting to get back to the air.

Surfacing, I cough, "Cash!"

He drags my flailing arm over his back. "Done being a hero now?" He says between pants.

"I'm sor—"

"Save it. Just keep your arm around me and kick your legs."

I watch my respirator float down the river, out of my reach.

When my toes touch the slimy bottom on the other side relief rushes over me. We haul ourselves out of the water and make for the trees.

"Are you insane?" Cash shouts at me. "Like, are you *actually* certifiably insane? You almost killed yourself and your respirator is gone. I might as well have left you there." He starts off further into the brush, not waiting for any response.

I look back, hoping to see Knox in the river, coming to join us. Other than the pull of the current, the water is still. Lights flash in the distance and the alarm is still sounding. There's a pull in my chest and an emptiness in my stomach. *He's coming. He'll find us.* I'm not so sure. If there wasn't a river between us, I'd go back, make sure he's alright.

A gun fires somewhere close by, the sound ricocheting in the night. It's the push I need to keep running, to help

Knox keep his promise to my mother. Even if it was the last thing he did.

PART TWO

"The world breaks everyone and afterward many are strong at the broken places."

-Ernest Hemingway

FIFTEEN

NO EXIT. That's what the sign says as we make our way at a brisk pace down the road, and I find it ironic. There's no turning back now. We know too much, everything has changed. I'm not the same person I was last week. Ignorant. Naïve. Happy to conform to a society that is so corrupted it makes my head spin. No, that Joanna is long gone.

Odd though, how I should be happy we made it, but I can't help thinking I've taken one step forward and two steps back. Knox is still somewhere out there. My respirator was swallowed up by the river. I could've already contracted the air-borne virus. Maybe I won't be able to help Knox keep his promise to my mother. Maybe I won't even get the chance to meet her.

"We have to find the trail," Cash is telling me.

The road ends abruptly. In front of us is a wall of trees and a cluster of overgrown weeds that goes as far back as I can see into the dark.

I walk along the edge of the jagged pavement, looking for an opening. "I think this might be it over here."

"Must be," Cash agrees, scrutinizing the small gap in two bushes where the earth looks more traveled. "Let's go."

I'm careful to step only on the trail as we walk deeper into the forest. Each step I take is mated with a squishing sound, my shoes still sopping wet. Branches tug at my damp clothing and pull at my hair, the hat I had to hide it lost somewhere along the way.

Cash stops, turning to face me. "I guess here is as good a place as any to wait."

I lean my body on the trunk of an old pine tree, the bark rough beneath my fingers. "Can you climb?"

A shadow obscures his face. I can't read his expression, but I hear him sigh, "I'd rather not."

"Afraid of heights?"

"Makes more sense than being afraid of small spaces and water."

I reach up and take hold of the lowest branch, just tall enough to get my hands around it. "Well, I'm going up. You can stay here if you want."

It's familiar. The scent of the pine, the way my hands know where to hold for the best grip as I heave my body higher and higher. Dreams are only that, dreams. If I'm careful, I won't fall. To give credence to an illusion is to make it real. Dianna said that to me once. Now I'm finding more than one meaning in her words.

I find a solid branch that faces south and tuck myself in close to the trunk. Before long I can hear Cash coming up, cursing and grunting the whole way.

He positions himself on an equally thick branch below me and to the left. He's trying to appear flippant, but his slow, shaky movements betray him.

The river is a small glint of silver from afar. The sirens have stopped, or we can't hear them this far away. On top of a hill to the south is the institution. Spotlights illuminate it enough I can see a cloud of smoke coiling into the sky, but nothing else. I can't see what's happening on the ground. I can't see if Knox is alright.

It's like someone's shoved sandpaper down my throat, my chest hurts and it's making my eyes sting. "Do you think he got out?"

"I don't know, Jo. All we can do is wait."

IF IT WEREN'T for the fact that I'm twenty feet above the ground in a tree, I would be unconscious right now. Gravity has become a tangible entity. Its pull draws my limbs towards the earth, and tugs at my eyelids until they're drooping and I can't force them open anymore. We've been sitting on these rough branches for at least an hour. The humidity of summer is dwindling as the hours push us further into the chill of early morning.

A sudden movement below jolts me back into wide-eyed alertness.

Cash folds his body in closer to the tree. "Someone's coming," he whispers.

Two identical lights jar and bounce in the distance, casting shadows on the trees. An engine whirs and roars as it accelerates down the road. It's coming this way.

"Jo, come on!" Primed for action, Cash's eyes are wild

circles of blue in the moonlight. "We have to run!"

I shake my head. "No, we should stay. They won't find us up here. If we start running they could catch up to us." I reach for his hand. He doesn't take it. "We could get lost out there, Cash! Knox will never find us!" I'm almost yelling now and I try to reign in my frustration, speak calmly, "Just—Cash, would you come up here. Please. There's better cover."

He looks to where the vehicle is now rounding a bend into the dead end, the engine quieting. The lights are steady. He curses. It's too late now, we have to stay here. He climbs up and I give him my spot against the trunk, pulling myself up one branch higher. We hear doors opening and closing. Hear the soldiers' boots leave the pavement and enter the woods. Two men.

Knox said he had a man on the inside, it's possible they've both gotten out safely and come to find us. I'm hopeful, but not optimistic. I whisper, "Maybe it's Kno—"

"Shh!" Cash is pointing down. The soldiers are getting closer. They're talking, their words becoming clearer the closer they get.

"...I never trusted that fucking kid. If I find him, I'm going to shoot him myself," one declares.

Knox. He must be talking about Knox, and if they're looking for him, that means he got away. My heart is singing, there's an electricity shocking me back to life. The blood that had congealed in my veins flows freely again.

"What about the blood bags?"

A short laugh in response, and then, "If we don't find them they're as good as dead out here."

They're right below our tree now and I'm clutching the

branch with all my strength, trying to stay as still as possible. Hardly breathing.

"Think about it man, they've never been outsi—"

Something small and shiny falls from Cash's pocket. It rings as it hits the branches on the way down. Drops at their feet. Cash is squeezing his eyes closed. My stomach drops.

"Wha—" one starts, but the other silences him with a movement.

A beam of light shoots up into the branches, then another. Flashlights. *They can't see us. Walk away. WALK AWAY!*

"Find what you were looking for?" A new voice, a deep monotone.

A thump as a fist connects with bones. There is a flurry of movement below us and I'm powerless to move. One flashlight drops to the ground, casting its beam on the men. His jaw is set, his eyes are savage, hungry for blood. *Knox.* My fingernails dig into the bark.

"Shoot him!" I hear someone yell.

No! There's a loud clap, the sound expanding around us. Then another, louder. A strangled cry as a body falls to the earth.

Cash is trying to tell me something, but I don't care what it is. I'm already halfway down the tree.

I drop to the ground, the impact coiling up through my heels. I'm swaying, struggling to stay upright, straining to hear a sound. Anything.

"Jo." I whirl around to face him. A smear of blood stains his lower lip, dirt streaks his face in haphazard lines and there's a long tear in his pant leg. At first, I'm paralyzed. I can do nothing but stare at him. His chest is heaving with the effort of inhaling and exhaling.

"Knox…"

He smiles. It's a small smile, but it's enough to break out of my self-constructed tomb. I clear the space between us in the matter of an instant and throw myself at him. His arms are around me. Strong. Sure. I allow myself a second to breathe, to really breathe. The oxygen seems foreign to my lungs and I cough, pulling away from him.

He looks at me, a crease forms in his brow. "Where's your respirator?"

"I-I lost it. In the river."

Cash jumps from the bottom branch of the tree, falling onto his back.

Knox pulls his gun out, aiming it at Cash, the menace back in his eyes. He stops, lowers it. "Oh, good, you're still alive. Now I can kill you myself."

"She's alive, isn't she?" Cash says, trying to brush the dirt from his back, a smart-ass look on his face.

I finally take notice of the two forms laying limp on the ground, "Are they…" I clear my throat. "Are they dead?"

"One is," Knox says matter-of-factly and a sudden urge to vomit tightens the muscles on my sides. "He'll be waking up soon, we have to move." He gestures to the other guy, but I'm not convinced he's breathing either.

Cash steps in closer, putting himself between me and Knox. "You're going to leave him here? What happens when he wakes up and tells everyone where we are?"

"Would you like to finish him off, tough guy?" Knox steps in, holding his gun out for Cash, who remains still. "That's what I thought. They'll be coming up here whether he calls it in or not. I've got enough blood on my hands for today."

Knox pulls the respirator from the dead man's face and hands it to me. "Put that on." I take it with shaking fingers.

There's something shiny on the ground next to my feet. I bend to pick it up, but Cash beats me to it, shoving it deep into his borrowed pockets.

"What's that?"

"Hmm? Oh–that, it's nothing."

Knox is already walking away, heading in what I think is a northern direction. "Keep up!" He calls back.

SIXTEEN

THE HOUSE IS nothing more than a shack. It squats in a small clearing in the woods. The roof is caving in on one side, and a mixture of moss and vines cover the other in a sun-beaten blanket of green. The wood paneled exterior is faded and worn. One window is broken. A pair of antlers hangs precariously over the door frame. It looks like the place dreams go to die. It's early morning now and we're almost there, closing the gap with clumsy steps in the glow of sunrise.

Knox told us he was taking us to a safe house to rest and then we'd keep going in the morning. We'd stepped off the trail and continued walking into thick brush and prickly pine trees. I wonder how he remembers where to go. The pitch black of night made it impossible to see under the canopy of condensed trees, but Knox knew exactly where to step. I held the back of his shirt to keep from falling while Cash crashed through the foliage behind us.

Knox shoulders the door to open it and we step inside. A dusty orange couch and chair surround a big black box with a glass screen in a room to our left. A plush carpet cushions our feet as we enter. To the right is a kitchen. The cupboards hang open, some falling from their hinges, their contents utterly bare. I imagine it for a moment. What it must have been like, to grow up in a home with a family. To watch moving pictures of adventure and romance. To eat at the dining room table laughing and sharing jokes.

It's a fantasy only realized through the pages of story books now. This broken world can't sustain the luxury of easy laughter and home-cooked meals anymore.

Knox pulls the refrigerator out of its nook in the kitchen, revealing a jagged opening big enough for us to squeeze through single file. A flight of stairs leads us downwards. An automatic light flickers to life as Knox waves Cash and I to go first while he pulls the refrigerator back into place behind us.

"What is this place?" Cash asks, steadying himself with a hand to the stucco wall.

"It's one of our safe houses. We have three in this Zone. This one's the closest to the compound."

"How many of you are there?"

"A lot, but it's still not enough."

As I step off the stairs I'm greeted by an older boy. Older than I am anyways, but not by much. His mouth is hangs ajar, and his glasses are two seconds from falling off his face.

I point at my respirator, assuming I'm able to take it off now. This far from civilization, the air is likely as safe as it can be. He nods. I unbuckle the mask and place it on an old school-desk that's pushed against the far wall, relieved not to restrict my air intake anymore.

A radio crackles on the other side of the room.

"About time you showed up," is all the older boy says. He nods towards Cash. "And who is that?" He rolls his eyes, "You know what? It doesn't even matter. You're here, you look like shit, but you're alive. And you got her out."

He steps closer to our group of three, putting himself in front of me. "And apparently, I have no manners whatsoever. I'm Liam," he says, holding out his hand for Cash to shake. He does. Then onto me. "It's good to finally meet you." I shake his hand.

"And this is the part where you say, 'I'm Joanna, nice to meet you too,'" he laughs, I don't have the energy to do anything more than force a pained smile to my lips.

"Ooookay. Guess they don't teach you what humor is over there."

"They're tired, we all are. It's been a rough night Li," Knox says, pulling his guns out of their holsters and dropping them to the desk.

"The room is all yours, get all the rest you need. You know where shit is."

An empty doorway takes us into an adjoining room, there are six cots spaced evenly around. I pick one and sit down.

"Do you need anything?" Knox sits next to me. He brushes a matted piece of hair from my face, seems to realize what he's doing, and immediately jerks his hand away.

It's been hours since the last mealtime, but I'm not

hungry. My throat is dry, but I'm not thirsty either. I'm not sure what I need. A shower definitely, but I don't think I ever want to stand up again. "No."

I can't bring myself to meet his eyes, I'm afraid what I'll find there. The savage who killed a man, the man I should be afraid of. Or the one who saved my life, the little boy I used to play with.

I notice a smear of red on the floor and follow it to Knox's leg where there's a tear in the thick fabric. "You're bleeding!" I'm shocked at the pitch of my voice. He's not just bleeding, *he's been bleeding this whole time.* "How bad is it? Let me see."

He smiles at me and my heart rate slows. "I'm fine Joanna." He stands, his face is pale, and I don't know how I didn't notice before. How I didn't notice how his hands are shaking at his sides.

"You're not fine."

Cash is laying on a cot in the far corner of the room. If the rise and fall of his back is any indication, he's somehow already asleep.

"Liam!" I call, hoping I got his name right. He's here in a flash, teeth bright in a wide smile... until he sees the panic written on my face.

"What's up, everything alright in here?"

"It's fine." Knox.

"Do you have a first aid kit? He's hurt."

Liam's scowling. "What the hell Ethan, why didn't you say something?" He's stomps out of the room.

"Ethan?" I never thought to ask what his last name was, since us 'orphans' don't have them. Surnames are replaced with our birth month and a number to serve as identification in the system. My name is Joanna August 638. Or so I thought. His name tastes familiar on my tongue, *Ethan.* Ethan Knox.

He is looking down at me, condescension in the sarcastic way he's set his jaw. "That was a little unnecessary."

I'm getting angry now. Angry at myself for not asking him earlier when I noticed his pant leg was torn, if he was alright. Angry at him for thinking it's perfectly fine to put his life in jeopardy to save mine, to keep a promise to someone I've never even met. "You could have bled to death. Don't be an ass."

He's grinning like an idiot. My skin burns everywhere he's touched it with his eyes and there's a warmth spreading like an ache inside my bones.

"Quit looking at me like that." I snap at him though without any mirth.

"Got it!" Liam calls from the other room.

Knox raises his eyebrows at me. "Admit it, you think I'm amazing."

I'm laughing, the sound is strange, strangled, but it's real. He winks at me and lets go of my hand. "Get some sleep, love. Liam will stitch me back up good as new."

SEVENTEEN

I WAKE UP to silence. Knox is asleep in the cot next to mine. His pants are cut off at the knee, and a white bandage circles his calf. A pinkish color stains the mesh gauze in a line running six inches to his ankle.

In sleep, ~~Knox~~ *Ethan* looks so peaceful. You'd never think he'd throw a punch at the slightest provocation. Or that he could kill a man. The latter thought dishes out a heaping pile of revulsion. How can I fault him for having the sense to pull the trigger first? Does it make him a monster because I can't say I would have been able to do the same? Or does it make me a coward?

Liam is awake when I come out of the room, he's set himself up at a desk. A pair of big black headphones cover his ears, their cord snaking into a big black box. *A radio?* There's a mug of black liquid giving off little wisps of steam. It smells of cocoa and toasted nuts and indulgence. It smells similar to the treats we used to get twice a year, little pieces of melty chocolate and slivers of cake with burnt caramel sauce.

"Hey," I venture, stepping into his view.

He pulls the headphones off, letting them rest on his collarbone. "Hey there. Did you sleep ok?"

"I think so." I say honestly, "I don't even remember laying down, just waking up."

He smiles.

"What's that?" I ask, pointing at the cup on his desk.

His eyes are wide. "You're kidding, right?"

I shrug.

"They really do torture you over there, don't they?" He takes the cup by the handle and places it in my hand as though it were a precious jewel. "This, my sweet girl, is called coffee. Also known as liquid gold. The nectar of the gods. Call it what you want, but I couldn't survive long without it." He's making wild hand gestures and I get the immediate sense that this guy doesn't have a single serious bone in his body.

It's hot, but not too hot that it burns my tongue. My first reaction is it's bitter and I must make a face because Liam says, "There's sugar over there if you want to add some. Lots of people do that."

I'm not sure what time it is when Knox and Cash come out of the room, but I've been sitting here next to Liam, listening in to enemy radio for at least an hour. They're still searching for us. They seem to have widened their perimeter, but Liam assures me we are well outside those boundaries for now, and well-hidden anyways. I'm happy to listen to him drone on about military protocol and radio waves so I don't have to think of anything else.

"What are you two doing out here?" Ethan asks, coming over to stand by my side.

"Don't get jealous, she's all yours. Smells like a dead fish anyways."

My face is hot, the blush spreading all the way to my temples.

"That was a joke!" Liam says, giving my shoulder a playful shove. "But seriously, you do need a shower, I'm pretty sure a bird just nested in your hair."

"Quit being an asshole." Knox says to him, holding out a hand for me to stand up, "Unless of course you want to get punched."

I can tell they're joking, there's no urgency in their expression, no real fire in their eyes.

He's put his headphones back on, takes what's left of his third cup of coffee and drains it in one gulp. "Lighten up. You're both alive, right? Start living a little."

"SAY HI TO the boss man for me!" Liam is calling after us as we climb the stairs. We've showered, if you can call splashing yourself with water from the sink a shower. We've eaten, if canned beans and coffee count as adequate food consumption. And now we're dressed in simple clothes found in the dresser drawers of an upstairs bedroom in the house.

"Nervous?" Knox asks me.

I understand what he means, and I am. Who wouldn't be nervous to meet a mother they didn't know they had? It doesn't feel right. How can I remember Knox, but I can't remember the woman who gave birth to me? A swarm of butterflies has migrated to my stomach. "I'm fine."

"So how far is this place?" Cash asks, jogging to catch up as we pass through the hole behind the fridge.

"A couple hours' drive."

"We're driving?"

Ethan takes us around back of the house where an old truck huddles under an overhang. It's rusted from hood to tailgate. Wooden planks fence in the back and one of the headlights is smashed. He jumps in the driver's side and turns a key in the ignition. The engine sputters at first, but it starts. Guess that answers his question.

"Get in," Knox says, shifting over to make room in the cab.

"After you."

I get in first, squishing up against Ethan, Cash piles in after me.

"Isn't this dangerous?" I ask him, "Won't they be able to see us on the road?"

He shifts the metal beast into drive and sets his hand on my knee. Cash notices and turns his eyes out the window, flexing his jaw. "This is no man's land. They don't usually come out this far. We'll stick to the back-roads for a while anyways."

He looks at his hand on my knee, looks into my eyes. An unspoken question is legible in the fine print of his stare, he seems to ask, *is this okay?*

I give him a small smile and he takes it as a *yes*, turning his focus back to the winding road ahead. I'm not sure if I understand this new feeling. It's something I've only read about. Now that the words are more than an imagination, more than just letters printed on paper to elicit a specific emotion, I'm not sure if this is real or right. He makes me feel safe. Sort of. But also, unsafe in a way I can't describe. He makes my heart beat faster and my body ache with the desire to be touched.

Studying his features from the cover my lashes, I take in his strong jawline. The way that you can still sort of see his dimples even when he's not smiling. The way his hair shines copper in the sunlight. His lips part and I have the sudden urge to touch them.

Cash elbows me in the ribs, whispers over the clamor of the engine, "Why don't you take a picture, it'll last longer."

I jump in my seat. Glare at him. The embarrassment staining my cheeks all sorts of unflattering colors makes me squirm in my seat. "You know what, I'm glad he punched you. I hope it hurt," I say, not too quietly.

Knox is laughing, a laugh that starts somewhere deep in his belly, his eyes are gleaming. "Shit Jo, did I miss something?" He has to stop talking to laugh some more. "Remind me not to piss you off, love."

EIGHTEEN

WE'VE BEEN DRIVING for about an hour when I notice the landscape has changed. I pull my head from the clouds and sit up a little taller. We've left the wilderness. The streets here are paved, small buildings and dilapidated houses dot the sides of the road. Old power lines hang limp and lifeless from their weathered posts, and a few stray cats chase each other through overgrown hedges. It's so quiet, it's as though we could be the only people left on this earth.

Knox is telling us about where he's taking us, "It's a refugee compound." He says, "We call it, 'The Inn.'"

The Inn houses upwards of one hundred people, young and old. Some escaped the institutions, and some are families; mothers, fathers, and their children who fled before their babies were born, unwilling to give them up. The one thing they have in common is that they were found by scouts The Inn sent out and given refuge within the walls of their compound.

The New Terra Alliance has been collecting O-Negative children for almost fifty years now. There's a mandatory blood test whenever a baby is born. If they're found to have O-Negative type blood, they're 'confiscated.' Their blood and organs keep the rest of humanity alive while scientists try to find another means for a cure, but, "They stopped looking," Ethan tells us, "And after almost fifty years of searching, of testing, they decided there was no cure.

"The institutions are a show. They're designed for one purpose, to keep you placated, focused until you've reached your full growth potential."

He's ripping bandages full of infection and lies from my mind, but I only feel more and more sick.

His hand tightens around the wheel, knuckles turning white. "Well that and somebody decided it was *inhumane* to harvest a child. As if the instant you turn eighteen you become an adult and that somehow makes it okay." He laughs, and it's a pained sound, full of anger and sorrow.

"But there's a cure. My mom found it. Right?" I say, confused now.

He sighs, "It's not exactly a cure." He meets my eyes for an instant, imploring me to understand. "The cure Amy—er, your mom, developed still needs some work. It only has about a sixty percent survival rate. We dropped her findings at a lab run by the NTA, to the attention of an old friend of your mom's, but I doubt they even looked at it."

"Why the hell not?" Cash asks, eyes accusing. "That doesn't make any sense, if there was even a chance, they'd look at it."

"You don't understand this world we're living in. Amy is a fugitive, we all are, why would they listen to us?" He's visibly shaking. "We lost one of our own getting them that information. Since you're so smart," Knox says, glaring at Cash, "you tell me why they didn't listen. You tell me why they're still killing teenagers by the hundreds."

We're quiet after that.

Lost, that's how I feel. Ethan has driven word after word into my mind, and its chaos. It's a traffic jam of thoughts with no off-ramp out of the boisterous stand-still. They kill people. They're murderers. People live like that? People give up their children for the so-called 'greater good,' no questions asked, no fighting for what's right. They relent. *Weak.* That's what I think. This government, the NTA, has bred a nation of cowards too hell-bent on surviving that they'd give up their own children for slaughter.

I think of Danny, of her boyfriend or boy *friend* Greg. He didn't get sick, he didn't leave her hanging. He may have kept his promise to her if he could've. But, no. He's been bled, harvested and incinerated. There isn't even a headstone for him somewhere. He's gone. I cringe thinking about what that will do to Danny when she finds out.

We turn onto another street and follow the road through a tunnel under a bridge. I'm about to ask Knox more about the plan. About how we're supposed to save the others when all thought of the NTA and the institutions is flung from my mind.

A white van speeds out from the right at the end of the tunnel, its sides smeared with red paint. Antlers jut out from its front grill. It grinds to a dead stop in front of us. A screech from behind us and I can see in the rear-view mirror that another car, black with the same red paint is blocking us in.

The side door of the van opens and five people jump out, holding big guns, aiming them at us. They aren't NTA. Tattered clothing hangs from their bodies, two aren't wearing respirators, two have hair formed into lengths of matted cords, and the last is a woman. She has eyes like the devil and hair as red as a seven o'clock sun.

"Get out!" She yells and her men fan out around us, rifles trained on our windows, inching closer.

My body has gone rigid, fingernails digging into the bottom of my seat. *No. No this isn't happening.* I didn't escape to die now, to watch my friends die with me. Cash is ducking down, looking as if he's trying to disappear into his seat. Ethan stares at them, his eyes jerking to each of the men around us, seeming to analyze each one.

"Who are they?" I breathe. They're drawing closer, only a few meters from us now, but the shadows of the tunnel under the bridge hide us well enough. I don't think they can see my lips moving.

I watch as Ethan moves his right hand under his seat, watch as he pulls a slick black gun out from under it. He places it into my lap. The weight of what it implies is crushing. "The Exiled," he whispers, the words laced with poison, pulling another gun out of the holster at his hip. "Scum who were thrown out of the cities for their crimes." His hand hovers over the shifter. "When I say, you both need to get down."

"We'll shoot!" One man hollers from the right.

The woman advances from the front, holding her gun

out, eyes wild. "If you get out now, perhaps we will let you live," she says, an unusual lilt to her speech.

"NOW!" Ethan yells and punches the truck into reverse. My hands instinctively clutch the gun in my lap and Cash and I throw our bodies forward, bending so the dash and doors form a barrier to the bullets. Gunfire is all around us, the reverberations shaking our seats as each one hits the truck. I'm thrown back as Ethan rams the car behind us.

"Get down!" He throws the shifter forward and the tires screech as we barrel headlong back through the tunnel.

"BRACE!" Ethan says as a bullet cracks the windshield and another blows the side mirror clean off. I hold onto the seat just in time for him to ram the rear end of the van. I see it spin off the road into the concrete and he keeps driving, aiming his gun out the window firing two shots. I sit up and whip my head back, expecting to see bodies in the wake of his bullets, but he's shot out the van's tires instead.

He pushes the old pickup to its limits, the engine protesting in roaring distress. They're still firing at us as three of them climb into the mangled car, barreling down the road after us.

"They're chasing us!" I'm yelling, my heart slamming against my ribcage.

Cash is still folded over, hugging his knees. "What do they want?"

Knox's eyes are trained on the rear-view, only looking away for seconds at a time to keep us on the road. "They're scavengers. They'll take everything we have."

"Well let's give it to them!" Cash says, and I notice a

trace of tears in his eyes, his voice is unsteady. I'm wondering what happened to the sarcastic tough guy I had made him out to be, wondering when he became this weaker version of himself…

"It's not that simple you idiot! It's not just stuff that they want. They don't play by the same rules."

They're gaining on us now and the road ahead is open, with fields of dying wheat for miles, all but barren. There's nowhere to run.

The gunfire starts again and I duck in time as a bullet shatters the glass behind my head. It explodes around the cabin, leaving small lacerations on my arms and legs.

"*Damn it!*" Cash cries, ducking even lower in his seat.

Ethan unbuckles his seat belt. "Take the wheel," he tells me and I must look as terrified as I feel because his eyes soften, "You can do this."

I nod, holstering the gun in the waistband of my jeans like Ethan did when we escaped, lean over to take hold of the wheel. He turns in his seat and leans out the window. He's shooting at them and I can hear the *chink* of bullets hitting metal on both sides and I pray that none of those bullets hit him. I pray if anyone gets out of this alive that it's him. He's the sort of person meant to survive in this world. I'm just a girl who's never even held a gun.

I keep the truck as steady as I can, ducking low enough to have the illusion of safety, but only so much so that I can still see the road. The growl of the engine in the car behind us is getting louder, closer. Too close. It rams us from behind. Knox is thrown back into the cab, knocking my arms away from the steering wheel. The truck careens off the road into the wheat fields. The tires chew the earth, spitting up loose dirt behind us until the truck stops dead, teetering to one side.

It takes less than a second for Ethan to reach over both me and Cash and open the door, "Run!" He says, every muscle in his body tense, his eyes betray no sign of fear, only an apology.

I look out the door, see a barn in the distance, turn back to Ethan. "No."

Cash is already out the door. "Come on Jo!"

I'm pulling the gun from my waistband, not moving from where I sit. Trying to appear strong, trying to seem as if I'm not ready to collapse in fear.

"Joanna, *get out*," Knox says so harshly that each syllable of his words sting my flesh. "Now."

I pull my mouth closed, grind my teeth together.

"Get the hell out of here!" He yells at me.

Somehow, I'm out of the truck and I don't even remember how I got here. Cash is pulling on my arm. Ethan is putting a new clip into his gun, cocking it back.

He puts his hand on the handle of his door, "Take care of her." He says to Cash, not sparing me another glance, "And keep heading east."

And then he's gone. Running through the field. Running into the fray.

NINETEEN

IT'S SO QUIET, too quiet. The only sound is our heavy breathing and the swooshing sound of dead wheat stalks as we squeeze through them. I've taken one hundred and eighty-eight running steps away from where we left the truck. I'm counting because it's the only way I can keep focused, the only way I can keep going and not turn around.

We're running east like he told us, keeping the barn in the distance to our right. Cash is slowing and I almost run into his backside.

"What are you doing?" I hiss, out of breath, unable to contain the panicked fury running through my body, causing my fingers to twitch. "Don't stop." But it's not the stopping I'm afraid of, it's the thought that if I stop I won't be able to start going again.

"We should go to that barn. Catch our breath, form some sort of plan. If Knox gets away, he won't be able to find us."

I hate how he says *if*, I hate how he's giving credence to the thought we might not see him again. He knows as well as I do without Ethan we have no idea where we're going, that we could wander east for days and never find The Inn.

It doesn't matter now.

"What? Stop there and hide?" I'm in awe of his utter stupidity, "That's exactly where they think we'll go." I throw my hands up. "And that's exactly where they'll be able to find us."

His eyes are pleading. "Then what do you propose we do?"

"Keep—" a gunshot fires in the distance behind us. Then another, the sounds echoing around us like some twisted song.

I'm running. I can hear Cash yelling after me. Begging me to stop, telling me to come back, but I'm not listening and his voice gets further away.

Their voices are becoming clearer as I near the road. I can hear an engine running somewhere close by. I slow my pace, gripping the weapon in my hand, keeping my finger near the trigger, but not on it. The mingled feelings of power and dread coursing through me from holding the weapon are revolting. Considering the length of smooth metal, I realize I haven't slightest idea how to use it. There are big guns and small guns, that I do know, and they have bullets in them that shatter lives.

I hope it doesn't come to that.

"Where are the others?" The woman yells.

I crouch lower in the grass, creep closer, careful not to

make a sound. I can see the road through the reeds, see their bodies flashing in and out of view. They're only a pocketful of meters away. My breath is coming in hitched gasps and I fervently work to quiet it.

I inch closer. Move to the left where their car sits diagonally beside the brush. I move as close as I dare, using its size to shield me from view.

The woman is standing with her back to me. A man lies dead and bloody next to her. She is facing Ethan. He's on his knees, his hands hovering a couple inches off the ground. Another man with enough girth to swallow a piglet whole holds him there with a firm grip on his shoulder, his fingers digging in. Ethan is sizing up the gun holstered on the man's thigh out of the corner of his eye.

Don't, I think, imagining too many scenarios where he grabs that gun and they all end up with him dead.

"Where are they?" She yells again.

Ethan spits at her, the saliva falls short of its mark, landing unceremoniously in front of her weathered black boots. The man holding him swings his long gun, landing the butt of it into Ethan's ribs. He cries out. The woman points her gun at his head.

I explode. I'm up and around the car in a millisecond. I'm too fast for them to react. I plant my gun into the back of the woman's skull, pressing on her fiery red hair. My whole body shakes, but I force my gun hand to remain still.

She drops her gun immediately, hands up in the air.

Knox's eyes register shock for a split second before he uses the commotion to his advantage. He pivots, pulling the man's gun out of its holster at his thigh. Not wasting another instant, he fires. The shot barrels a hole through the man's skull, cutting up from under his jaw. A stomach-turning mist of red erupts from the exit wound into the breeze. It's all I can do to keep my gun pointed straight and not expel the contents of my stomach onto the woman's back.

Knox is on his feet, he spins, his weapon now trained on the woman.

"Stop," I shout before I can even make sense of what's happening. I don't want anyone else to die.

He ignores me. His sights fixated on the woman in front of him. Her shoulders shake with laughter and I'm thinking she must be insane.

"She may not have shot you, but I will."

"No Ethan, stop!"

"Joanna.." he growls. "Move away." He puts his finger on the trigger. "She'll follow us. I'm sure her *minions* are not far behind now, they'll probably be here any minute."

The woman is still laughing. I wish she would shut up. "I know who you are." She says between bursts of laughter. "You are the rogue soldier and your friend here is one of the ones who escaped The Mill."

"You know nothing about me," I say, forgetting for the moment I owe this woman no explanation.

She lowers her hands a few inches, "You got out just in time."

Ethan closes the gap between them in a flash, leaving two—one foot of space between his gun and her face. "And what exactly," he breathes, "do you mean by that?"

I've lowered my gun now, the ache in my arm the only trace of memory left that I may have shot it.

She's stopped laughing. "Oh, you have not heard." She

says, sounding amused, "Some soldier you are."

"Talk!" Knox bellows.

"They have changed the age requirement for harvest. Too many smart children figuring out what's going on behind the curtain." Her accent is so strong it's difficult for me to understand, but not so difficult that I can't grasp what she's telling us. What I don't understand, is *why* she's telling us.

My lungs collapse, orange spots obscure my vision. *They what?*

"*Seize*. Sixteen." She says simply as if it was the most normal thing in the world. As if she didn't tell us something so repulsive it makes my skin itch. "They have been building another harvest plant. They will enforce the new law next month."

Knox has gone pale. "*Enough!*" His finger moves to squeeze the trigger and I do the only thing I can think to stop this madness.

I ram the heel of my gun as hard as I can into the back of the woman's head. She slumps to the ground, unconscious, but at least she isn't dead. Enough people have died today.

Dropping the gun, I fall to my knees, weaker than I've ever felt in my life.

Knox kneels in front of me, puts two fingers under my chin. "I'm sorry," he says, and I'm not sure why he's sorry but I nod anyways, unable to meet his eyes. He saved us, but two men lie dead at our feet. Their lives for ours. It doesn't feel right. He picks up my gun, inspecting it before he slips it into the back of his waistband.

"It helps to have the safety off if you want to shoot

someone, right?"

I wretch into the dirt at the side of the road and when I'm finished Ethan lifts me up and tucks me into the backseat of the Exiled's car. It smells faintly of alcohol and sweat, making me want to throw up again.

"Joanna?" A voice calls from the wheat fields, Cash emerges, his movements jerky, looking like he's seen a ghost.

I don't answer him. I don't have the strength for words.

"Get. In. The. Car." Ethan orders him, enunciating every word.

TWENTY

"WE'RE HERE."

Across from us is only one building that stands out. Off-white pillars stand tall in the entrance and the doors behind are wide panes of glass. A patch of green, overgrown with shrubbery and littered with specks of discarded tin and other trash is in the middle of the roundabout driveway. I rub the sleep out of my eyes, unsure of how long I've been out, how long we've been driving. The afternoon sun reflects off the sign on top of the building, it reads *Holiday Inn Hotel.*

"And where is here exactly?" Cash, asks, looking a little green.

Knox sighs at Cash's attempted sarcasm. "Home."

Pulling around to the back of the building, we park in a row of other vehicles, all pockmarked with rust and coated with a film of dirt. Knox turns the key back and the car rumbles to a stand-still, but the vibrations are still coursing through me.

Past the door marked, 'employees only,' there is a dingy hallway filled with a haze of sunlight that traps the dust in its net. We enter a stairwell and begin descending downward. My legs are like stilts, propelling me too far from the ground, my head lives in the clouds. A strange numbness seeps into my blood, buries itself in my bones. Knox offers me an encouraging smile. I can't return the sentiment, can't smooth the crease in my forehead. I'm lightheaded, and so tired I can hardly keep my eyes open.

Over the course of a week, I've left the only home I remember, lost my best friend, found out the world as I've known it was a façade, could've been killed by The Exiled, oh and that I have a mother. The walls of my life, the bricks I've placed each day that make up who I am have come crashing down around me. Strangely, I'm not afraid, or sad, or any of the emotions I would imagine a person to have in this situation. I've been cheated out of a normal life, tricked, betrayed, lied to and drugged.

I'm *furious*.

It's odd, there's a peace to the anger, a numbness that settles over the surface of a fire building below. With only the slightest provocation, I might explode. Even the claustrophobia that would normally plague me in such an enclosed space has evaporated.

Knox jars to a stop at the bottom of the stairs. Cash stumbles forward, looking greener than ever. Knox takes my respirator and places it in a bin in the corner. "Ready?" He asks, his stature strong, sure, his jaw set, his eyes relay messages of reassurance, sympathy. You'd never think he killed a man not more than a couple hours ago.

A shiver rolls up my neck, making me simultaneously hot and cold at once. "As ready as I'll ever be."

We step out into another world. There are people, young and old, milling around an open space. Couches and chairs line the walls; a long table sits in the center where people are looking at what appear to be blueprints. The air smells of bleach and lemon. Within the space of a single breath, they stop what they're doing. Their eyes meet mine, each displaying shock, excitement, and another emotion I can't place. A girl who was sitting in the corner bolts from the room, the papers she was working so diligently on left scattered on the table.

"Everyone, this is Joanna," Knox says, pride evident in his voice. "And this is Cash."

The stunned stupor of a moment ago fades in an instant, their faces break into wide smiles.

A guy in his late-twenties, I'm guessing, and built like a pickup truck moves across the room and offers me his hand. "Name's Ace," he says, eyes wrinkled with joy. "Glad you made it home."

Home?

"Amy is going to lose her shit!" A girl says, wrapping her arms around me. "I'm Erica." And then to Cash, "Hey hot-stuff, you're looking a tad pale, why don't you come sit down." He follows her without a word, slumping into a chair at the table.

"Is he?" She asks Knox. *Is he infected* is what she's implying, I can tell by the sudden fear that freezes her in place.

"Motion sickness I think, but keep your distance, they'll both need to be tested."

She exhales, slumping into the seat beside him, edging it a few inches further away.

It's like this for what can only be a few minutes, strangers telling me their names, shaking my hand. I offer them small smiles and say little. My hands have begun to shake, breathing seems like a chore. One by one they greet me, a line of dominos falling at my feet. Their names swirl around inside my skull until I'm not sure I can remember my own anymore.

"Oh whoa, back off," Knox says, his voice laced with worry. He pulls me to him, cupping my face in his hands. He pulls away as if stung. "Jo, you're burning up." He looks like he might puke. I might join him.

A woman darts into the room, her white lab coat swirling around her hips. Dark hair is spilling out from a loose bun on top of her head. Her skin is pale, brown eyes wide, brimming with tears.

She looks at me. Doesn't say a word, stoic still, a look of anguished joy on her face. My heart feels like its beating through sludge. My fingers have gone numb, tingly. Knox is working harder to hold me up. I register him pulling my arm around his neck, supporting my weight with his. *What's happening to me?* People stop advancing to say hello, instead, they back away very slowly, smiles disintegrating.

I hear someone yell at the others to get out. And someone else calls for someone to fetch the respirators.

Only Knox and the woman remain. All at once the joy vanishes from her face, replaced with a fear so intense it'd be impossible not to return the feeling. "Joanna.." She says, her voice strangled.

I move my lips to answer her, to answer this woman who reminds me so much of someone I know, but I can't. Someone's turned out the light in my world and I don't want them to turn it back on.

TWENTY-ONE

THE DARKNESS STRETCHES on for miles. It claws at me with talons of heat and a biting cold that sears my flesh. There are lights out of reach and voices speaking in disjointed echoes. Someone has glued my eyes shut, stuffed cotton in my ears and dried up my insides. I'm powerless to stop the waves of pain coursing through my body, so I lie here in quiet agony, wherever *here* is, somewhere between awake and asleep.

There is a sharp stabbing pain to the back of my hand. "It's alright," a woman says, "You're going to be fine." There is a conviction in her words but I think she knows it's false.

Even in my fevered stupor, I can piece together what's happening, I have contracted the virus. TEN. That's the number of days I have left to live. If I'm lucky it'll take me faster. If I'm very lucky, the cure will work on me too like it worked for Knox, but a nagging suspicion in the back of my mind whispers, *there is no cure.* It also whispers dark things, terrifying things, as if there is another voice in my head. *This is your end. You are mine,* it echoes in the abyss of my torment, as if the virus is a living thing, with hands and teeth and the voice of psychopath.

Hallucinations. This is stage three. That's what that voice is. It's not real.

I am *real,* it says.

I cringe.

Footsteps, someone is coming. "Is she going to live?" Cash asks.

A crashing sound, broken bits of something rain onto a hard surface. "If she dies, you had better start running." Knox, it must be him, but there is so much pain in his words, so much malice. I'm afraid he might not give Cash the chance to run at all, afraid he might shoot him right where he stands.

Footsteps retreating.

"Ethan, this wasn't his fault. There's no one to blame. It could have easily been that boy lying here—" The woman says, a beacon of calm in the storm.

"What are you saying? That's your *daughter* Amy! I told him to take care of her. I told him to make sure nothing happened to her."

"The virus doesn't discriminate, you can understand that as well as anyone."

The voices become farther away until they're only garbled noises in the distance.

I'M RUNNING. Someone is chasing me. I weave between the trees, leap over fallen branches. They're gaining on me but I can't go any faster. There's only the moonlight to see by. I look back, I see him. No, I see it; a mass of shadow the size of a man, moving through the forest without a sound. My breath comes in labored pants as I push myself harder. I nearly run into something. An obscure shape hangs from a tree. My heart stops, stomach-turning. Bodies. There are bodies hanging from the trees. Dianna, Ethan, Cash, Amy, Ace, the other people from The Inn, Danny, Sophie.

It's too much. Tears stream from my eyes, blur my vision. I blink them away, force myself to run through the pain. The Shadow Man is on my heels, and I have a mind to let him take me. I almost stop, but see a break in the trees, an edge to the ground I'm running on. A cliff. I see my chance. To die how I choose, not how it *wants me to, and I take it. I jump. My arms open on my sides like wings and I relish every second of the long fall. I don't know what lies at the bottom, my eyes are shut, welcoming the end.*

Open your eyes, *the shadow hisses inside my head,* you're a coward, *it says,* open your eyes!

An awful sound assaults my ears, it's a shrill, blaring, broken sound.

"Open your eyes!" Someone urges.

The sound is coming from me. I manage to make it stop, manage to peel my eyelids back enough for the lights above me to scorch them. I'm lying on a soft bed, a beeping sound pulses from somewhere to my right. There's a man near the end of my bed, but my eyes are filled with a glue-like substance and I can't quite make him out.

"Cash, get Amy! Knox, say something to her,' the man says.

The vague shape of a face appears above me, blocking

the light enough that I can open my eyes a little more.

"Jo." His green eyes are gentle, they welcome me into their calm waters. "Jo, wake up, it's me." His eyes are filling with tears, his jaw is hard, straining with the effort of holding them back. "You're alright. It's over now." He brushes the hair from my face, his touch cool against my cheek. "I'm going to take care of you."

"How?" I don't recognize my voice, it's rough and frayed like the edges of a cloth. *How am I alive,* is what I meant to say, but my throat is like sandpaper and the words can't scrape past.

He smiles, understanding what I'm trying to ask. "The same way as me."

So, it is real. The cure. It saved Ethan and now it's saved me as well. I'm warm but no longer scorching, the pain is all but gone from my body. Only a throbbing remains in my head and a weakness borne of too many hours spent without food or consciousness. I wonder how long I've been in and out of the suffocating blanket of darkness.

"Joanna," she says as she enters the room, a tentative smile drawing up the corners of her mouth. *Amy,* my mother. She crosses the room, her steps careful, measured, as if she's afraid the floor might open and swallow her whole.

Knox moves away and she takes his chair beside the bed. I count the seconds of silence that pass between us.

I try. I try to remember her, but only manage to capture a few glimpses of memories before the rest flit away. A woman tying my shoes, brushing my hair, twirling me around a living room filled with warm colors and shelves of books. Then I remember her eyes, deep brown with a light hazel inside, fringed with thick black lashes. I remember those eyes smiling at me in a memory so far back in my subconscious I'm not even sure if it's real or if I've created it myself.

She exhales a gust of carbon dioxide, seeming to blow out her tensions with it. A sense of peace washes the unease out of my mind. "Thank you," I say awkwardly, not knowing how to begin.

My mother smiles. "Welcome back."

TWENTY-TWO

IT'S BEEN THREE days since I woke up. My mom comes each day to tell me a bit more about the life I've forgotten and the life I've now stumbled into. My name is Joanna Rose Claymore, and I was never meant to be in the institutions.

She's known since I was born I was O-Negative. She also knew that by the laws of the New Terra Alliance she had to give me up to further the lifespan of humanity. But she couldn't. *Wouldn't,* is what she said. She falsified my blood test. She's an incredible pathologist Ethan tells me, so I'm sure that was an easy feat to accomplish.

She told no one. If ever I was ill, she took care of it herself, having had experience in the field of medicine. I never saw the inside of a medical center, never attended a daycare, and never left my house unless escorted by my mother by the sounds of it. It only took one mistake and I was taken away. She told me, hands shaking as she recalled the happenings of such a day as one to scar her forever.

She had to go away, only for a day, to investigate a case of the virus that had somehow miraculously healed itself. That day she left me with her neighbor, a woman she trusted wholeheartedly, but who didn't know the secret hidden in my blood.

I was hurt, badly. The neighbor, not knowing what would lie in the aftermath of her actions, did the only thing she thought she could. She took me to the medical center. I needed a blood transfusion.

They tested my blood type.

I never came home.

The neighbor reached my mother in time to warn her before the authorities. She had no choice. She fled, never to return to the home where she raised me.

"It was all I could do," she told me, trying to make me understand, her eyes pleading. "I was just one person. I wanted to find you, to get you back, but it was too late. You were in the system."

All of it is so strange. I expected to be elated, buoyant even when I finally met my mother. I expected to find a place where my misshapen puzzle piece of a soul would finally fit. I wanted it to be like coming home. And it does. And it doesn't.

I don't know how to be a daughter.

I asked her about my father, wondering why she never mentioned him, why no one ever mentioned him. That was when her expression changed, her forehead creased, her hands balled into fists beside me. It was at that moment that a younger woman in a lab coat came into the room and asked my mother for her help with something.

He must be dead. The virus has claimed so many lives. Why not the life of my father?

A knock at the door and Ethan walks in. He's wearing a tight-fitting black tee shirt and tapered blue jeans. The scruff I had grown accustomed to seeing on his face has been shaved off, leaving his jawline looking smooth and defined. "Hey."

"I need to get out of this room."

Three meals a day have been brought in for me, and about three times a day the doctor—who is Ethan's father I've found out—comes to test my vitals. For three days, I've been staring at the same walls. I'm sick of three's. I'm sick of this bed, and I'm sick of being useless. It's time to get up. Get out. It's time to make a plan, to fight back.

"Slow down love, we should probably check with the doc."

"No, I'm fine," I say, too harshly. Calming myself, I say as nicely as I can, "I need to move, I need to help."

His eyes chastise me, and I have to hold back the urge to scream at him. "You need to rest."

"It's been three days Ethan." I roll my eyes. "Tell me what's going on. Have you come up with a plan? We still need to get everyone else out of that place."

He squints his eyes at me, a smirk playing at the corner of his mouth. "We? What's this 'we' business? You have *zero* training. You're staying right here."

"Then train me."

"Train you?"

"Yes, that's what I said."

He sighs, runs a hand through his tousled hair. "Ok, let's take a walk. See if you can manage that first."

I snort, practically leaping out of bed, hiding the slight wobble in my step, give him a look that says, *I told you I'm fine.*

He shakes his head, appraises me from tip to toe, "You look ridiculous in that hospital gown. How about you put some clothes on first." He gestures to a pile of neatly folded clothes sitting on a tall table beside the bathroom. I try not to meet his eyes as I walk over to pick it up, acutely aware of how the thin material covering my body is blowing open above my tailbone, cool air licking up my lower back.

"I'll wait outside." he says and I hear the door shut behind him.

TWENTY-THREE

ETHAN APPRAISES ME as I fall into stride next to him, smiles wide. And it's odd. I've only known him for thirteen days and somehow there is already an undeniable connection between us. There is an ease to our friendship, a comfort I have yet to find anywhere else, except perhaps with Dianna. It's a stark contrast to the awkward tension between me and the woman I now know to be my mother.

She's come every day to my little room, telling me things about her work and about how she and Ethan's dad started the whole movement here at The Inn. She never tells me anything I'm truly curious about, like if my father is still alive or what's happening outside. I don't tell her what it was like to grow up in the institutions. She doesn't ask me and I don't ask her. The way she reacted the last time I asked about my father tells me it's not a subject she's ready to talk about. So, though the air is filled with words between us, it's also filled with unasked and unanswered questions, leaving it stale and empty.

"Hungry?" Knox asks me as we walk by a room filled with people, the smells of burnt butter and something sweet coiling around us.

I shake my head, my stomach rebelling against the scent and the idea of eating. "Not at all," I say, noticing Cash sitting with a group of girls at a table in the far corner of the room.

"What's Cash been up to?"

"He's taken over as the resident asshat, flirting with all the girls. There's a rumor going around that he saved us both," he chuckles, looking amused, and now I'm laughing too, a little guilty for it.

"Is that so?"

"Yep."

"You going to set the record straight?"

"No." He shrugs. "I figure it'll blow up in his face, eventually."

"You get that it wasn't his fault, right?"

"What?"

"Me losing my respirator and leaving him to come back for you when the Exiled found us. It wasn't his fault. Those were my choices. He couldn't have stopped me even if he'd tried."

"Well, he should've tried."

I shake my head. "Just let it go. He may be a lot of things, but he isn't stupid. He knew what was going on before I ever did. If it wasn't for him, I may not have ever listened to what you had to say."

He says nothing, opting instead to stare down the hallway in brooding silence.

"Hey," I say, grabbing his arm. "I trust you now. I trust you more than I think I've ever trusted anyone before."

"You don't have to do that. You don't have to try to make me feel better," he says, eyes light again.

"Well don't look so damn morose." I lightly punch his arm and he can't hide his grin.

I haven't been paying attention to where we were headed so when Ethan's dad walks up to us I pull away from him, feeling guilty of something.

"Dad," Knox says, seemingly surprised as well.

"Ethan," he says in greeting, turning to me. "How are you? I was coming to check on you." Ethan's dad is the resident doctor. He's been poking and prodding me for days. He has a wide chest like Ethan does, with lighter hair and a perpetual smile that never touches his eyes. There's a pain there that I'm afraid is so deep-rooted, it can never be extracted.

"I'm great," I lie, though the more I walk around, the stronger I feel. "Thank you for all your help."

He wasps the sentiment away. "Always happy to help. Take it easy for a couple more days, lots of fluids, you'll be right as rain by week's end. I'd like to speak with you after you get settled in and run some simple tests. The cure Amy gave you can have some strange side-effects, nothing to worry about right now, but do tell me if you experience anything odd."

I nod, wondering what sort of side-effects I should expect, but minor headaches or nausea are the least of my worries right now.

"Ok, I will."

He smiles, gives me a tight nod. Something haunts this

man. He looks as though he's ready to go sleep and never wake up. Dianna would have said he's just 'going through the motions'.

Then it hits me. Dianna is his wife. She's been away from him, working in the Institute for years. That might account for the pain I see in him. I make a mental note to ask Ethan why that is. Why his father is safe away from the confines of a twisted government while his mother has relegated her life to prison.

"Ethan, I know I didn't say it before, but I should say it now, I'm proud of you," Charles says, and I suddenly feel like I'm eavesdropping. Ethan looks mildly shocked. I see his shoulders tense. "You made it right. After all this time. Now your mother can finally come home." And then again, "I'm proud of you." His hand falls on Knox's shoulder, squeezes it, before he walks away.

Knox is silent and still for too long, I think I see a threat of tears in his eyes, but then it's gone and he's walking again.

"What did he mean by that?" I ask, realizing too late I'm prying into matters that are none of my business.

He clears his throat. "Something about my Mom, don't worry about it."

"When's the last time you saw her?"

"Hmm?"

"Your mom."

"Oh," he says, coming back to the present, "Um, a couple of months ago, but my Dad, he hasn't seen her in years."

"Is she–I mean, is she coming here?" I can't hide the need, the excitement in my voice. I miss Dianna more than

I could say. It would be so much easier, be more *right* if she were here with me.

"She was supposed to leave after you and the others were carted to The Mill. If everything went as planned she should be on her way here right now. We've been sending out scouts every night to see if we can find any trace of her. I went out myself last night, but I didn't find anything."

"Could I go with you next time?"

He shakes his head, "No, you need to recover."

"When I get better, then?"

He doesn't answer. Sighs.

When we come to a fork in the hallway, he pulls me to the left, but there's something to the right, someone coughing. At the very end of the hallway, and around the corner, there's a light on, throwing its glow onto the wall. It looks like the light is shining though bars.

"What's over there?"

"You don't want to go down there. In fact," he says, taking my elbow to guide me in the other direction. "That hallway is off limits, and if you have to go down it keep walking."

I stop mid-step, forcing him to stop with me. "Who's down there?"

"Joanna."

"No. I'm sick of the secrets and being lied to. If you won't tell me then I'll go see for myself."

I can tell he's suppressing the urge to roll his eyes at me. "Why do you have to be so damned difficult?"

My eyes widen. "Why can't you be honest with me?"

He's taken aback, the muscles in his jaw tense. He won't look me in the eyes. Finally, he tells me. "It's one of the Exiled."

"One of the–what? Why?"

He struggles to stay calm. "He got in while I was away. My dad found him scavenging for food and supplies upstairs. He gave himself up, didn't fight."

"So… what? You guys are going to keep him here?"

"For now."

A part of me knows how this will end. They can't let him go. They'll have to kill him. And maybe that's the best thing, even if it doesn't seem like the right thing.

"So, can we go now?" He asks, turning to continue down the hall.

The inside of the room is an open space. There are large sacks hanging from the ceilings and some equipment for weight training in the corner. In the middle is a big white circle painted onto the floor. The floor itself is springy, like a hard sponge.

Inside the ring, there are two people fighting. One of them I recognize to be Ace, the first one to introduce himself when we first got here. Their skin is shiny and slick with sweat and their eyes are hard, focused as they grapple and swing and kick at one another. I have half a mind to turn around and go back the way I came, but Ethan puts a light hand on my lower back and the small gesture makes me stronger and weaker all at once. *I need to do this.*

"You said you wanted to be trained," he says.

"Let's go before I change my mind."

He laughs.

"Ace!" Ethan yells, and four eyes turn towards us, the fight forgotten for the moment.

"Oh man!" Ace laughs, throwing his gloves off. "Has

the great Ethan Knox come to see the show, or are you here to join in? I wouldn't mind a quick throw down, you know, for old times' sake." His eyes are sparkling. "You even brought an audience!" Ace stops in front of us, "Glad you're feeling better." He nods in my direction.

I nod back.

"I'm not here to kick your ass," Ethan says. "Joanna wants to train."

Ace's eyes widen. "No shit."

I construct the most serious face I can muster. "I need to know how to fire a gun. I need to know how to protect myself."

He nods, thin lips puckering, considering. "Okay," he says. "Okay, grab some gloves, let's see what you got." He points to a supply closet beside the door.

I freeze, lightheaded. The sickness still lingering in my bones pulses, more dominant in an instant.

Ethan steps in. "She just got out of bed today man. We'll come back in a few days. I wanted to make sure you were up for it or I'd try to train her myself."

Ace turns to me, an earnestness crinkling his forehead. "A person with a gun pointed at your head isn't going to wait 'til you feel better doll face."

"I know that. I'm ready," I say, trying to trick my body into being stronger, into being as ready as I am in my mind.

Knox looks at me with patronizing eyes. "No, you're not ready."

"It's not your choice," I snap.

"You see?" he says to Ace. "You see what I'm dealing with here?"

Ace whistles. "You two sound like an old married

couple. Quit bickering." He walks back into the ring, pulling his gloves back on. The other guy guzzles some water, waving him over as if to say, *bring it on.* "Come back tomorrow around one," he calls over to us, circling his opponent, fists raised. "We'll take it easy for the first day or two. Wouldn't want the hubby to get all bent outta shape."

"You wouldn't know *easy* if I hit you over the head with it," Knox hollers back, already retreating. Then to me, "Come on, I'll show you your new room."

TWENTY-FOUR

WE TAKE THE stairs up two levels and walk down a wide hallway lined with doors, little gold numbers decorate the walls above them.

"Don't mind Ace," he tells me. "He doesn't know what he's talking about."

"Right."

"I think I'll train you myself. Ace may seem friendly, but his military background makes his way of training too hard-core, especially for a beginner."

I ignore the first part of what he's said, knowing full-well that training with Ethan would yield little results. Where Ace might go too hard on me, push me to my limits, Ethan will only worry I'll break. I see the way he looks at me, like someone who needs protection, like if he touches me in the wrong way I'll shatter.

"Ace was in the military?"

"Yeah, he enrolled when he was seventeen, took the

oath without knowing what he was getting himself into. By the time he was nineteen he was promoted to sergeant. They stationed him at the Phase One Institute in Zone Two for a few months. He oversaw the transport from there to Phase Two."

A fire burns under the surface of my skin. I don't want to train with someone like that. I don't even want to live under the same roof as someone who was an accomplice to murder.

"Why? How could he do that?"

He blows out a breath, slowing as we reach a door with the number 125 marked above it, "He hated it." Runs a hand through his hair. "He took the oath. If he tried to leave, he'd be executed or exiled."

He looks into my eyes. "The things he saw, they ate at him every day. Every time he had to bring a new batch of fresh blood into the Phase Two Institute he wanted to order the driver to take them the other way, take them somewhere safe, but he couldn't."

"Oh."

"Yeah."

"How did he leave?"

"He ran, and he never looked back. He didn't know there was anything outside the city's perimeter, but to him, it was better to be alone in the wild than be a party to NTA. His sister is still there though. He told her he was leaving and she refused to go with him, even though they were all each other had left in the world. That was five years ago."

I understand now. I understand why the people stay. I understand why they don't fight back. They think there's nothing out here. They think the only way to feed their families, to live, is to stay where they have access to all the securities they need to survive.

"But that's how a lot of the people who are here got out." Ethan continues, "They left. It's easy to get past the city limit patrols. It only gets hard once they're on the other side of that imaginary line."

He opens the door and we step inside the dimly lit room. It's simple, a bed with two night-tables, a desk and chair pushed against the wall in the corner. Floral wallpaper covers the far wall, peeling off in places. A window sits in the center of it with heavy green curtains pulled tight over top.

"Is this okay?"

I sit on the bed, the coils of the mattress poking me through the thin blanket covering it.

"It's perfect."

He sits down next to me on the bed and I stare at the millimeters of space between our bodies, willing it to disappear.

"I'm through there." He points to a door on the opposite wall. "You can get into my room from the other side of the bathroom."

Convenient. I swallow back my first comment, instead saying, "Thank you."

"There's a no light rule up here," he says. "We can't be attracting attention." He pulls two candles, matches and a candlestick holder from the drawer on the nightstand. "If you need some light, use these, and make sure both sets of curtains are closed tight. Dinner should be in about an hour. I'll come back and get you."

He gets up to leave.

"Wait."

He turns, surprise pulling up his brows.

I swallow again, unsure how to ask him. "I want to know about my father."

"Amy hasn't told you yet?"

I shake my head, "I deserve to know."

"You're right."

I wait as seconds of silence die in the air between us. Until I can take it no longer.

"Well? If he's dead, just tell me. I can't remember him anyhow."

He looks at me with a mix of sympathy and I steel myself for the worst, waiting to hear that he's gone, that I'll never get to know the man who is *was* my dad.

But then he says. "You've already met him."

I'm sure my face must register the shock rushing through me, because Ethan places a hand over mine, sobering me back into the present. "He's alive? Is he here?"

"No."

"Then where?"

He squeezes my hand and I wonder why he looks like he already regrets what he's about to say, like he wishes there was another way to say it. "He's the Commander General of the NTA. Tobin Rivers is your dad."

I shake my head, laugh a little, though the sound comes out strangled, without mirth. "That's a joke, right?"

He doesn't say anything at all and it's so much worse than him answering my question. It's worse because I know he isn't joking. My father, the man responsible for bringing me into this world is working for the NTA. *Wait, no.* He *is* the NTA. It's sickening, no, more than that—it's *obscene*.

It's a chilling winter frost creeping up my arms, prickling the flesh on the nape of my neck.

And then a new thought dawns on me. "How could someone like my mother be with someone like him?"

"That's something you'll have to ask her. The only thing she's told us is that he wasn't always that way. When she met him, she was working as a lab assistant and he was starting out in the military. She said he was nice, charming."

"Nice?" I hiss. "*Nice?* Charming? How deluded do you have to be to not realize your boyfriend is a monster?"

"Calm down. She didn't know, not until after you were born, how he really was, and by then it was too late. Why do you think she never told him your blood type? She was protecting you from him."

I pull my hand out from under his, stand up, start pacing. I need an outlet for the frustration, a distraction from the storm clouds forming around me. "How could she stay with someone like that? How could she *love* him at all?"

Ethan stands up. "You should talk to your Mom about this Jo. I probably shouldn't have been the one to tell you. I don't have all the details."

My hands are turning to claws at my sides. "The details don't matter!" I stop dead in my tracks, scowling at Ethan, the picture of tranquility, waiting for me to process what he's told me, waiting for me to calm down.

I don't care.

"What matters is that my *father,*" I spit the word, "Is a sadistic psychopath!" I'm laughing again, but this time its hysteria, a savage sound. "Let's change the harvest age to sixteen. Let's start killing more kids!" I mimic what I would imagine his brutish voice to sound like. All business, no emotion. "I'm sure he had a say in that too."

"Joanna."

"I'm sure he had a say in it!"

He steps closer, arms half raised to embrace me.

"Just, don't."

He turns to leave. "He's only a man Jo, and your blood doesn't make you his daughter. That doesn't matter. You can choose who your family is."

I slump back onto my bed, suddenly exhausted, like I've been dragging around cement blocks all day.

My eyes water and I curse the tears that fall, thinking I wish Knox would've told me my father was dead.

TWENTY-FIVE

MY MOUTH IS full of sawdust and my bones as heavy as lead when I awaken the next morning. I haul myself into the bathroom and splash cool water on my face in the dark. Guilt turns my stomach when I look at the door leading Ethan's bedroom, to where he's likely still sound asleep. I shouldn't have reacted the way I did. He was right. Just because we share a blood-line does not make Tobin Rivers my father.

Taking a deep breath to steady myself, I knock on the door and wait several seconds before thinking Ethan must still be asleep. Biting my bottom lip, I decide it couldn't hurt to have a peek inside. I didn't take him for one to sleep in and the clock in my room says it's already after 9:00am.

He's not there. I open the door wider, looking through the shadows to see his bed covered in rumpled blankets. The whole room smells of lemongrass and something tangy, like sea salt or citrus. It's sparse. The only things he's added to make it his are a target full of darts on the far wall and a photograph on his nightstand. I walk over and pick it up, the frame lighter than I expected.

Where everything else in his room seems covered in a thin sheet of dust, this photograph is pristine, not a single fingerprint taints the glass. It's a picture of his mom and dad, I recognize them both even though the years have somewhat changed them. They're smiling brightly. Charles' arms are around Dianna, his eyes gazing at her lovingly. Behind them stands a small white house with blue shutters and into the distance a forest thick with tall evergreens.

My breath hitches when I notice off to one side of the photo are two children playing in a sandbox. One, a boy of about eight years, with dirty blond hair that is scintillating with streaks of gold in the sun. And a little girl, no more than three, with blue eyes and hair the color of faded mahogany.

It's us.

I take a moment to caress the photo, wishing I could remember this day, wondering in an offhand way, why neither of my parents are there. Why is it that I recognized Ethan right away when I first saw him in Phase Three, and I had to work to remember my own mother?

I put the picture back where I found it, stroking the frame one last time.

WANDERING THE HALLS of the lower level I am greeted with warm smiles and nods, though no one approaches to ask me how I'm doing. I'm grateful.

I find the dining hall and see Cash, looking depressed,

sitting alone at a table near the front. His eyes are glazed and staring off into the distance, his fingers fiddle with something deep in the left pocket of his hand-me-down jeans. I slip into the seat opposite him and he snaps out of his stupor.

"Hey," he says. "You look better."

"I don't blame you, you know, for any of it."

"Glad we got that out of the way." He smirks, taking a drink from his mug, clears his throat. "So, what's up? How are you adjusting to life at *The Inn*," he says, putting air quotes around his words.

I think about it for a second and realize I'm not sure how I feel. "It's different," I reply.

He nods, understanding.

"How about you?"

He fiddles with the collar of his shirt. "Fine. But I wish I knew more about what's going on outside. Like, what's the plan? Are we just going to sit here with our hands under our asses?"

Strong words for someone who gets queasy from a car ride.

"I know," I say, looking around, noticing for the first time a group of children sitting at a short table a few meters away. They wave at me and I offer them a smile. My mom walks over to the table and busies herself talking animatedly with two of the little girls. She's so happy it's hard not to smile.

"There's a meeting the day after tomorrow to get a plan together," I tell him, relaying what I learned from Ethan last night at dinner.

"See!" he says, throwing his hands up in the air. "Why

doesn't anyone tell me anything?"

I shrug. "Maybe it's because you don't ask."

"Maybe," he relents. "Or maybe it's because I'm asking the wrong people."

Cash is surprised when I tell him I'm starting training today. He looks at me with an awestruck expression, mixed with something that looks like jealousy. I tell him some people are built to fight and some people simply aren't. Some people are more useful for what they can offer in ways that don't involve fists and guns. He seems placated by this and resolves to see if he can help decipher the radio transmissions with Liam. He should be back soon.

After a few bites of breakfast, I leave him to his own devices and go in search of the training room. I'm not meant to meet up with Ace until noon and it's only after 11:00am. Problem is, I can't remember where the room is. Walking aimlessly seems like as good an idea as any. I should get my bearings if I'll be spending all my time in this hole in the ground.

There's not much to see, and the fact that I'm thinking about Ethan makes me realize my wandering *did* have a purpose after all. But after inspecting the innards of several all but barren rooms and saying a few hasty hellos to unfamiliar faces, I still haven't seen him.

This place is big, but it isn't that big. I'd have seen him by now if he were here. Unease cramps my muscles. I chastise myself, knowing Ethan is a valued member of this community and he's likely been sent on some errand.

I've rounded several more corners and retraced my steps twice when I come upon a hallway. *The* hallway. The one Ethan told me not to go down. I almost turn around, but then I don't. This guy, the Exiled, he's behind bars. There's nothing he can do to me.

I walk past, but then I stop and retreat a step. He's asleep. And it's strange. Strange how even the most messed up of people seem so peaceful, so innocent while they sleep. His hair is longer than I've seen on any man. It's a tawny brown color, a mangled mess, hanging over a tan face that should belong to someone more deserving of its beauty. With strong and yet gentle birdlike features, he could almost be mistaken for a girl from the wrong angle. But the shadow of russet stubble on his jawline and the broad span of his shoulders make him too hulking to pull it off.

There's a thin mattress to lay on in the small space, but he's stationed himself directly across from the door instead, propped against one wall. The entire room is no larger than one of the janitor's closets at Phase Two.

"How long do you plan to stand there?" He lifts his head, quirks a brow at me. I teeter backwards, pivot on my heel and hurry in the opposite direction.

He can't be much older than I am. I almost feel sorry for him. Almost. His voice sounded different, the way it lilted, melodic. There used to be a large population of French-speaking people in this area, but that was over a century ago. The language should be dead. It's not legal to speak anything but common English anymore.

A bright light dumps into the hall up ahead. It comes through a small rectangular window near the top of a tall metal door. I hover outside, stand on tip-toe to peer inside.

Long metal countertops surround most of the expansive room. Microscopes and other machinery as well as glass containers and notepads litter the top. Whiteboards scribbled with numbers and letters in multicolored marker cover the walls. A girl with hair so light a shade of blonde it's almost white sits silently, a nurse's mask and clear glasses covering her face as she drips a white liquid from a syringe into a test tube.

I open the door and step inside, expecting to see my mom somewhere I couldn't see from the window. This is a lab after all and she's a pathologist.

The girl stops what she's doing, places the test tube into a holder on the countertop, the syringe next to it. She looks up, her initial expression of alarm makes way for one of an annoyance.

"Amy isn't here," she states, pulling off her mask and pushing up her glasses to rest on top of her head, flips through one of her notebooks.

"Oh."

A muffled rattling sound starts up somewhere behind me and I turn around, nearly tripping over my own feet trying to put distance between myself and what's in front of me. A huge tank dominates most of the floor and wall space. It's home to at least ten snakes slithering over one another, their scales patterned in shades of grays and browns, tails up in the air, tongues out.

I find I'm drawn closer to them, I've never seen a snake before. They're sort of beautiful in a vicious way. Their eyes are pearly black, staring at me. One strikes at the glass and I suppress a squeal.

The girl behind me is appraising me when I turn around, seemingly pleased with what she finds.

"Why are there snakes in here?" I ask. When she

doesn't respond, I try a new tactic. "I'm Joanna by the way."

"I know who you are." She turns her back to me and continues to drip a clear fluid into a neat row of test tubes.

"Have you seen Ethan at all today by chance?" I ask, thinking this place is so small, everyone must know everyone else.

Her eyes snap up to meet mine so fast you'd think I asked her to stab herself in the foot.

"No, why should I have seen him? You're his *girlfriend,* why don't you tell me where he is?"

Heat builds in my chest, throwing my heart beat out of its rhythm. I have no idea what I did to piss this girl off, but I'll be damned if I'm just going to sit here and listen to her condescending tone.

"What is your problem?"

"My problem?" She asks, eyes narrowing at me. "My problem is—"

My mom walks in the room, looks up from her clipboard, stops in her tracks.

"Oh," she says. "I wasn't expecting to see you today, Ethan said you'd be with Ace in the gym." She smiles, but it falters as she senses the energy in the room. "Naomi, why don't you take a break hmm?"

She needs no more coercion, she stalks out of the room, glaring at me as she goes.

"Did I do something to offend her?"

My mom closes the door behind her and leads me to sit on a stool opposite her at a workbench. "No, Naomi has been grumpy lately. I don't think it's anything to do with you. Don't take it personally."

I nod.

"So, how are things, how are you feeling?"

"Better," I say, thinking about what Ethan told me last night, deciding to keep it to myself that I know about Tobin Rivers, even though I have a burning desire to understand how someone as kind and smart as my mother could have ever loved a man like him.

"That's good." She tucks a stray strand of brown hair into her loose bun. "I'm not sure if Ethan told you, but now that you've had the virus and lived, you can't contract it again. We've never had an instance where someone who was sick survived via our methods and got sick again."

I vaguely remember him saying the chances of his getting the virus again were low the night we escaped, but I never thought what that could mean. "No more respirators?" I ask, my voice elevating a few octaves. Suddenly I can't wait to go outside, swallow the wind, feel what it's like to take an unrestricted breath without fear.

She shakes her head. "At least something good comes of all that suffering, huh?"

"I don't get it." I fold my hands together in my lap. "How? What is the cure?" And then the real question. "How is it that so many scientists in the cities have been searching for it for years and you managed to make one on your own?" My voice takes on a tone of disbelief and accusation, I try to reign it in. "And where did this equipment come from? You couldn't have carried it with you all the way here."

"Ok," she says, placing her clipboard on the table, looks at me with understanding eyes, "I can see you have a lot of questions…"

I wait while she considers how to answer them. Takes a deep breath, "The equipment came from an abandoned research facility in the next town over, we *borrowed* it," she smiles. "And I stumbled on the cure out of luck."

"Luck?"

"After we got the lab set up, Charles got sick." A sadness drags her features down as she remembers. "It was just the two of us here, the lab was in shambles, and we hadn't gotten anything set up. I thought he was going to die and I was going to have to watch him. He was my best friend's husband. And it was my fault they were separated. Though he never blamed me for anything."

"How did he survive it?" I ask, incredulous.

She stands and walks over to the tank full of slithering bodies in the corner, facing away from me, she continues. "It was early on. The virus was taking its toll but he was still mobile. We were running out of food and he insisted on coming with me to gather supplies." She turns, hesitant. "About ten miles from here there is an old nuclear power plant. We stopped to see if they had any supplies we could use. We were in the building for less than five minutes when he was bitten by a rattlesnake. There was a nest of them inside, they were everywhere. It was so dark in there. We couldn't see them."

"I didn't piece it together at first. I brought him back to The Inn, tried my best to clean the wound, tried to extract the venom. I even went on a raid by myself to find a clinic or anything that might have carried an antivenom. But I knew it was useless, the virus would eventually consume him anyways."

"So, the snake bite? Something in the venom?" I'm

lost.

There's a gleam in her eyes now, an unabated excitement. "Yes! When I got back, he was unconscious, with a fever and nothing I did woke him. I set up an IV, praying for a miracle. He woke up. The next day he just woke up. The fever was gone. He was weak but alive. It took months of studying, but we figured it out. The snakes were exposed to radioactive phosphorus or what we call P-32. That compound combined with the venom creates antibodies that kill off the virus."

"But it's only sixty percent effective, right?"

She picks up her clipboard again, absently studying what's written on it. "We've tweaked the serum, we've run tests, we've done all we can with our limited resources. It seems the cure either heals you or for some people, it kills them faster. We can't figure out why. We were able to save Ethan with a shot of epinephrine to the heart. The venom did its job, but it was almost too late for him. If we didn't have the epinephrine on hand, he would have died."

"You'll figure it out." I swallow against the tightening in my chest, not wanting to imagine what could have happened if they didn't have the adrenaline to kick-start his heart.

I wouldn't even be here right now.

She gives me a small smile that's more of a grimace. "In time, I think we will, but time is not on our side. The Exiled have been infiltrating the NTA camps, raiding for supplies, the General," she says, looking away and I'm reminded she doesn't know I've found out about my father. "Has put up a search and destroy perimeter that misses The Inn by half a mile, if they come too close…" She trails off.

I bite my cheek. "Where's Ethan?" I'm still reeling from the fact that there will be NTA soldiers not eight-hundred meters from our door, but now I'm more worried if Ethan has left The Inn, he may not be able to get back.

"Ethan? I thought he would've been with you, you haven't seen him?"

"No."

My worry is now mirrored in her eyes. "I'm sure he'll be back soon." She covers my hands with her own. "He's spent his entire life looking for a way to make it right and now he has. I bet he's taking some time for himself, letting it all sink in."

My eyebrows knit together. "Making what right?"

"The fact that you were taken away, and he wasn't."

"Wait, why would he have been taken away?"

"There you are!" Ace says, busting through the door to the lab. "Not chickening out on me, are you?"

The clock above the door says I'm fifteen minutes late for training. "No. No, I'm ready."

"I'm sorry, what are you two doing again?" My mom interjects, suddenly tense.

"Training," I explain. "I want to learn to defend myself."

"I don't think that's nec—"

"Awe come on Amy, everyone should learn. I wish more of the women here had the same attitude as her! I swear most of them run for cover when I'm around." He winks at me.

Amy doesn't seem pleased, she glances at me. "Well, I'm certainly not in a position to tell you what to do. But be careful, you're still recovering."

I wonder what it must be like to have a daughter you know so little about. A pang of guilt hits me in the chest. As glad as I am to have a mother, as happy as I am to be out of the clutches of the system, it's true; she is in absolutely no position to tell me what to do. Maybe if she hadn't left me alone to begin with, or if she'd run when I was little, maybe I'd have gotten to grow up knowing her. Maybe then she'd have a say. The guilt takes another swing and the angered grief subsides.

"I will."

TWENTY-SIX

"AGAIN!" ACE HOLLERS, pushing the heavy bag towards me. I've changed into sweatpants that sit snugly on my waist, the elastic band now sufficiently saturated with my sweat. My hair is up in a long ponytail, but pieces are falling out, sticking to my forehead and my neck. I swipe at them to move them out of my eyes, wishing for a pair of scissors.

"Is that the best you've got?"

We've been at this for only fifteen minutes and already my arms are sore. Even with the gloves covering my hands I know bruises are forming on the ridges of my knuckles.

I strike the bag again, trying to keep my one fist up, covering my face like he showed me. Feel ridiculous. The bag barely moves when I hit it.

"Ok, stop," he says, moving so he's standing behind me. Moves my legs so they are apart, squared towards the target. "Keep your weight on your heels." He moves my hands into the proper position. "When you go to punch, don't reel back, you aren't throwing a ball."

I blush.

"You don't want your attacker to anticipate what's coming. If you have to move your arm way back here before you swing." He moves my arm to show me my mistake. "By the time your fist gets anywhere near them, they'll either have moved out of the way or blocked it."

"How do you expect me to do any damage if I can't swing?"

"You use your body."

I raise an eyebrow.

"Watch closely."

I move out of the way. He takes the stance he's been trying to make me replicate. "Watch my body, not my fist."

So, I do. I watch his body. I never noticed before but I realize in the shorts and shirt he's wearing I can see every individual muscle snaking around his bones. I don't think there's an ounce of fat on his body, though he must be close to double my weight. He hits the bag, hits it again. I watch how he uses his shoulder to propel the hit, how his body tenses and turns, just slightly, into it. He doesn't reel back, doesn't look like he's going to tip over. And the bag moves a solid two feet along the line, the chain holding it up chiming as it moves.

"Ok, let me try again."

We go on like this for another half an hour until I've managed to move the bag a half a foot and my knuckles feel like they're bleeding. Ethan was right, while Ace seems like a nice guy, when it comes to his training he doesn't comprehend the meaning of 'go easy.'

I'm a sweaty, heaving mess when he says it's time for a break. I guzzle the entire bottle of water he hands me in ten seconds flat.

He snorts.

"What's so funny?"

He shrugs. "You."

I'm on the defensive right away, all that punching has left remnants of unspent adrenaline coursing through my muscles in spasms. "What about me?"

"You're just this tiny thing... no offense." He's more serious now. "I half expected you to give up or quit by now. But you," he says, points at me with both his index fingers. "You look like you wanna kill someone."

Two weeks ago, before I knew everything, before I had been through everything I have to get here, he might've been right. I might've given up. But he doesn't know me, the old me or this mirror image of myself that's somehow stronger, fiercer. I'm not even sure I know what this mirror self is capable of yet. "I don't want to kill anybody. I want to be able to protect myself so no one else has to. I want to be useful."

He looks pleased with my answer, nods his agreement. "Admirable." He sits on the mats and I follow suit, peeling my gloves off. "But it won't be easy, it takes time to learn these things. You aren't only training your body to be stronger and faster, you've gotta train your mind to anticipate the moves of your opponent, to evaluate every situation for danger."

"I understand," I say, though I'm not sure I do. "Is this how they taught you?"

I've struck a nerve, his easy smile has faltered, his

shoulders tense.

"Sorry, I—"

"No, it's alright, I take it Ethan told you I was in the military?" He doesn't wait for me to answer. "I started training with my dad when I was twelve."

My eyes widen, trying to imagine him as a young boy, learning how to kill someone with his bare hands.

"The day after my sixteenth birthday my dad was killed in a raid on one of the Exiled's camps. I enrolled the next day. It only seemed natural at the time to follow in his footsteps."

"Oh. I'm sorry."

He stands back up, holding out his hand for me. I take it and follow him into the ring. "It was a long time ago, don't worry about it."

An understanding settles in my mind, he thought he was doing the right thing. He wanted to be like his father, probably looked up to him, not knowing exactly what his job entailed.

We're quiet for a few minutes while Ace rubs chalk dust on his hands, tells me to do the same. I change the subject, now noticing how red my knuckles are, but they aren't bleeding like I thought. "Have you seen Ethan? I didn't see him this morning."

"He went on a mission last night."

"A mission?"

He claps his hands together, the excess chalk coming off in plumes of white. "Our man on the inside at Phase Three was compromised. He's been radio silent for 'bout forty-eight hours now. Ethan went to find out what's going on." He says it so casually I want to punch him.

"But the NTA is patrolling around the—"

He cuts me off. "Don't worry about Ethan doll-face, if there's one thing that guy knows it's how to get outta a tough spot. He'll be back before you know it."

"But—"

He's amused by my worry and it makes me self-conscious, his eyes laugh at me. "But nothing. Keep that emotional shit in check, you can't fight with that kinda mental baggage." He knows Ethan better than I do, if he says he'll be fine, he's probably right. I'm overreacting.

His fists are up, he's circling me, his eyes gleaming, crinkled on the sides. "Now come on. Try to hit me."

TWENTY-SEVEN

THE MOON HANGS low in the sky tonight. Its glow is a stark contrast to the black canvas it's pinned to. The lights are out in my room, the smell of burnt wicks still lingers from when I blew out the candles. I think I can see lights in the distance but I'm not sure, I've only pulled back the curtain enough to squint through the slit in the fabric.

It's past nine at night and there's still been no sign of Ethan. I've showered and then paced and then laid down only to start pacing again. My body is heavy, like someone's injected my muscles with liquid stone. There are veins in my hands I hadn't noticed before and it hurts to open and close them. The red tinge that colored my knuckles earlier has turned to shades of yellow and purple. Even though I'm weak from exertion, I also feel stronger, like I could crush a steel pipe with my bare hands.

Someone left clothes for me in the closet while I was gone. I'm glad to see there are no dresses or frills or flowery patterns inside, like I've seen the other girls wear. It's stocked with cotton basics, jeans, and other pants, black, in a clingy fabric that stretches to fit my legs and hips like a glove.

I'm wearing those now with a white t-shirt, wishing I had this outfit earlier. It would've been so much easier to move and lunge without the bulky fabric of the sweatpants and loose t-shirt hanging off my frame. It all seems to fit too perfectly, even the simple cotton bras. I wonder absently if someone took my measurements while I was sleeping.

Two knocks on my door and I've dropped the curtain shut. Fumbling, I relight the candle on my nightstand and call to whoever is on the outside to come in.

The door opens and he's standing there, perfect, not a scratch on him, but his soft green eyes tell me he could sleep for days and the exhaustion filling them might still be there. He's wearing jeans and a sweater that hugs to his frame, leaving nothing to the imagination. His hair glistens like burnt caramel in the light filtering in from the hall.

"Ethan," I breathe his name.

I've crossed the room in what seems like a single stride, wrap my arms around him. His posture tenses with momentary shock before he hugs me back, molding his body to mine. I bury my face in his chest.

"I'm happy to see you too."

Hi chest shakes with silent laughter.

I pull away, pressing my lips together.

"Ace said you were looking for me," he states. I can do nothing but stand there. So relieved, so inscrutably amazed that he's back in one piece, that he's completely unharmed.

LEA MCKEE

"I would've told you I was leaving but it was late, after two a.m. And you're so peaceful when you're sleeping."

He has the audacity to wink at me, a sneaky grin slithering across his mouth.

I shove aside the mortifying image of him watching me as I slept, knowing I'd have been drooling. Ignore the blush clawing its way up my neck, indebted to the darkness for hiding it so well. "Did you find out what happened? To your um–that guy you had on the inside at Phase Three?"

He whistles low through his teeth, falls onto his back on my mattress, stares at the ceiling. "No. There's no trace of him, it's like he fell off the face of the earth."

I sit next to him, trying not to stare at the gap where his jeans and sweatshirt have come apart. Unsure what to say. The way his skin looks in the candlelight is so distracting. "What about Dianna–er–your mom, any sign of her?"

"No, nothing. But she's smart, she'll find a way."

He sits up, lays a hand over mine. I pull away reflexively, the bruises covering my knuckles screaming at his touch. His eyes snap up to meet mine, he grabs for my hand again, gentler this time. Examines them.

"It's nothing. A little sore, that's all."

His green eyes are almost black in the absence of light. "I'm going to *kill* Ace." And then in a softer voice, "Are you okay?"

"I'm fine," I say, a little too defensive. "I'm not a porcelain doll."

Shock, hurt, guilt, cross his features all at once.

I rub my fingers over the back of his hand, exhale. "I'm sorry, I'm just tired of everyone thinking I'm this weak little girl who needs saving all the time." A small voice in the back of head tells me I'm still that same little girl. I tell it to shut up. Wonder when I grew a backbone.

"You're kind of sexy when you're angry."

I glare at him.

"What? You are." He looks at me for the first time since he came into the room, really looks at me. Takes in my clothes, the way they cling to my body like a second skin, eyes hungry. It's all I can do not to shiver.

We stare into the gloom for what could be a lifetime before either of us dares to say something.

"Joanna?"

I look up, wait.

"Do you remember," he's tripping over his words now, unsure of himself and I think of how I've only ever seen him nervous around me. How he's always composed, ready, sharp with everyone else. "Do you remember anything from before?" He swallows. "From before you were taken away."

"I wish I remembered more. It's weird but I remember you more than I remembered my own mother." I choke out a laugh. "I knew there was something about you I recognized from the start, but I wasn't able to place it until that day in the green room." I pivot on the bed so I'm facing him head-on. "I remember a little boy with blonde hair and green eyes. I remember the smell of campfire and running through fields of tall grass, chasing you."

A smile works its way onto my face at the pictures being painted in my mind, cut short by something I hadn't realized before. "But we weren't wearing respirators, I don't think, how is that possible?"

"Most people live inside the city, they have

underground facilities where people don't need respirators, and lots of them live in the old apartment buildings too and wear respirators almost all the time. We were the lucky few. We have our parents to thank for it since your mom was indispensable to the labs that were looking for a cure and my dad was probably the best doctor in our Zone." His smile doesn't touch his eyes. "We still lived within city limits, but on the outskirts, the houses there are on small acreages, fenced in with tall gates."

"And the air there, it was safe?"

He shrugs. "As safe as it can be I suppose. Honestly, we should've been wearing our respirators anyway, but when we played outside, just the two of us, my mom figured it was safe. There was no one else around who we could contract the virus from."

"How can I remember so little?"

He rubs his eyes and I'm reminded of how tired he looks. He probably hasn't slept in over twenty-four hours. "You were young, almost five years younger than me."

I motion to the door that will lead him to his bedroom. "You should get some sleep."

He shakes his head, stands, but doesn't get more than a few steps. "You aren't at all how I imagined you'd be when I found you."

"What do you mean?"

At first, he won't look at me, his voice sounds pained. "You're strong. And you're brave. You're not the same awkward kid who used to chase me around the back yard. You're all grown-up."

"So are you."

He drags in a shaky breath. "You're incredible Jo. And

strong. So, so strong… And you're so goddamn beautiful it hurts to look at you."

When he finally looks at me, I see real pain in his eyes, the kind of torture you'd think only a knife could inflict. I'm completely still, but there's a war raging inside of me. Two sides of a battlefield hell-bent on colliding in a blaze of glory. I can't stop looking at his lips, wishing they were closer, wishing they would say more, wishing they would stop moving altogether.

His hand comes up, fingers lightly brushing the curve of my neck, leaving a trail of flames everywhere they touch. My knees are jell-o. His eyes are hungry. My heart is running a marathon. I'm amazed at how it feels to be touched, to be wanted. He leans in, leans his forehead against mine.

"I don't know what I would've done if anything happened to you. I can't lose you again Jo," he whispers.

"You won't," the words stumble out, sounding oddly broken. I pull him closer and it's the only invitation he needs.

His lips are on mine before I have time to register what's happened. So soft at first, and then with an urgency bordering on desperation. My hands are clutching at his clothes. My body is a live wire, the electrical current passing between us is throwing sparks into my blood, lighting every inch of me on fire. There's a beautiful ache spreading through me from somewhere deep inside. He's pinned me against the wall and I hear myself gasp, our lips are apart for a millisecond and it's too long. I yank him back, drinking him in like he's liquid life and I've been dead for a century, like he's the answer to every question

I've ever had. His hands are tracing the curves in my body, writing stories in my skin.

He pulls away and it's all I can do to keep myself on my own two feet. We're both gasping for air, but when I see the expression on his face, I stop breathing entirely.

He looks mortified, like he might throw up. A million thoughts are racing through my mind. Could he not feel the same way? Does he think I'm too young? He said he was five years older, is that too much older? Maybe I did that wrong, I've never kissed anyone before.

"Are you alright?"

He won't meet my eyes and it's making everything so much worse. "I-I can't do this."

He looks like he might cry. I've never seen him so vulnerable in all the time I've known him. I want to wrap my arms around him and tell him everything will be ok. But something inside me is breaking and the fire I felt in my blood only a moment ago is quickly turning me to ice, freezing me in place.

"Did I do something wrong?" I'm biting back to urge to scream.

"No."

"Then what?"

He's visibly shaking now, backing away from me. Every step he takes is putting an ocean between us. He's mumbling something to himself, his fists raking through his hair.

"Ethan!" I'm yelling now, I'm so confused, I don't understand what's happening and I need him to talk, to stop moving so far away.

"It's my fault okay!" He's shouting at me. I know he

doesn't mean it, I know the hostility in his words is aimed at himself, but it hurts nonetheless.

I've moved two steps from the wall and he's backed up two more steps in response. It's like someone's switched our magnets to polar opposites and there's an unseen force pushing us apart.

"What's your fault?"

It clicks.

I'm afraid I already know the answer. The jagged pieces of my life are coming together and I realize I never asked how *exactly* I ended up in the hospital. I never asked how Ethan and his family are so inextricably connected to mine. Why everyone seems to keep saying things like, 'Ethan finally made it right.'

I realize now I didn't want to know.

"If it wasn't for me," he says, eyes downcast, looking like he's aged ten years in this moment. "You never would have been taken away."

TWENTY-EIGHT

LAST NIGHT I dreamt of the tree, climbing, chasing the shadow above me, falling to the earth, the sound of a woman screaming in the distance. Except this time when I woke up, I was crying. Because now I know. Now I know it was never just a dream. I was right all along. It was a memory. Ethan told me as much as he could before I couldn't take anymore and I yelled at him to get out, to leave me alone. I could see the hurt in his eyes, but I didn't care. I wanted him to hurt.

We never should have been climbing that tree. We weren't allowed. Ethan didn't listen to his mother's warnings and made me climb it with him anyways. I was three, of course I followed him. I'm surprised I even made it up as high as would've been needed for the fall to do as much damage as it did. He and his family were our neighbors and I gather my mom and dad were away a lot. We climbed that tree every day when his mom wasn't watching.

I fell. They didn't know I was O-Negative. They called an ambulance. I was taken.

End of story.

Except it wasn't the end of the story for everyone else. This one incident created a domino effect of catastrophic proportions. Ethan's dad and my mom were away, investigating a case together. Dianna was able to get word to Charles to tell him and my mom what happened. My mom knew she'd be charged with treason and needed to flee if she was ever going to have a chance of getting me back. Charles went with her, expecting his wife and son to follow as planned.

They didn't.

The NTA got to them first. They had to pretend they knew nothing, had to pretend to be disgusted with what my mom had done in forging my blood test. They were moved into an apartment in the city where they could be *monitored.*

When Ethan turned sixteen, he and his mom formulated a plan. He joined the military and his Mom volunteered to work in the institutions. Each riddled with guilt for their actions. Dianna, for not paying closer attention, and Ethan, for coercing me into following him up that damn tree day after day.

Every time Ethan pulled a patrolling shift he'd come out to The Inn and see Charles and my mom. He promised them he'd make it right, he promised my mother she would have her daughter back if it was the last thing he did.

So, for almost fifteen years a mother went without a daughter. A husband without a wife. And I sat there in that institution thinking I had no family in all the world.

"You were kids. Ethan was only eight years old. Kids do stupid shit."

The gun kicks back in my hands as I fire it, missing the target completely *again.* The sound of the discharge rings in my ears. When I came into the training room this afternoon Ace had moved all the equipment out of the way and had set up a paper target on one side of the room. We'll alternate days, one day of physical training and one day of target practice, no days off.

"It doesn't matter."

It doesn't matter that I've only seen Ethan once today and he walked past me as if I wasn't even there. It doesn't matter that even though I had no desire to talk to him, he didn't even acknowledge me. Didn't even slow down.

Ace sighs at me and I try to ignore the sound, widening my stance as I take aim again. I wish I hadn't told Ace what happened. I don't want to talk about it. I don't even want to think about it. I want it to go away.

"It does matter." He places a hand on top of my gun and I take my finger off the trigger. "That kid cares more about you than I think he's ever cared about anything in his entire life. He spent the last fifteen years blaming himself."

"Well it was his fault." My tone is cold. I don't even recognize my own voice. A small part of me whispers Ace is right. We were just kids doing stupid shit. And he *has* paid for it. In some form or another, he's lost both his mother and his father.

At least he knew they were alive.

"Can we talk about something that matters? Like what the plan is to get everyone else out of Phase Three. I've got friends there, Ace, I won't leave them to die. I'll go back for them with or without you people."

I put my finger back on the trigger and Ace moves his hand so I can fire. I hit the outside ring of the target. Not good enough. I aim again.

"The plan has gone to shit. Since our man on the inside is MIA, there is no more plan."

I empty the clip into the wall. "So that's it? You're just giving up."

He puts his hands up, blocking my advance. I catch myself. I'm not thinking straight. I need to calm down, but I can't.

"It's not my call. There's a meeting tomorrow to see if something else can be done."

I'm breathing hard and I feel like I want to rip all the hair out of my head. My frustration quickly morphs into anger, and now I'm teetering on the edge of rage. I force myself to stand still. Take deep breaths through my nose, push them out through my mouth.

Ace takes the gun from my hand and I let him. "Go cool off. Come back when you're good, or take the rest of the day off." He puts it down on a table and I turn away, embarrassed by how I'm acting. I know it's not his call what the plan is. I know he's right about Ethan... but I'm not ready to hear it. There's a sense of control that comes with the rage, and if I let it go I might fall apart.

TWENTY-NINE

I'VE GOT TO calm down. I'm not sure if it's because I'm so angry with Ethan that I want to do something that would upset him, or that I'm being a complete idiot. But somehow, I'm on my way to the prisoner's cell.

I need more information about the Exiled, about the woman who almost got us killed on the road. Now that I've started to get answers, I find I'm starving for more. It's not enough to have half-truths and part of the story. I want it all. He must know something about the new law which will allow the NTA to harvest at sixteen. And maybe, just maybe, it's not even true, it's possible that woman was lying, isn't it?

"Hi!" Two little voices squeak, almost making me jump out of my skin. I was so focused on something inside my head I didn't even notice them skipping along behind me. Two little girls. One blonde, a stick of a girl with freckles sprinkled over the bridge of her nose and the other, a little younger, about seven, with muddy brown hair and a baby face. Complete opposites in almost every way.

"Um, hi. What uh—what are you girls doing down here?"

"We're pirates!" The one with brown hair says.

The other girl smiles at me. "Yeah! We're looking for buried treasures."

I bite my lip, the frustration I felt only a moment ago dissolves into nothing. "Well that sounds like fun, but I don't think you guys should be down here, it's not safe." If they go ten steps down the hall and turn down the other hallway to the right, they'll be finding a lot more than buried treasure. Are they even aware we're holding a prisoner here?

The blonde one scrunches up her face at me, ignores what I've just said. "You're Auntie Amy's baby, right?"

I stifle a laugh, wondering if these girls somehow are actually my mother's nieces, and what that would make them to me... cousins? "Yes, I'm her daughter. What're your names?"

"Lily," the blonde one tells me.

"I'm Rosie," the other chimes in.

"We're sisters."

I kneel to get to their eye level, suddenly feeling too tall. "Where are your parents?"

"Our daddy's working," Lily says.

Rosie crosses her arms. "And mommy's an angel now, so we don't get to see her anymore."

"I see," I say, swallowing back the urge to cry. They're so innocent, so blatantly ignorant of the world around them. I hope they never have to find out what it's really like.

"Do you want to play with us?" Rosie asks, looking up at me like I'm some sort of goddess.

Lily elbows her sister. "She's a *grown-up* Rosie, they don't play stupid games."

"Auntie Amy plays with us!"

Lily looks condescendingly at her sister. "That's cuz Auntie loves us."

This is too much. My heart can't take it. "You know what? I've got some things to do, but maybe after we can play together okay?"

I hear a soft moan coming from the direction I was headed before these little girls ripped all the hatred out of me. Remember what I was coming down here to do.

"Why don't you girls go down that way and play, maybe your Auntie has treasure for you?" I tell them, wanting to put as much distance between them and the prisoner as possible.

"Ok," they both say and skip away.

I've already started walking down the corridor to the prisoner's cell, the sounds of them skipping the other way still echoing behind me. Another moan, louder this time, propels me to go faster.

He's laying on his thin mattress on the floor, face buried in it. His fists clutch at the sides; his hair looks matted and wet. He moans again and my instant reflex is to back away. When he turns his face towards the light, I can instantly see how pale he is, how his face is slick with sweat. Another moan rips from his chest, he half sits up and falls back down. He's sick.

Infected?

No. *Shit.*

Wait, I can't be infected again. I race up to the bars, trying to find a way to open them. There's a deadbolt on the latch, I can't open it. I tell myself I don't care that he's sick, it shouldn't matter if someone like him dies. But if he's infected, he could get everyone else here sick. It could become an epidemic. The girls. The *girls!* They're down the hall.

There's a key, it's hanging high on the wall, just out of my reach. I jump to grab it, hurriedly undo the lock.

Now what, genius? I can't carry him all the way to the medical wing.

"What the *hell* are you doing?" Someone shouts behind me.

It's Ace, looking like he might strangle me, eyes burning.

No, not Ace. "Get back!" I yell at him as he tries to advance.

He takes exactly two seconds to evaluate the situation, sees the prisoner.

Throws his hands up. "Damn it."

"Ace, get away from here. Get help!"

He nods, takes off at a full sprint.

THIRTY

IT'S A MINEFIELD out there. It's night and I'm looking through the scope of the sniper on the roof. NTA patrol cars are dispersed in a wall of blinking lights not three hundred meters from The Inn. Logan, who is the resident sniper, and Ace stand behind me, they've already seen what I'm seeing. This is not what I meant when I said I needed to get some fresh air.

Turns out the prisoner, Adrien is his name I found out, wasn't infected. He was just sick, normal sick. Lucky guy. He should be back in his cell by now. All that chaos for nothing. And not to mention a waste of precious medical supplies.

The meeting is tonight. I spent most of yesterday in my room, only leaving to get food and a clean towel, avoiding Ethan at every turn, which is easily done since he seems to be missing again. *I don't care.*

Except that I do. I care more than I should.

"They're everywhere," I say, lifting myself up off the ground. "How the hell are we supposed to get past that? Is there a way around that won't put us within their perimeter?"

"Nope," Logan says. He's a tall, skinny guy with skin like chocolate pudding and eyes like black coffee, he almost seems to disappear in the dark. The perfect sniper.

I brush the dirt off my jeans. "Well that throws a wrench in things."

"It does." Ace.

"Roman will think of something, he always does."

Roman is their lead gunman. He leads all the missions, whether they're simple supply runs or assault missions. He was there the night we escaped, he was the one responsible for the explosion that distracted everyone while we ran in the opposite direction. Apparently, Ethan threatened to do it on his own if Roman refused to help. Now he's paying for it. Roman is so pissed off he sends Ethan on every mission they have just so he doesn't have to look at him. I'm told this guy is someone you don't mess with, never mind threaten.

I haven't met him, but the way everyone talks about him, from what I gather he's someone they all respect and maybe somewhat fear.

I'm both excited and nervous to meet him, but more so to hear what he has to say about the plan. Danny and Sophie are still in there, and all the others. They have no idea that in two weeks they'll be harvested and soon after *discarded* or worse. The note I left Danny, was vague. I didn't want her to ask any questions, just to be ready when the time came to get out.

Logan needs to stay here, in case the patrols get too close, so he can notify the others.

Ace and I make our way back down the stairs. It's time to meet with Roman.

It's me, Ace, Charles, and Liam, who got back from the safe house this afternoon. We're all sitting around a wooden table in a room that barely fits us. There are only five chairs, the rest of the space is standing room only. The meeting should've started ten minutes ago. Ace told me I'm not even supposed to be here, so I must stay quiet and listen. I told him I would try, but we both know that's not how this is going to play out.

Ethan is the first to walk in and I try not to over analyze why there's a cut above his left eyebrow. A shorter, stalky man enters behind him, rolled up sheets of blue paper in his hands. He has a receding hairline and eyes the color of steeped tea, faded tattoos in black ink cover his right arm down to the wrist. Two others I don't recognize follow them in, both tall with blonde hair. They could be brothers, no more than twenty-five.

Roman doesn't waste any time. He spreads the blueprints out on the table, using the guns from his holsters to keep them from curling back up again. "As you know, we've lost all contact with Pete." He looks at each face in the room, hesitates when his eyes rest on mine for an instant, before moving on to the next. "And the NTA is patrolling all 'round the city limits. We have our work cut out for us boys, this shit's not gonna be easy."

Everyone is quiet for too long. Every second of silence passed filled with unspoken words of defeat, the lights have gone out of their eyes.

"Damn it!" Roman says, pounding his hands against the table. "Let's go! I wanna hear what you've got! We don't have time for this. We've waited too long to do something 'bout this and I'll be damned if I'm going to sit here and let another hundred-odd kids die."

I wonder why they've never attempted something like this before. Why did they wait until now?

"Pete was our in, he was working to get that placement at The Mill for the last two years. And since you fucked up your cover," one of the blondes says, pointing two fingers at Ethan. "Without Pete, our plan doesn't work."

"That's not true," Ethan counters. "Pete may have been our eyes on the inside, but you forget, I was stationed there too, and Joanna knows the layout as well. We can do this without him. We don't have to wait any longer than we already have."

I stand up quietly in the corner, try to get a closer look at the blueprints.

The other blonde smirks at Ethan. "Enlighten us then, what's your brilliant plan?"

"A diversion, like we did the last time."

"You really think that's going to fool 'em a second time?"

"What else can we do?"

"How can we even get past the patrols undetected?"

"It's a suicide mission."

There are so many voices echoing around the room I feel like my head is going to explode. There *has* to be a way. We have to save them. I could never live with myself knowing I escaped, that I have the chance to live, to fight back, while all the others die.

"You," Roman says and everyone else shuts up at the sound of his voice. He's pointing at me. "What do you think we should do?"

"Me?" I'm in absolute shock. I'm back in second grade, the kid in the classroom who never raised their hand but the teacher calls on them anyways. Except this time, I don't know the answer.

His eyes challenge me to speak. "I know who you are, but I don't know why you're here. If you don't have anything to say that can help, there's no reason for you to be in here."

I swallow hard, fighting the urge to lash out at him. I have just as much a right as anyone else.

"She's been training with me, and she's been inside The Mill—"

Ace starts to defend me, but Roman cuts him off with a glare.

Stepping closer to the table, I scrutinize the map. They've marked off our location, as well the locations of the Exiled encampment, Phase Three, or I guess they call it 'The Mill,' and several other unlabeled locations. An idea is forming in my mind, but I have no way of knowing if it's viable.

No backing down now. "Do we have any more explosives? Something big enough to make a lot of noise and smoke?"

Roman's eyes widen, he nods, apprehensive, "We can't blow it up, we'll kill more than we'll save."

I shake my head, "No. I don't want to blow up Phase—er, I mean, The Mill, I want to set it off at the Exiled encampment."

A wave of understanding rolls across his eyes.

"Two birds with one stone. We attract the NTA to the camp, let them deal with each other. While they're busy doing that... we go around." My index finger traces a red line on the map that would take us a safe distance from the fight, but still get us to The Mill.

"And then?"

I look to Liam. "Can you take out their communication, block their radio signals so the soldiers at The Mill can't call for help?"

"I can do that, not sure how long it'll last though. I mean, what you're saying is doable, but how do we get them out once we're there?"

"Those buses I saw on the road when we were driving in, do they run?"

"Probably not," one of the blondes says. "But we can fix that, what are you proposing?" He has a smirk on his face that says it all, he's waiting for me to crucify myself, hoping I do.

I steel myself against the dozen sets of eyes penetrating my skin, "We armor them with whatever we can find, we put snipers in the trees around The Mill and drive right through their front gate."

Ethan is smiling. Roman is laughing. I scowl at them both, "What?"

"You're certifiably insane, aren't you?" He's still laughing.

An angry red blush claws its way onto my face. "But we can—"

"Stop, stop." He looks more serious now. "I was laughing 'cause I thought you were dumber than a stick, growing up in the system and all..." He waves his hand absently in a sweeping motion.

I'm unsure whether to be insulted.

"I was wrong, these worthless sods couldn't come up with a damn thing." He jabs a finger at the men behind him, eliciting himself some murderous stares. "Five minutes in this room and you've given me something more solid than any of them have."

I don't know what to say so I just stand there, feeling proud and slightly berated.

"But I've got one question for you," Roman continues, leaning closer to me. "How do you propose we get a hundred somethin' kids to leave with us when they think they're on their way to a bigger and brighter future? We don't exactly look like missionaries you know."

I have an idea, but they won't like it and we haven't got time to come up with another. "Take me with you."

"No," Ethan says.

"Shut up," Roman retorts, never taking his eyes off me.

"They know me–the others. They'll trust me. If you can get me to the P.A system in Dunne's office, I can get them out."

Roman shakes my hand, and Ethan's hands curl into fists. Everyone else nods, though none speak.

We have a plan. It might not work. We may not all make it back. But it's the first step, and I'm both exhilarated and terrified to take it.

Roman claps his hands together, a sinister smile spreads across the width of his face, "We've got thirteen days boys. Let's get to work."

PART THREE

"Only those who will risk going too far can possibly find out how far one can go."

-T. S. Eliot

THIRTY-ONE

ETHAN HAS BEEN a ghost for five days. I tell myself I don't care. He's left The Inn long before I wake up and I've heard him come back as late as two in the morning. They're all busy putting the plan I helped concoct into action. The buses are running now. The team is armoring them using scrap metal foraged from the towns north of here. The others, including Ethan, have been stocking a secondary location about thirty kilometers from The Inn.

Roman says it's too dangerous to bring them to The Inn, to jeopardize almost fifteen years of work. It's a miracle they haven't been discovered already.

Everyone has jobs to do. Everyone except me. Get the respirators from the front of the building when we arrive. Drive the bus. Take out the guards. And me, try not to get killed on my way to the PA system. Ace will be with me, keeping me safe, much to Ethan's annoyance I've heard.

While the others are spending their minutes and hours

on making sure this works, all I've been tasked with is to keep training. So that's what I'm doing. Twice a day now. Hand-to-hand combat in the mornings and shooting practice in the evenings.

Erica takes aim at the target. The gun looks awkward in her hands. She's been training with Ace and I for the last three days. I guess I won't be the only girl who knows how to defend herself here anymore. The shot goes wide, missing the target entirely.

"Keep trying Erica, remember to keep your feet shoulder-width apart, right slightly forward." Ace turns her hips to face the proper way, she blushes. His hands are still on her hips when he says. "Exhale on the release." She nods, shoots again. Hits the target. Her lips twitch into a half smile of pride[A1].

My mind slows as I take aim. The bullseye coming into perfect focus. My bullet buries itself into the wood half an inch outside the little red circle.

Ace's mammoth hand clamps down on my shoulder. "Well would you look at that, you're not completely useless anymore." He winks at me and I shove him off with a grin. I'm doing well I overheard him say to one of the blond brothers that I shoot better than he does already.

"Maybe I won't need a bodyguard when we get to The Mill."

Roman gave me two choices; Ace or Ethan would be in charge of getting me to Dunne's office to use the PA system. He made me choose one. I think he enjoyed watching me squirm. Going alone was never an option.

"Nice try, but your skinny ass is stuck with me. Besides, you can't take all the credit. Fancy side-effects and all."

"What's that supposed to mean?"

He stares at me for a few seconds, a stupefied look on his face, "Hasn't Charles spoken to you, or run tests yet?"

I shake my head.

"Ah, well apparently, you lot who've survived the venom injection get some pretty sweet advantages. Faster reflexes and shit like that. Pretty sure most of it's a load of crap, but I'm no scientist."

"That's ridiculous."

He shrugs, "Trust me, I'm with you, but I've seen it first ha—"

Ethan kicks the doors open to the gymnasium. We all freeze in place. Guilt burrows into my chest and I don't know why. He glares at me. His jaw is taught, a vein is protruding out of his neck by at least two centimeters.

If he wasn't the reason I grew up as property rather than person I might ask him what's wrong. Instead, I square my jaw right back at him, put my gun down, and shove my shaking hands into the pockets of my hoodie. Try not to remember his lips on mine. Try not to remember how I felt around him before I knew the truth.

Ace steps towards him, but Ethan's eyes never leave me. "Hey Ethan, what's—"

"Shut up Ace." He breathes in deeply. I see his adams apple bob up and down. "Can I talk to you for a minute in private?" His voice sounds much calmer than he looks.

My lips part, but there's a burning in the back of my throat and I don't trust myself to speak yet. The ugly mix of guilt and betrayal is digging a hollow pit in the bottom of my stomach. I pull my eyes from his and walk past him into the empty hallway. He's half a step behind me.

"What is it?" I ask, leaning against the wall far enough from the doors that Ace and Erica won't overhear. The words come out strong and yet soft like I couldn't care any less. Foreign, not myself, but this other self I'm becoming. The Joanna who can shoot a gun and take down a grown man with her bare hands. This Joanna can't be hurt.

"What is it?" He mimics, a smirk on his mouth. "If you play dumb we'll be here all day love. How could—"

"Don't call me love."

The hurt in his eyes is causing me physical pain. I grit my teeth against it. Why should I feel bad?

"You know what I'm talking about Jo."

Of course, I do. Obviously Roman or someone else told him I'd chosen Ace over him. Either way, I didn't expect this reaction. He hasn't so much as glanced at me since he told me the truth. What does he care who I picked? He should be happy I didn't force him to babysit someone he doesn't care to be around anymore.

"I'll be safer with Ace." A lie. I've never been good at it.

"Bullshit!" He smashes his palms against the wall on either side of my face. I don't give him the satisfaction of flinching, but my breathing is coming faster now. My chest is too close to him, only inches away. He's searching for something in my eyes. Doesn't find it. I want to push him away, but I don't.

I want to pull him closer, but I don't.

He moves so I don't have to, taking two steps back, putting a canyon between us. If there was a ledge I might jump off. Anything to escape the hurt, the accusation and the betrayal crumpling him like a piece of tissue paper. I've never once thought of Ethan Knox as weak. Until now. And it's my fault. I'm his weakness.

I don't want him to be mine.

He rubs a hand over the stubble on his face. "Just tell me why. You know I'd never let anything happen to you. Answer me this, if it came down to it, would he take a bullet for you?"

My eyes narrow at him. "What, and you would?"

"Yes." One word, but the conviction in it is enough to shake the ground.

Standing straighter, I stare straight into his eyes. "I can protect myself."

He snorts, his expression bordering on condescension. "Do you really think you could shoot first? Could you take someone's life to save your own?"

I don't know the answer to his question. It's not that simple. What I do know is I'm done with this conversation. "Why are we even having this conversation? It's not your problem." I walk away, not back into the gym, but down to the stairwell that will take me back to my room.

"Joanna wait. Please."

I stop, but don't turn around.

"I'm sorry." His shaky intake of breath makes me tighten my fists. "I should have told you everything sooner, before…" he trails off. I know what he means to say, before he kissed me, before I let my walls down and invited him in.

My eyes burn. I don't turn around, I don't want him to see how much he's hurt me, instead, I mutter, more to myself than for him to hear. "Yes, you should've." And force my legs to keep walking.

I listen to the heavy metal door to the stairwell slam shut behind me and slump down onto the first step. My fingers run along the soft skin of my scar. The 'O' tattooed on my wrist makes me want to chop my own arm off.

A part of me understands how unreasonable I'm being, blaming him for something that happened almost fifteen years ago, something he did when he was only eight years old. That same part of me knows it would have happened anyways, some way, somehow, I'd likely have ended up in the system. He should've told me. But would I have trusted him enough to escape if he had?

And then it's obvious. I wish I could hold the hand of my younger self. Tell her everything will be alright, that she's not alone. But that time has come and gone. And not knowing has made me who I am today. I wanted to be angry. I *want* to be angry. I wanted to hate him. Hate is easier, you can't get hurt from hate, and the anger has been my fuel.

The truth is scarier than the lie.

Because the truth is I forgave him as soon as the words came out of his mouth. It's a terrifying revelation, but one I've known all along, even if I couldn't admit it to myself. I was filled with so much fury, so much confusion. I needed a reason, I needed to make sense of why I had to spend *fifteen years* thinking my family was dead. Ethan painted a target on himself and I jumped at the chance to take aim.

I'm an idiot.

Ripping the door open, I race back into the hallway. "Ethan!"

The hallway is empty. I'm met with utter silence.

Ace comes out of the gym, leans on the doorframe, seems to examine something stuck under his nails. "You're an idiot," he says and I wish he'd told me sooner. I wish I'd have listened to him.

Wishing won't get me anywhere.

"Where is he? I have to talk to him."

His eyebrows unknit when he gets a good look at my face, the way the tears are pooling in my eyes. I rub them away.

"He's gone Jo," Ace says softly.

There's a knife in my gut. "What do you mean *gone?*" When he doesn't answer me right away, I walk up to him and put my face in his. "Where the hell did he go Ace?"

He shakes his head at me, sighs. I get the sudden urge to hit something. But it's not him I'm angry with, it's myself.

"He's going with the crew to stock the secondary location. He won't be back 'till the night before we leave."

Ace grabs my arm as I move away. If I'm fast enough I can catch him before they leave. His eyes soften enough to keep me from ripping myself away and tearing off down the hall. "I dunno what you said to him, but if I were you I'd let him go. You've done enough damage for one day. Give him time to cool down."

THIRTY-TWO

IT'S QUIET HERE.

I try to imagine the hotel lobby as it once would have been. Soft music playing, a reception clerk awaiting the next clients. Everything pristine. Now it's just a dusty old foyer with discolored yellow paint. The once-plush green couches are sagging and smell of old socks. No one is waiting to check in, there's no music playing, only the sound of a plastic tarp flapping in the wind coming through a broken window.

But there is one redeeming quality. To the right of the desk is an old bookshelf, filled seven feet high with tomes. The cash register stands open, emptied, the place where a television would've stood on its little stand in the corner is bare. They took the money and the electronics and left the books. I smile. And it's the first real smile I've had in a while.

I run my fingers over the volumes. Some I recognize

and some I don't. Once the mere sight of a book I haven't read before would've made me infinitely happy. Back when all I had to look forward to was lunch-hour and my weekly test-scores. Now, that joy is diluted, forced under layers of stress and guilt. Even though there isn't any way I'll have time to read them, I take a few, tempted to stay here. Alone. No one would bother me. I could read all day.

But then again. I have shooting practice in an hour and I don't want Ace to think because I'm upset I won't show up. What we're doing is bigger than any of this. It's bigger than my relationship, or lack thereof, with Ethan. I make my way down the stairs. I won't allow myself to be *that* girl. The one who cries in the corner over her feelings.

Feelings don't matter anymore. Proper aim does.

And then there's the doc. He's been patiently waiting to for me to come in for my 'check-up,' and I've been putting it off for days. Since I seem fine, other than my self-induced soreness from hand-to-hand combat training with Ace, I haven't seen the point.

The hallways are uncommonly empty as I make my way to Charles, and I'm again reminded how everyone is preparing for the heist of the century. And here I am, going for a check-up. I stifle a laugh that's more of a sigh.

I don't even realize where I am until it's too late. I'm outside his door. Why did I come here? The books under my arm are suddenly heavier. I steel myself and move into full view, peeking through the bars.

As soon as he sees me he stands, back to the wall. His hair has been washed and appears softer and thicker. There's a little more color in his cheeks than there was the last time I saw him. His ochre eyes look bright, red-rimmed, almost like he's been crying.

He takes a deep breath. "Thank you," he says, and I can tell he means it.

I don't know what to say so I nod, licking my lips which seem to have become chapped in the last two minutes. I suppose he was conscious enough to remember I was the one who got him help, who helped carry him to the medical wing. Oddly, I'm more relieved than I thought I'd be to find he's alright.

I'm both glad and a little disappointed to find my heart hasn't completely turned to stone.

I'm about to walk away when he comes over to the bars caging him in, wraps his hands around them. He's tall, a head taller than I am, I never noticed before. "Do you know what they are going to do with me?"

"No. No, I don't." But I do. Even if no one will man up enough to make the decision and even though it's wrong. There's only one thing they can do unless they plan to keep him here in a cell for the rest of his life. Otherwise, they risk him giving away the location of The Inn.

His eyebrows draw together. "Why help me?"

That, I don't know the answer to.

"They did not need to use the things—the supplies for me." It's easy to tell English is not his first language. I remember there were Zones in which they spoke mostly French before the NTA made it illegal to speak anything other than common English. That must be his native tongue. I wonder what their words sound like.

Shifting the books over to my other arm, I tell him, "Not everyone left on this earth is a horrible person. Some of us can't sit back and watch another person suffer."

He backs away from me, going back to sit on his mattress, exhales loudly. "Well, if it is the same to whoever is in charge, I would like to stay here for a while."

He might just get his wish, if only for a while. He doesn't seem crazy, not like the other Exiled we ran into. He seems normal. Nice, even. *I shouldn't be here.* I don't like how the idea of his impending death is making my chest ache. He's too young to die. There's no way he's any older than twenty.

"Here," I say, passing him a book through the bars, it's a mystery I've never read before, but maybe it'll help him pass the time.

When he takes it from my hand, he smiles at me. I've never seen teeth so straight in my life, or so white. Our fingers brush and I've just now realized I'm still holding the other side of the book, I let go too quickly. Clear my throat.

"Thanks. This is one of my favorites. My name is Adrien." The way he says it is different than I would've imagined it to sound. With a soft *Ah* sound, instead of a hard *A.* "I never asked, what is your name?"

"Joanna."

"Joanna." He repeats my name, making it sound exotic, smiles as if he likes the taste of it on his tongue.

Leave Joanna, you have to leave. "I uh—I have to go. Enjoy the book – I mean... well, you've already read it, so..."

"See you around."

I've never walked away from a conversation so fast in my life.

THIRTY-THREE

THE DOOR TO Charles' office is open. The word 'Medic,' scrawled across the top in thick permanent marker lines. I clear my throat as I enter, pushing the door a little wider. He closes a file on his desk and rubs his eyes.

"Oh, Joanna. I wasn't sure when I should be expecting you."

A photo peeks out from the manila folder, and I immediately recognize half of Dianna's face in the ink. "I'll come back." I say, taking a step back towards the door. Feeling like an unwanted intruder at a funeral service. Except the person he's mourning isn't dead, or at least, I refuse to believe that.

"No, no. Please, come in and have a seat."

I nod reluctantly, and wait as he puts the file-folder into a drawer on his desk, replacing it with another labeled with my name.

"I was really just stopping by to tell you I feel fine.

Great, actually."

He smiles, but it looks more of a grimace, "Don't worry, I'm not going to stick you with a needle or check your vitals."

My eyebrows pull together, until it dawns on me what exactly this 'check-up' is about. "So, you want to know if I've had any side-effects from surviving TEN?" The words come out sounding more condescending than I meant them, and I attempt to rein in my judgement.

"Precisely."

I'm having trouble meeting his eyes. "Charles, don't take this the wrong way, but Ace told me about the kinds of *side-effects* you think I might have, and–"

"Some are more noticeable than others," he interrupts, pulling another file onto his desk. It says Ethan Knox on the cover. "For instance," he says, opening to a page filled with notes and other data. "Ethan's eyesight has evolved. He can now see nearly four times better than the average person. Even in pitch-darkness, he can tell you exactly what you're wearing, down to the smallest detail."

"That's impossible." *He would've told me.*

"That's what I thought as well."

He pulls another file, lays it on top of Ethan's, "Caroline," he says, clearing his throat, "Lost her sense of touch. She couldn't feel heat, cold, pain, pressure, anything."

"Who's Caroline?"

He closes the file again and puts it back into the drawer, runs a shaky hand through his tousled blonde hair, "She took her own life before you arrived."

I can't imagine what it would be like not to feel

anything. A kiss. The warmth of your bed when you fall asleep at night. Awful, it would be utterly unbearable.

"Well," I say, folding my hands together, "I can still feel everything. And when I blow out the candles in my room, I can't see any more than I could before."

He looks disappointed, pulls out another file, "Liam has been the most effected, though not in a way you'd notice."

"Liam? I didn't know he'd been infected."

Charles shakes his head, "He doesn't like to talk about it, makes him feel like a freak, he says. But Liam has become something of a human battery. He can use any electronic without needing to plug it in, as long as he's touching it, it has power." He has the gleam of a mad-scientist in his eyes as he tells me, "Now that his ability has evolved even more, he's able to charge our batteries when there isn't much sun for the solar panels. Takes a lot of out him to do it though. It's incredible, really."

I cross my arms, "How is any of this possible? It's like something from a story-book."

"Your guess is as good as mine. But it seems these *special* side effects only affect about half of survivors." He puts the files back where they belong, continuing on as if he hasn't just told me super-humans exist, "There are a few smaller side-effects that everyone who has survived TEN seems to have."

He moves so fast he's almost a blur, and I don't even realize what I've done until I see the pencil, sharpened side an inch away from my eye, and my hand gripping it. I drop it as if burned. "Why the hell did you do that? You could have taken my eye out!"

He laughs, "Faster than average speed, and quick reflexes are some of the smaller effects. Don't worry, I knew you'd catch it. Or knock it out of the way."

"So, it's true then?" I cringe, deflated. All this time I thought I was improving in my training because of *me*. Because I was trying so damned hard. But, no, now that accomplishment has been taken away from me too.

"What else?" I ask through gritted teeth, not wanting to have any more surprises.

Charles jots down a few notes, telling me, "Well, an elevated body temperature seems to be common. Also, a heightened sense of hearing, though not always."

I stand to leave and gather my books from where I dropped them on the floor.

"That's not all." He says, stopping me mid-step. "Caroline's, Ethan's, and few others' *special* side-effects didn't manifest until a couple of weeks after treatment. And they only strengthened over time."

"You're telling me I could lose the feeling in my body tomorrow? Or next week?" I spit, standing on the balls of my feet, ready to run, to get as far away from what he's telling me as possible.

Looking more like a father-figure than I've ever seen him, he tells me, "For your sake, Joanna, I hope not."

THIRTY-FOUR

IT'S AUGUST 24th TODAY. There are only four days left until we attack and all I can seem to think about is Ethan. And how I should've gone after him. Once I explained to Ace why I needed to talk to him, he apologized for making me feel worse, called me an idiot again and gave me a hug. It's nice to have a friend like him. Someone who'll always say it like it is. He reminds me of Dianna.

Not for the first time, I send out a silent prayer she's alright and hope she's somehow making her way back to us. I can see the lines in Charles' face deepening every day she isn't here. Ethan's been trying to convince Roman to let him sneak back into the city to find out if she's still there. Roman says there isn't time, he'll have to wait.

Taking the clip out of my gun, I set it down and admire my handiwork. All but two of my bullets made their mark. *Side-effects* be damned, I'm taking the credit for this one. Even Erica is getting better, her bullets are on the target, even if the majority aren't near the center.

"You're getting good at that."

She smiles. "Thanks."

I never noticed before, but her eyes are so dark brown they're almost black, fringed in thick lashes. I've seen Ace staring at her when she isn't paying attention. She's very pretty in a simple sort of way. I wonder if she likes him back. Without meaning to, my mind wanders back to Ethan. I shake my head.

Ace is pulling a bag out of his locker, Erica keeps peeking at him under the cover of her lashes. She's been grinning all day. Everyone has been acting weird today.

When I went to see if my mom needed help with anything between training sessions, she practically jumped out of her skin. Cash brought me lunch in my room and sat with me while I ate every bite, rambling on about codes and how deciphering radio transmissions is 'super fun, really, it's sooo badass. I'm like a super spy.' Even Charles, who I thought might be upset with me about the way I acted during our check-up, stopped by just to say hello. He was about to ask me something when Ace grabbed him and dragged him out the door, giving him a pointed look and telling him, very loudly, that I had training to do.

"Heads up." Ace tosses me the bag from his locker. "Hope it fits, I told the guys to check the sizes of your other clothes."

Opening the bag, my eyebrows raise. Inside is a wad of thin navy fabric. Pulling it out, I let the bag fall to the floor. It's a dress. Thin straps, flowy, with a deep cut 'v' in the top. A tag hangs from the side. The words are faded, but it seems to say Armani. Once upon a time this dress would've cost four-hundred and fifty-nine dollars. As far as I know, the world doesn't run on dollars and cents anymore, but on rations doled out based on how much you can contribute to the NTA or how useful they deem you.

"What's this for?"

Ace is fighting to keep the smirk off his face. Erica is rushing around getting everything put away.

Picking up the bag, I shove the dress back inside. "Ok. What's going on?"

Erica takes the bag from me, I let her. What the hell am I supposed to do with a dress anyways? It's completely impractical.

"Don't look so disgusted, it's a dress, not a straightjacket." Ace pulls his shirt off and tosses it in his locker on a pile of other dirty clothes. Erica stops to stare at his chest. If I didn't know any better, I'd think he was purposely flexing his muscles to impress her. No one walks around like that. I know what a six pack is, but he must have something closer to eight, or maybe ten. "It's a surprise. Now go grab a shower and meet me in the cafeteria."

"Erica…" I say, hoping she'll be the weak link and tell me what's going on.

"Nope," she says. "I'm not ruining the surprise so forget it." She's suppressing a smile, trying to look serious. Failing. "I'm holding this hostage by the way. I'll meet you in your room in twenty minutes. Shower fast!"

The clock says it's 6:45pm. I'm so confused. "For what? Why are you meeting me in my room?"

Her enthusiasm is infectious. My facial muscles are traitors.

"Make-up!" She squeals and sashays out of the gym, becoming someone other than the Erica I've come to know. Someone who cares about make-up, and whose voice can reach octaves only dogs can hear.

AT EXACTLY 7:05pm there's a knock at my door. Still cocooned in my towel, I rush over and open it. "Well, you're punctual."

Her hair is still damp from the shower, and she's wearing a dress that's the color of a peach, somewhere between orange and pink. "Yeah, well, we don't do this a whole lot. It's nice to dress up every once in a while." She unslings a small duffle bag from her shoulder and drops it to the floor. I don't say what I'm thinking, that whatever 'this' is it seems like a big waste of time and effort given the current state of things.

Instead, I ask her what's in the bag.

She unzips the top, revealing a small lamp, something black and bulky that says *Conair* on the side and every kind of make-up that exists on the planet, at least I'm assuming so. Aside from lipstick and mascara a girl at Phase Two stole from Mrs. Tyson and proudly showed around, I've seen no other kind and definitely never put any on. Involuntarily, I flinch at the sight. Only half serious, I ask her, "Does it hurt?"

I'VE BEEN BLOW dried, plucked, trimmed and painted.

I'm stifling the urge to itch my left eyebrow. If I so much as touch my face, Erica has threatened to kill me.

"And you're telling me people used to do this every day?"

She applies another coat of deep red stain to my lips. "Yeah, before the whole world went to crap. Most of this stuff is probably expired but Liam gets it for me when he can. What are big brothers for?"

"Wow, wait a second, Liam is your brother?"

"Half brother." She tells me, wrapping another length of my hair around the barrel of her curling iron. "I didn't even know he existed until a few years ago. My mom had been fighting the virus for a long time. I stayed home a lot to take care of her. She was a higher-up working in some kind of tech for the NTA when she got sick."

Erica deftly weaves another chunk of my hair around the iron, she could be talking about the weather, and not about her mother, who I must assume is dead.

"She never really talked about it, but her status made it possible for her to afford to set up a quarantine room in our house and stay at home." She pauses and I can't decide on a proper response, 'sorry your mom was sick', or 'sorry your mom worked for the government responsible for the deaths of thousands of innocent teenagers'. Neither seems appropriate. "There was a shortage of blood at the clinic when I went to pick it up for her. She died a few days later."

A wave of agony washes over her features. "I'm sorry," I tell her.

"I wasn't allowed to listen to the radio. I could only leave the house to go to the clinic. I took my courses at home with a tutor." She stops what she's doing, sets her mouth in a firm line. "So, no, *I'm sorry*. I lived a very sheltered life with my mother in our big empty house. I was so oblivious to the world around me. I had no idea where the blood came from. She lied, told me it was synthetic."

I find this hard to believe, but if she's telling the truth, I wonder if there are others out there who don't even know.

"I was still a minor when she passed. The NTA sent me to live with my dad. I never met him, but he was my closest living blood relative."

"That's when you met Liam then?"

She nods. "He was training to go into surveillance and communications. I was bitter for a long time when I found out what was actually going on. But me and Liam didn't know the full extent of it until Dad got sick. He refused the treatment, said he wouldn't be a part of it anymore." She looks down. "I hated him for so long. He left me and my mom when I was a baby. And I didn't forgive him until that day. I didn't realize who he was until that day."

She didn't have to say anymore. If he refused the treatment, he died. I may have been raised in an institution, tricked, drugged, brought up only to die or become an involuntary test subject. The thing is, I knew none of that. My biggest concerns were whether I'd pass exams and finding out how the books Dianna gave me would end. I didn't have to watch anyone die. I didn't have to make any tough choices. You could almost say I had it easy until a few weeks ago.

"Liam started his new job at the Phase One institute of our Zone a couple weeks later. He came back from his first day and wouldn't talk to me. He wouldn't even look at me. He pulled two backpacks from the closet and started packing. Told me he was leaving and that I should too. He never told me what happened and he didn't try to force me to leave with him. But what was I supposed to do? He was the only person I had left. And it was like Dad said, he didn't want to be a part of it. Until then, I didn't realize I had a choice."

"You made the right decision, Erica."

"I know we did. But I'm not sure what we would've done if Roman hadn't found us and brought us here though. We were holed up in an abandoned cottage, running out of food and clean water."

In this moment, she is back in that cottage, her gaze resting on a memory in the air. Placing a hand on her knee brings her back to earth. "You're okay now, you're safe."

Her eyes darken. "It's not enough. We have to fight back."

I nod.

She shakes her head, pasting a smile back on her face. "That's enough depressing chit-chat. This is supposed to be fun." She jumps up and claps her hands together. "Tell me what you think." She moves the lamp from the floor beside me to the countertop in front of the mirror and helps me stand in my borrowed heels.

My hair falls in soft waves over my shoulders and down my back as it normally does, but the waves are more structured, shinier, and somehow my mousy auburn hair seems to shine like polished mahogany. The thin black liner and mascara she put on my eyelids and lashes makes the blue of my irises appear electric. The matte red she painted on my lips makes them seem fuller.

The reflection in the mirror is beautiful, but she's not really me. She's a version of me that has no right to exist in this world –but for just one night, I get to be her. The Joanna I could've been in a parallel universe where TEN and the NTA didn't ravage the earth.

THIRTY-FIVE

AS WE APPROACH the cafeteria a miasmal feeling creeps over me. It's quiet. The lights are off. Something's wrong. I put my arm out to stop Erica. "Wait, something's not right." I inch along the wall, Erica has her arms crossed behind me, fighting back a laugh.

"You are so paranoid." She strides over to where I'm standing, grabs me by the arm and drags me the rest of the way into the dark cafeteria. My body tenses, ready for an attack. Dark shapes surround me, crouched down. Adrenaline is a flash fire in my blood. The lights flick on and it takes a second for my eyes to adjust to the orange glow of a thousand twinkling lights on strings.

"Surprise!" The dark shapes spring up.

My mom's face is the first I recognize and my tensed muscles start to relax. She wraps me in a hug, my pulse slows. "Happy birthday," she whispers.

I'm struggling to pick my jaw back up off the floor.

Somewhere, music has started playing and Erica is squealing next to me. She throws her arms around me as soon as my mom lets go. "Happy birthday Jo!"

Once the initial shock wears off, I laugh.

And then to cry.

"No, no, you can't cry! What's wrong?"

"It's her birthday, she can cry if she wants to," Ace says, coming up from behind me.

Wiping my eyes with the back of my hand, my cheeks inflame. "I'm fine," I say, wrapping Ace in a tight hug. "I just never knew when my birthday was. I've never had one before."

"Well technically you have, you just didn't know it," a voice says from behind me, I spin around, suddenly anxious. It's Liam. If Liam is here then maybe…

"Is Ethan here?"

Scanning the bodies around me I quickly discern he is nowhere in the room. But everyone else is, all of them from The Inn, many I don't even know by name. I sense that this birthday party was a good excuse for everyone to blow off steam before the big event. It's so nice to see so many people smiling at the same time. It's hard not to smile in return, and why bother trying not to? "Happy to see you too birthday girl," Liam says, rolling his eyes.

"He's not with you?" I try to sound light, like it doesn't matter.

"No, I've been monitoring the radio communications from the NTA. I've barely left my room. Been training Cash on a bit of it. He's a quick study."

"Sorry Li, it's good to see you. You look exhausted. I can't image how much you had to charge the batteries to make this possible."

He clears his throat and I can tell he's immediately uncomfortable, "It was nothing. You look sexy as hell by the way." He halfway hugs me and I notice for the first time the wrapped package under his arm. "Oh right, this is for you. From me and Ace."

"Well I'm the one who picked it out, Li just gave it *pizzazz*."

I tear off the brown paper, judging by the weight and odd shape, I already have a solid idea of what's inside.

I'm not wrong.

It's a gun. The exact same as Ethan's. Or close enough. Sleek, shiny silver with a black grip. Slightly heavier than the one I've been practicing with. Engraved on the side in a script-like font are my initials. My full *real* name J.R.C. Joanna Rose Claymore.

"I love it, thanks guys."

"No worries. We all have our own piece. It's about time you had your own too."

"And that's not all," Ace cuts Liam off, pulling a bottle off the table behind him and pouring the contents into a glass. "You're eighteen now. It's about time for your first *real* drink."

It's a clear liquid, and when I get a whiff of it I shove the glass back into Ace's hand, afraid the smell alone singed my nose hairs off. "What is it? It smells like peroxide."

"Moonshine. Old family recipe. Chris and Doug make it." The blonde brothers, the sarcastic ones. Of course, they make alcohol. Ace hands it back. "Don't knock it till you try it, you could stand to loosen up a bit."

GRAVITY IS A STRANGE *thing,* I think to myself as I tip the contents of my third cup of moonshine back. My head is full of air, yet my limbs and body are heavier than normal, more difficult to carry without swaying or tripping.

Birthdays are strange too. People give you things and sing you a special song. My mom gave me a bracelet, shows how well she knows me. She left an hour ago.

Charles gave me a book on first aid, at least that's useful.

"Dance with me!" Erica calls over the music, pulling on my hands.

So, I do, for what is the first time in my life, I dance. Terribly, I think, but since I'm sure the alcohol has replaced most of the blood in my veins, I don't care. In fact, I don't care about much of anything right now.

"Mind if I cut in?" Cash asks, taking my hands and swinging me around. He gave me a book as a gift, I didn't have the heart to tell him I'd already read it three times.

Cash's hair is slicked back and he's put on weight under his grey wool sweater, but in all the right places. I wonder how long he starved himself, afraid there were drugs in the food. Turns out he was right anyways. Ethan told us they put a small dose of something called lorazepam in our food. Not enough so anyone would notice any effects, just enough to keep us calm and complacent. It's sickening.

"Are you having fun?" Cash hollers at me over the music, someone must've turned it up.

I nod, trying to emulate how Erica is dancing, all hips and grace, right in time with the beat. Fail miserably. Don't care.

"I've been meaning to talk to you. Do you think we could meet up for lunch soon? It's important."

I nod and he pulls me closer, his body swaying in perfect time with my off-beat movements.

"I'm sorry," he yells. "I feel like I haven't talked to you in weeks."

"That's because you haven't, well aside from—from some mumbo jimbo—er, jumbo about radio trans—transmissions."

Words are hard.

I'm surprised when a pang of guilt lances through me. I haven't gone out of my way to search for him either. And now, seeing him here, holding his hand in mine, I know I *have* missed him. But missing him is easy, almost an afterthought. Missing Ethan leaves a hollow feeling in my chest. *Ethan.* No matter how much moonshine I drink or how much I try to push his face out of mind, I can't seem to do it.

I leave Cash on the dance floor with a dumbfounded expression, waving him off when he tries to follow me. I make my way, with little steps, into the hallway. The lights are out and no one has followed me. Good. I just need a second to myself. My head is spinning and my legs weak. I sit with my back against the wall, the cool cement floor feels incredible. My head falls between my knees, hot tears well behind my eyelids. *Wait, why am I crying?* I don't remember.

Someone's coming. Breathing deeply, I fight back the urge to cry for no apparent reason and hope whoever it is can help me get back to my room. I'm done with dancing and trying to be happy.

"Joanna…" The shadowy figure calls, and then closer and louder. "Jo!"

Rubber soles slapping the cement floor and then he kneels in front of me.

I can't breathe. Forgot how.

"Are you hurt, what happened?" Ethan stares into my eyes for an eternity, and I'm lost in his, still trying to draw a breath. The green of his irises in the darkness are almost black, two oceans gleaming in the soft light flowing out from the cafeteria. I'm caught in the undertow. I manage to shake my head, try to find my voice. There was something I needed to say to him but my brain isn't functioning properly. "I'm sorry," he says, pulling me to my feet. "I tried to stay away but I had to wish you a happy birthday. It didn't feel right not being here."

I remember what I wanted to say. I'm watching his lips move and I want them to stop. My fingers come up and rest gently on them. His eyes widen as if my touch has shocked him. "Stop talking." My voice is a whisper. His hands shake where they hold my arms. "I'm sorry. I should never have said those things to you."

His eyes widen. His breath is coming fast now. He smells of fire smoke and spice. I want to taste him. There's only inches of space between us and it's too much.

Reason has taken a sabbatical.

I want to be *un*reasonable.

His fingers trail up my arms, rest on either side of my neck, sending a shiver of pleasure down my spine. Hot, it's so, so hot in here. I swear I can almost hear his heart beating, or maybe that's my own. "Ethan…" I whisper, leaning into him.

He breaks. Any bit of composure or restraint he was trying to maintain falls away. He pulls my lips to his. My fists are curled into his leather jacket. His hands are in my hair. His tongue circles mine. His body presses into me, and I can feel – I can feel *everything*. I want more. So close.

Not close enough.

I slip my hands under his shirt, revel in the strength of his body against my fingertips. He moans and dips his head down, leaves a pattern of kisses like warm summer rain along my collarbone. I'm dizzy. Elated. Drunk on his touch. I pull his lips back to mine. He catches my bottom lip between his teeth and I am two seconds away from collapsing in a heap of desire. I've pulled his jacket off and am starting with the hem of his shirt when he breaks away.

"Jo," he says between ragged breaths. "We're in the hallway, love."

Oh. Right. "I'm sorry," I whisper against his hair and he starts, circling me in his arms. Holds me there. Both of us are breathing as if we've just run a marathon while standing still. "I'm so sorry, Ethan."

He makes shushing sounds and strokes my hair, holding me tighter, holding me together. I could melt into him. Stay like this forever. "It's ok, Jo. Stop apologizing. Please."

When he lets me go, all my remaining strength goes with him. I stagger back and catch myself on the wall, slip on something wet in my heels. Crashing to the floor, a glass shatters under me. The smell of the remnants of moonshine in my cup makes my nose wrinkle.

"Shit!" Ethan lifts me back up. "Are you…" He starts

and tilts my chin up to look him in the eyes before finishing. "Are you drunk?" A flash of anger crosses his face before he notices the blood that is steadily leaking down my leg. It's funny, I can feel the blood dripping down my freshly shaved leg, but there's no pain. A muffled laugh sneaks past my lips.

Thank you, moonshine.

Ethan pulls my arm over his back and wraps his other around my waist, supporting my weight with his. "Come on, let's get you cleaned up. That might need stitches."

At first, I think he's taking me to the medical wing, but when we round the corner he takes me to the stairs instead.

Bed. Good idea.

"Whoever gave that 'shine to you is going to get real well acquainted with my right fist." He lays me in bed and closes the door behind us. He lights a few candles, readjusts the curtains to make sure they're closed and grabs a wet cloth from the bathroom.

The room is spinning. I close my eyes, but that just makes it worse. Ethan sets to cleaning my leg, it doesn't feel like much, but when I prop myself up to inspect the damage the sight makes my stomach turn. There's a gash in my leg a good three or four inches long, blood covers my calf, running in small rivulets to my ankle. My stomach lurches. I close my eyes again, preferring the spinning.

"This'll probably need stitches. I'm going to get my dad."

"No!" I grab his hand as he moves to leave. "Stay with me. It's fine, just wrap it with that tensor bandage over there."

He sighs. "I'm not a doctor Jo, we should make sure."

Now it's my turn to shush him. "It doesn't hurt, and it's not bleeding anymore, see?" A sharp pain lances through my skull. "Why are you making me talk so much?"

He laughs. "Ok, but my dad's checking it in the morning."

"Fine."

He wraps me up and tucks me in, puts a glass of water on my nightstand, makes a joke about me trying not to break that one too. My eyelids are heavy and with each candle he blows out they get heavier, the darkness a tangible force weighing them down.

A soft kiss is placed in on my forehead, reviving me back into wakefulness. I pull his face closer, touching his lips to mine, he kisses me gently, a haunting shiver prickles along my skin, all the way to my toes.

"Stay," I whisper between kisses.

"I don't think—"

"Stay."

He hesitates for only a moment, then takes off his sweater and his t-shirt, pulls the covers back, and settles in next to me. Ethan lifts me so my head it's resting on his bare chest. It's unlike anything I've ever felt before. This sense of absolute calm. His body is so warm, so strong. I could stay here, right here, forever. The soothing *thump thump, thump thump* of his heartbeat lulls me into sleep.

THIRTY-SIX

I'M SOMEWHERE BETWEEN awake and dreamland when Ethan gets out of bed and I hear the door open.

"Oh, Ethan, I didn't know you were back—is she alright?"

"Yeah, she's asleep, going to have one hell of a hangover tomorrow though."

"Well you can thank your friends for that."

"They aren't going to like how I intend to say thank you. I don't get it. I mean, why didn't you stop her?"

A sigh. "I haven't been her mother for fifteen years, I have no right to try to control her now."

An awkward silence. I try to move my head to hear better. It feels like a block of cement.

"Ethan, I have to ask you something."

More silence.

"I can't stop her from going with you." *That wasn't a question*, I think to myself. "I couldn't take it if anything happened to her."

"Amy, I would never let anything happen to her, never again. Ace may be assigned to get her to where she needs to be inside The Mill, but that won't stop me from following them." His voice changes, deepens. "I promise you, no matter what happens, I *will* bring her back."

"You love her, don't you?"

My pulse quickens. At first there's no reply, and then he says, "Trust me Amy, I'll keep her safe."

THIRTY-SEVEN

I AWAKEN WITH a head full of fog and eyes covered in a fine layer of glue. But when I sit up, I find that other than being overly tired, I'm completely fine.

Joanna 1, Moonshine 0.

"Ethan?" I pull back the blanket covering his sleeping form. Pillows, no Ethan.

The events of last night are all in torn, smudged pieces in my mind. I'm thinking it's possible I imagined him being here or maybe it was just a vivid dream when I see a folded piece of paper on my nightstand, "Good morning, beautiful," it says on the front. I smile.

Sorry I had to leave. I needed to get back before Roman noticed I was gone. I'll be back in a couple days. Try to stay out of trouble. Miss you already, love.

P.S. my dad is expecting to see you this morning. Drag

your hungover ass downstairs. No excuses.

-E

Heaving a loud sigh, I stand up and stretch, suspiciously eyeing the bandage covering my calf. It doesn't hurt at all. Starting to peel it off I find that even the skin around the red stained fabric isn't tender. I stop, secure it back in place, better to leave it on until I get downstairs. Twisting my hair into a knot, I scrub the leftover make-up off my face and dress in my regular sweat pants and tank top.

Breathing is easier today, as if no matter what happens I could breeze right through it. A quick stop to get checked out by the doc and then off to hand to hand combat with Ace, which I'm overly excited for today. If he's hungover I might have a chance. The sparring board stands a bazillion to one right now and the one on my side was a fluke. Ace assures me I'm doing good and getting better every day, but if my opponent is as well trained as Ace, I'm still not good enough to be able to take them down. Even with my so-called *advantage* of heightened senses and fast reflexes.

Taking the stairs two at a time, I listen to the echo of each footfall as they follow me, sounding like a hundred marching soldiers are right on my heels. Shoving the door open, my smile falters.

Chaos.

All the main arteries of the basement floor are clogged with people. All are wearing paper masks covering their mouths and noses. Running, shouting muffled conversations at each other. They're all congregating here in the common wing or heading for the stairs... Far away from the medical wing.

I spot Erica in the rush of people coming down the hallway, pull her to the side.

"What happened? Is someone infected?"

She nods, eyes wide and frantic. "Oh god Jo... I touched her! What if I'm..."

I shake my head at her. "You're going to be fine. Who's infected?"

She seems to calm at my empty assurance. "Charles found them this morning. They were hiding out in the parking garage. There was so much blood!" Only now do I notice the smell of bleach and see a women who helps take care of the laundry ferociously scrubbing at a red stain on the tile down the hall, rubber gloves to her elbows.

Every nerve ending in my body is instantly alive. "Who are they? Were they followed?"

Where is my gun? My memory is still in choppy pieces, but I can recall my mother saying she would bring all my gifts upstairs for me before she left. *Damn.*

"I don't know."

If anyone followed those people here we're going to have bigger problems than a few people getting infected. I wish Ethan was here, or Roman, they'd be able to sort this out.

"Ace! Have you seen Ace?"

She shakes her head at me, running on to the door leading to the stairs. "Not since last night." She pushes past people into the stairwell, probably going to go scrub her skin with steel wool and sanitizer. I would.

Weaving my way through the congested bodies, I whip around the corner into the hallway housing the lab and the medical wing. I'm about to rush into the quarantine unit to see if my mom has seen Ace when a man is pushed out. A respirator covers most of his face, but I'm almost certain I haven't seen him here before. He looks to be in his late twenties, possibly early thirties, with sandy brown hair to his earlobes and green eyes ringed in red from crying. His skin is a roadmap of red and purple. His once white shirt is torn and covered in dirt and something that resembles dried blood.

"Who are you?" Even though I'm not blind to his distressed state, I can't help sounding blunt. No matter what this man has been through, right now, he's a threat.

"My wife," he sobs. "Is she going to die?" He's heaving now, hunched over as if it's too much to even stand. "No! She can't die!" His voice is the sound of torture, unrefined, raw. It hurts to listen.

"Were you followed here?" I have to shout over his sobs. I have to quell the stabbing pain in my chest, try not to imagine how I would feel if someone I loved was on the verge of death.

He doesn't answer. I make the mistake of peering over his hunched form, through the rectangular window in the door. Charles and my mom are there, frantically inserting IV's and setting monitors beside the bed. But they aren't what I can't stop gawking at. The woman laying on the gurney is eerily still and covered in varying degrees of wet and dried blood.

Even more mortifying is the perfectly round shape under her shirt. Charles sets to cutting the fabric and my stomach drops to my toes. She's pregnant. Very pregnant. And from the way her hand hangs off the gurney and the greyish color of her skin, I'm afraid her husband is right. She is going to die. If she isn't dead already. I put a hand on the man's back. I don't know what else to do. I can't force him to say anything right now. I'm not even sure *I* can speak.

The amount of relief I feel when Ace comes barreling around the corner is immeasurable. He takes one look at my face and composes his own, discerning he needs to be the one to take charge. He also needs to be the one to keep calm, because I'm seconds from breaking.

"Grab his other arm."

I do. Together we half drag, half carry the man to the gymnasium. He's so consumed by his grief he doesn't fight us, doesn't speak a word. He just cries and winces every time his rib cage brushes against my side.

IT TOOK A COUPLE hours and copious amounts of coffee and water before he was ready to say something. His name is Ezra, the woman in the quarantine room is Summer.

"Look, I'm really sorry for whatever happened to you and your wife, but we're going to need to ask you some questions," Ace starts, crouching down to where the man is sitting on the floor.

He lifts his head for the first time since we entered the gym. Eyes all but blank, it's like looking into the soul of a dead man.

"I need to see my wife."

"We just have a few questions for you, if you answer—"

"I need to see my *wife*."

I bend down next to Ace and put a hand on the man's knee. "Ezra, our doctors are doing everything they can for her. If we go back over there now, we'll only be in the way."

He seems to deflate. "Where are we? What is this place?"

"We'll answer all the questions you have and I swear I'll take you to check on your wife as soon as we can. First, I need to ask a few things. There are a lot of people here, innocent people we need to keep safe."

Ezra nods. "I understand."

Ace looks at me as if I'm a completely different person than I was a minute ago, arches a brow at me. I sneer at him.

What? I can be civil.

"Where did you come from?"

"Zone Three. I worked in broadcasting there until about a week ago."

That's my Zone. Which means they came from the south where the NTA is patrolling. And where the Exiled's encampment is. I work to swallow the lump in my throat, curse the way my heart pounds.

"Why did you leave?" Ace asks him, but I can hear the underlying question in his words, *were you exiled...*

"My wife is eight months pregnant." He gives Ace a hard look. "That, and I got my hands on sensitive information they didn't want going public. I didn't agree with them."

Ace nods his understanding. So, they left before the child could be tested. I'm filing the second part of his answer away for later, hoping this 'sensitive information' can potentially be of use to us.

"Could you have been followed? Did you run into anyone? Did anyone see you?" I butt in.

"One question at a time Jo," Ace scolds.

"There was a patrol on the road a few K away from here, but we skirted around it. We only traveled at night. I don't know how they found us."

My blood turns to ice in my veins.

"Who found you? The NTA?"

He shakes his head. I can see the muscles in his jaw working as he grinds his teeth against the memory. "It was a group, not NTA. They were driving a white van. People with guns. A *lot* of guns."

I cringe inwardly. Ace and I exchange a knowing glance, he notices. "You know them?"

"They're people who have been exiled from the cities. Our people've had several run ins with 'em." Ace offers.

"What happened?" I ask.

"They found us, that's what happened."

It's obvious he doesn't want to elaborate, and frankly, I'd rather not hear it anyways.

"How did you end up here? Is it possible they could have followed you?"

"I honestly don't know. They took what they wanted from us and left us half dead where they found us. I don't think they would've followed us, but I can't be sure. We had to keep moving, there wasn't any time to cover our tracks."

"You're lucky to be alive," Ace tells him, but I doubt he's feeling so lucky right now. I hope his wife and child will be alright.

"That's what *she* said," Ezra scoffs, disgust twisting his mouth. "She made us *thank her* for letting us live. Said if she ever saw us again she'd kill us."

The knife twists in my gut. "Who?" I almost shout, remembering that day on the road, remembering the spray of blood drifting on the wind, the weight of the gun in my hand that I didn't have the heart to shoot.

"The bitch with the red hair."

THIRTY-EIGHT

I'M SITTING IN the cafeteria staring at the plate of food Ace put in front of me. I don't plan on eating it. In fact, I'm more likely to throw it across the room and watch it shatter and smear across the wall still adorned with my birthday banner.

It's two weeks ago. It's two weeks ago all over again and the barrel of my gun is pressed against a slice of red hair. The light of the dying sun glints off the sleek metal gripped in my hand. I couldn't do it. I was too weak. Maybe I still am. And now, because of my weakness, someone's wife... Scratch that, someone's *pregnant* wife might die, her unborn child with her.

She's in a coma now, she was never infected with TEN, which is a miracle, but it may not make a difference. She suffered a massive blow to the head and lost an ocean of blood. They told Ezra if she didn't wake up soon they'd have to deliver the baby by C-section. They don't think she'll survive the surgery.

They're leaving it to him to choose. Wait for her to awaken, if she does at all, and he risks the life of his unborn child. Or do the surgery, and risk losing his wife in the process. No one should have to make a decision like that. No one.

"You've gotta eat something," Ace tells me.

I resist the urge to jump down his throat. Clench my teeth. He doesn't know all of this could have been avoided. He doesn't know I had the chance to end a life that may have taken two others. Maybe more than that. How many people have they killed? *Why?*

Humanity is already so messed up as it is. This world has been pulverized and jammed into a box of hatred and lies. It's turned us into something more sinister than mere humans. It's become a contest of who's more ruthless, more deranged than the rest. The winners get to breathe another day, and us, the so-called sane ones, are being picked off at an alarming rate. We are mice in a cage staring down a hoard of feral cats.

I can't tell him.

I'm afraid to say it out loud. What would he think of his star student then? The truth doesn't matter now. The damage is done. All I can do is stop it from happening again. And that's exactly what I'll do. I've changed my mind, there are people who don't deserve to live. Red Hair is one of them.

"When are we leaving Ace?"

He cocks his head at me, squints his big brown eyes. "Leaving?"

"We have to take care of this before more people get

hurt. We're the only ones here who can."

It's easy to see he isn't happy, but his anger isn't directed towards me. "We aren't going anywhere, Jo." He says a little too harshly. "We need someone on the roof twenty-four hours to keep watch. I've gotta relieve Logan in a couple hours and right now you and I are the only protection The Inn has against an attack. As unlikely as that may be, we need to be here."

"So, what you're telling me is we're just going to let them get away with this?" I can't keep the disgust from pouring out of my mouth. My heart is cold and black, thoughts of revenge are building a concrete wall around it, making sure it stays that way.

I'm standing before I've even made the conscious decision to move my legs. My fingers are splayed against the table. My body leans into him. "They need to be put down." I can't believe what my ears are hearing, the consonants and vowels coming out of my mouth. I sound like a psychopath. I sound like what I imagine my father would sound like. But the thought doesn't sober me. It makes me angrier.

Ace looks around, on my back are the eyes of the other brave souls who left the safety of their rooms to have lunch in the cafeteria. He lowers his voice. "You think I don't want to go out there and rip their fucking heads off? Because I do." He drops his fork onto his plate with a clatter. "Don't do anything stupid. Two more days. That's forty-eight hours until we set off that explosive at their camp. Let the NTA take care of them. They *will* get what's coming to them. You've gotta calm the *hell* down and have a little patience."

My teeth grit against the chapped flesh of my bottom lip until it's on the cusp of bleeding. *Don't do anything stupid,* he says. The words on Ethan's note flash before my eyes, *try to stay out of trouble.* Why does no one believe I'm capable of making the right decision, of taking care of myself? I'm not a child. And I've got better aim, and more training than at least ninety percent of the people in this stupid hole in the ground. I grab my tray and stomp to the trash bin, shove it in.

Patience was never my strong suit.

THIRTY-NINE

"WHY WERE YOU EXILED?"

Adrien yawns, rubbing the sleep out of his eyes, "Good afternoon."

My skin is bristling. I need to know. I need to know how this person could ever be with the Exiled. Has he killed people too? Has he beaten pregnant women to within an inch of their life? It takes all my willpower not to scream at him.

"How? How could you be with a group like that?"

He sits up, looks me square in the face. "I did not think I had another choice."

I'm against the metal bars now, trying to hide the way my body is vibrating. "What did you do? Why were you even exiled?"

He shakes his head at me, preoccupies himself picking bits of lint off his black pants. I can see pain in his eyes, his voice is raw when he says. "And why would I tell you? It is not your business."

I slam the palms of my hands against the bars, the metal rings. I try not to cry when I tell him. "We found a man and a woman today. The woman was pregnant and your people—*your people* beat her half to death. She could die, and her baby too."

Adrien grits his teeth, stands, but doesn't move to come any closer. Smart man.

"We are not all that way," he whispers. "There is a reason I was alone when your doctor found me. It is because I left."

Oh.

A voice in my head whispers he could be lying. He's probably lying. He's just a crazy as the rest of them.

"Your people, the others, they almost killed us too. There was a woman, she spoke just like you. I could have killed her, but I didn't."

He doesn't say anything so I go on, wondering why I'm even bothering with him, why I feel the need to tell him, to tell *someone* what I've done. How all of this could have been avoided if only I was strong enough.

"If I had," I say, swallowing back the bile rising in my throat. "The people we found might have been alright. It was the same woman who did this to them."

He meets my burrowing gaze with a steady one of his own, seeming to recognize something within me. "She spoke like me?"

"Yes."

"Red hair?"

I nod. *He knows her.* Of course, he does. She'd be a tough person to forget.

He sits hard, props his head up with a fist connected to an elbow that rests on his knee. "If it makes you feel any better, she tried to kill me too. Many times. She's my sister."

I sit across from his cell in the hallway to process this. There are so many questions, but none of them matter. All that matters is hopefully soon she'll be dead. And if the NTA doesn't take care of her, I'll be making it my personal mission to dispose of her myself.

His sister?

This earth has shrunk, the people and places so reduced and closely compacted together that I wouldn't be surprised if someone told me Erica is my cousin and Roman is my long-lost uncle. My head is spinning.

"Would she have followed them here?" I ask him after a time.

He tilts his head, purses his lips, "Did she take much from them?"

"Everything they had."

"It depends."

"On what?"

He shrugs. "If it was enough. Or, if she thought they could lead her somewhere she could get more. She does not often leave people alive unless she is not finished with them."

FORTY

WALK FORWARD.
Turn around.
Walk back.
Repeat.

The carpet is wearing thin in a straight line from one end of my room to the other. I need a shower. I should eat. I need to stop pacing.

Two sharp knocks on my door.

Breathe in. Breathe out.

Need to calm down.

I yank the door open. Charles stands in the doorway with a flashlight, a red bag tucked under his arm. It's strange how I'm calmer at the mere sight of him, sobered from the high of blind desperation.

"Charles, is everything alright?"

His eyes travel the length of my arm, stop and widen. "Going somewhere?"

I follow his gaze, my own eyes widening in response. My gun. It's gripped in my right hand. I can't remember picking it up.

I'm losing my mind... I shrug my shoulders at Charles as if I'm not, shake my head. "No."

"Can I take a look at that?" He invites himself in, points at the bandage on my leg. I had all but forgotten it was there.

I'm still holding the door open when he pulls the chair over from the other side of the room, brushes off the dust and sets it beside the bed.

"You've got more important things to worry about right now. Besides, it's fine, I can't even feel it."

He huffs, tosses the bag on the nightstand, drops his bones into the chair and runs a shaky hand over the scruff on his face. I can see the stress, the exhaustion in the color of his skin, in the way his eyes don't seem to focus on any one thing, "Listen, Joanna," he says. "I could use the distraction if you don't mind. I've done all I can do for Summer, it's up to her husband now how we'll proceed. Giving stitches just might be the highlight of my day." He meets my eyes. "You look like you could use the distraction too."

I can.

I nod, set my gun on the bed and sit down beside it.

"Thanks."

He unwraps his kit from its coil, revealing a line-up of polished silver pieces that glint in the light from the candles. Charles readjusts his flashlight on the nightstand so it throws a circle of light over his equipment and the chair where he sits. Once, the mere sight of all this would have turned my stomach, but now I'm oddly unfazed by it. Maybe I deserve to hurt.

He takes a small oblong bowl and goes to the bathroom to fill it with water.

"So," I say as he sits back down. "How's he holding up?"

He glares at me. "Ezra? How do you think?"

Duh. Stupid question.

"Sorry, that was rude." He takes a long, shaky breath, seems to hold it. "I'd rather not talk about Ezra, hits a little too close to home, you know."

At first, I don't know. But then I do. He hasn't seen his wife in fifteen years. Up until a few weeks ago at least he knew she was alive. Now there's been no word, not even a whisper.

She should have been back by now. That was the plan; watch out for me as long as she could, keep me out of trouble, and then do whatever it takes to get the hell out of there and get here, back to her family. I wonder why he hasn't ever asked me about her. He hasn't seen her in so long, but I have. I've seen her every day for the last five years of my life.

"I bet she knows about the patrols, she's probably just being smart, waiting for the right time. She's always *so* careful. She wouldn't get caught."

He drops the cotton pad in his hand, regards me as though I've read his mind without his permission. Nods. "Here, lift your leg for me." I help him rest my ankle on his knee, he presses gently on the area. I realize, a little belatedly, that I'm not being a very good distraction.

"That tender?" He asks.

The blood stain on my bandage is the size of a small saucer. It's turned an ugly shade of burgundy, but no, "It doesn't hurt at all."

He purses his lips. Clicks his tongue. "Ethan said it was pretty deep." He's started to unwrap the bandage. His touch is feather-light even though I've told him it doesn't hurt.

"I don't remember." The back of my neck burns, staining my ears red. "I was drinking, maybe he just overreacted."

The last part of the bandage sticks to my skin, the crusted blood acting as a morbid sort of glue. He pulls it away in small increments until my leg is bare.

Charles snaps his neck up, narrows his eyes at me. My lips part and my brows furrow.

There's an abstract painting of blood smeared and speckled on my calf. That's it. There's no gory gash, not even a scrape. The skin under the layer of old blood is smooth, unmarked.

Impossible.

FOURTY-ONE

I'M RESTLESS.

I've been spending my days training and my nights with Logan on the roof helping him keep watch, or so I tell myself. He says he doesn't need the help. I say he does.

"They should have been back by now."

We attack less than twenty-four hours from now. They were supposed to be here an hour after sundown. That was three hours ago. Where are they? Where is Ethan? I hug my knees to my chest, put down my binoculars.

Logan's eye is fixed on his scope. "They'll be here. Relax."

"But what if—"

"*If* the Exiled were around, Id've seen them by now. They're fine," he draws out the last two words, clearly getting tired of listening to me.

I dare to exhale. It's uncomfortably quiet tonight. Even the wind is afraid to move.

There's a storm rolling in over the hills to the south. I hope they're ahead of it. The moon is blotted out with black clouds, shades of grey and blue glint around the edges. The atmosphere is charged with an electrical current and the threat of rain. I've always wanted to see a thunderstorm, but not tonight. I beg the skies to clear, wish away the imposing clouds. Thunder rumbles above us and the sound ricochets from one end of the universe to the other. Like there are giants playing dominos in the sky.

Logan's not much for conversation. It's ok, idle chit-chat isn't the reason I come up here. I come to get *away* from all the talking, all the questions. Charles has been coming up with all kinds of wild theories as to why I could heal overnight. He wants to run tests. They've noticed a slight elevation in healing times with Ethan since he was cured, but nothing compared to what I experienced.

I keep telling Charles maybe it wasn't as bad as it seemed. We both know I'm lying. The amount of blood proves it. I've asked him not to say anything about it to anyone yet. I have enough to worry about as it is, enough to think about. We all do.

A resounding crack splinters the sky, spears of light hurtle towards the earth, fracturing the ground somewhere over the hills. The sky brightens and darkens, brightens again. Beautiful. Dangerous.

"You see that?" Logan breathes, tightens his hold on the sniper rifle. My heart does a nose dive into my stomach. I duck, shuffle my body to the ledge beside Logan.

"What do you see?"

I can't seem to catch my breath. My throat's gone dry. Reaching through the hole I cut into the pocket of my sweats, I pull the gun from its holster on my thigh.

He doesn't answer.

"Logan—"

"It's gone."

"What was it?"

"Thought I saw someone. Hundred yards away. Ten o'clock."

My binoculars are up and moving, scanning the treeline and the empty road.

There.

A shadow moves between the trees. I hear Logan's sharp intake of breath, hear him exhale in one focused, slow breath. He saw it too, chambers a round.

There's a ringing in my ears and a prickling in my fingers. If I held the binoculars any tighter the lenses would shatter. The shadow moves closer. Another close behind it and third to the right. It's an ambush. How many are there? How many can Logan take out before it's too many?

"Ace," I whisper, wiggle the walkie off of Logan's belt. "We have to warn them."

"Wait."

For what? I want to scream at him, s*hoot!*

I grip the walkie in my hand like a lifeline. Flip the safety off on my gun. Wait. Watch the trees. It's too quiet, everything is too still.

The sky breaks in half, bleeds white light across the land. I catch a glimpse of a face.

It's Roman.

I feel more than see Logan relax beside me, pull the binoculars back onto my eyes. Chris, his brother Doug, and Ethan are behind him, making their way home through the trees.

I flip onto my back, drop the binoculars. Logan looks at me and smiles. A rumble from above proceeds the rain. At first a few drops and then a downpour. Neither of us moves. And then he starts to laugh. I'm so utterly relieved I join him. I want to dance in the rain, kiss the clouds. They're ok. Ethan is ok. And so are we. The sky is crying warm tears of joy and it's one of the most amazing things I've ever felt.

"Well, what are you waiting for?" Logan says between fits of laughter. "Get your ass down there."

FORTY-TWO

I MAKE IT down the stairs in record time. As I approach the underground entrance, Roman is just making his way inside. Lily and Rosie are waiting for him and he scoops them both up in a big hug, smothers them with kisses as they laugh and squeal. I do a double take. I knew Roman was their father, but I could never picture it. Could never picture him as something different from the time-hardened man I know. Until now. His smile is real, and brilliant. He may be even more elated to see his girls, than they are to see him. It's beautiful, and I am so glad the world hasn't stolen that beauty from them as it did me.

I nod at Roman, blinking back tears.

Chris and Doug are behind him on their way inside, their backs hunched and eyes dark-rimmed.

"Where is he?" I ask. He was with them, I'm sure I saw him.

Chris turns around, rolls his eyes as he tells me, "He

wanted to check the perimeter. Charles got a hold of us over the walkies 'bout fifteen minutes ago, told us what happened with that guy and his wife."

And I'm outside. It doesn't take me long to find him.

I'm so desperate for an escape, to feel something good that when our eyes touch, I don't hesitate. I close the gap between us, taking in the way the rain makes his black t-shirt cling to every one of his muscles, how his eyes glisten, and how his lips crack into a brilliant smile when he sees me.

He takes the last step, crosses that invisible line keeping us apart, takes my face in his hands, doesn't waste an instant. He kisses me hungrily, passionately, with a desire so intense it borders on pain. Warm rain drip drops down my neck, soaks through my clothes, my skin, doing nothing to the douse the flames raging within me. Ethan's hands are on my hips, simultaneously rough, and yet so, so gentle. They fumble with the hem of my shirt, slip over the contours of my bare skin.

Everything is magnified, charged, electric. My skin is hypersensitive. His touch is a drug, and I'm hopelessly addicted. I want to catch this feeling in a jar and keep it forever. My heartbeat is a primitive sort of music pulsing through me. He whispers something between kisses, something I'm too delirious to understand. A moan stumbles from my lips and trips down the length of my being. His hands grip me harder in response, run from my sides to my lower back, and then lower still, circling my thighs. He lifts me onto him, holds me like I'm the lightest thing in the world. I wrap my legs around him. He buries his face into my neck.

And it's like this. I'm holding a million possibilities in the palm of my hand, a thousand photographs of a future I never thought I could have. And yet it's here, this future I'd do anything to keep safe. Because no matter what happens, I'll always have this moment. If I die tomorrow, I'll die knowing what it felt like to be touched by Ethan Knox. Knowing what it felt like to be in love so irrevocably, so undoubtedly, that dying isn't even an option.

"Ethan!" Charles calls though the rain and the thunder.

Ethan sets me on solid ground, but doesn't let me go, says through ragged breaths, "We should get inside, love."

FORTY-THREE

"THIS IS BULLSHIT!" Ethan spits at Roman.

It's been decided two people need to stay behind tomorrow. With everything that's happened in the last couple days, it's no longer safe to leave everyone here without people who have been trained to shoot a gun. Roman has chosen Ethan to stay behind with Erica and Charles, who both have *some* training. No other bodies can be spared. Everyone has their jobs, Liam, to jam their radio signals and guard the bus, Chris and Doug, get the masks and herd everyone to the buses. Roman, to guard the other bus and make sure everyone gets on safely. Ace is with me, Logan is the sniper, he has to take out their transformer so all the doors will open. A guy named Seth is driving one of the buses, and a guy named Jerimiah is driving the other, both have military training and are tasked with taking down anyone who stands in our way.

There are a few others coming with us, guys who have

training and want to lend a hand however they can. Ethan is the only one without a job already designated to him, and the one Roman trusts most, aside from maybe Ace.

Roman rubs a hand over the blonde stubble on his face, exasperated, though seemingly not surprised by Ethan's reaction. "I need you here Knox."

Ethan changes tactics, glares at everyone else standing in the meeting room. No one jumps to his defense. Everyone is here save for Liam, who's been glued to his radio, deciphering transmissions around the clock.

"I know that place better than any of you! It would be stupid to leave me here and you know it."

Roman levels his gaze at Ethan. "This conversation is over. It's already been decided. You and Ace are the only two people with enough training. I wouldn't leave The Inn's safety with anyone else."

A murmur from Chris and Doug tells me they aren't overly happy with that last comment. I breathe a sigh of relief, brush off the pins stuck in my flesh. Ethan will stay here. Whether he likes it or not. And he'll be safe. Safer than the rest of us anyways. They'll barricade the entrances, and Liam has set up a few extra surveillance cameras outside. Cash has offered to man the control room and keep watch.

But then Ethan looks at me. And I know the conversation is not over. I know what he's going to ask me, I've been waiting for it. I'm not sure I can give him what he wants. No matter how mad he is about it.

"Choose me instead," he says, all traces of anger seeped away.

I don't answer right away, Ace shrugs at me. "It's up to

you."

"Please Jo. I won't be able to concentrate on anything knowing you're out there without me."

"You'll be fine."

"Joanna."

"No."

He starts to smile, and now I'm worried. "Ace is a wayyyy better sniper than I am. If Ace stays behind, everyone here will be more safe."

He's playing dirty now, I can see what he's doing. I don't like it.

"Tell her Ace."

"It's true, he's shit on the sniper."

Ethan's eyebrows cinch together. "Well I wouldn't go that far."

"I would, you couldn't hit an elephant at fifty yards on your best day."

This is so frustrating.

"Anyways." Ethan glares at Ace. "Your mom, Erica, Roman's girls... If something *did* happen, they'd be better protected wi—"

"Fine." I say against gritted teeth, picturing Rosie and Lily, I could never let anything happen to them. They're too young, too innocent, too blissfully ignorant of the violent world outside these walls. And I hope they never have to witness it. I hope they never turn out to be like me. Hardened. Angry. "You win. Ace stays. Are you happy now?"

Victory dances like flames behind his eyes. He comes around to my side of the table and wraps me in a hug I'm unable to return. "If anything happens...." I almost shout.

"Don't," he whispers back. "I got this. Nothing is going to happen, I've got you."

"But who's got you?"

"Well, now that that's settled," Roman starts. "Ethan, you'll take Ace's place with me tomorrow before we leave. You've got experience with explosives already, you and me are gonna—"

Liam crashes into the room, hair disheveled, eyes bloodshot and bugging out of his head from too much caffeine.

"Well? Spit it out Li." Roman curses under his breath, says something to himself that sounds like *what is it now...*

"I-it's Commander Tobin."

A gallon of ice-water is injected into my veins. I'm seeing spots, my body fighting against the sudden chill in the air.

"I just overheard a transmission, the Commander has stationed himself at The Mill. We–we thought he had left, but I-I don't know, he's back and it doesn't sound like he's going anywhere."

Breathe. Just breathe Joanna.

Ethan is searching my face, rubbing the cold out of my arms.

"Shit," Roman growls, knocks his knuckles against the table.

I swallow the razorblades in my throat, try to see the situation objectively. This man is nothing to me. It shouldn't matter if he's there. "He's just one man, why does it matter?" I say against the voices rising like waves in the small room.

At first, I'm unsure anyone has heard me. I'm a small

speck in the middle of an ocean, struggling to get to shore, but the current is pulling me away. Their voices get louder, some shouting, others whispering to one another. But Roman heard me, his eyes blaze into mine when my gaze falls on him.

"It matters," he says, the rest of the room quieting at the sound of their leader's voice. "Because he isn't just one man."

"Commander Tobin never travels alone. He's always got a personal entourage of anywhere from five to eight soldiers with him, sometimes more," Ethan explains.

Ace snorts. "Not just soldiers. They're the best in the bizz. Highly trained, no mercy. They're like dogs. The Commander says kill, and they go for the throat, no questions asked."

"Do you think he knows?" Chris asks Liam.

Liam shakes his head. "No. I mean there's no way he could. And besides, if he did, he'd have a whole battalion there and I'd have heard something about it."

"Nothing's changed," Roman says, "We're as ready as we'll ever be. This. *This* is what we trained for." His jaw is taut, eyes glassy. I've never heard him speak with as much conviction, as much raw passion as he is right now. "Tomorrow everything changes. We tear those fucks a new asshole. They will not get away with this, never again. This is the start of something boys. A show of force. We show them what we're capable of. We show them we will *not* back down. More will follow us. There are so many people who have been waiting for someone, *anyone* to challenge the Alliance. Too many lives have been lost… I'm ready– *I'm ready to fight back!* Are you?"

There are murmurs of ascent, they evolve, morph into all-out shouts and leather booted feet drumming the cement floor.

"We're with you!"

"Let's take those bastards down!"

"They won't know what hit them."

My heart swells. There's still ice-water in my veins, but there's a whisper of steam in the core of my being, thawing the frost covering my heart.

Roman puts up a hand to quell the noise, everyone waits for his next words with bated breath and clenched fists. Fury and passion gleams in their eyes. He pulls a sheet of paper out from under a pile on his desk. Walks over to the board on the other side of the room. Grabs a pin and shoves it through the paper, moves away.

A fist is punched through my stomach, reaches up and tears out my lungs.

"If you see this man?" His face goes red with an undiluted sort of hatred. "You shoot first."

On the board is a photo of my father. And my mother. And me.

I bite back bile. I'm just a baby, my mom is a ghost of herself. My father... he looks like the devil incarnate, eyes steel blue and piercing. He holds me on his lap. He's smiling. I can't explain why, but that only makes it worse.

FOURTY-FOUR

"CAN I TALK to you for a second?" My mom pokes her head out of the door to her lab. Ethan and I were just on our way to dry off our still rain-dampened skin and get to bed. But there's no point, really. I doubt anyone will be sleeping tonight.

"Of course," I answer, and then to Ethan. "I'll meet you upstairs," offering him a small smile.

"'Night Amy," he says to my mom and shuffles his tired feet to the stairwell.

She closes the door behind us and the fact Naomi isn't here makes me breathe a sigh of relief.

"Sit," she says softly, motioning to a stool. Only now do I notice the way her hands are flitting about, the tension in her shoulders.

"Everything alright, Mom?" It's strange to say the 'mom' word out loud. It's still a foreign language my mouth has trouble wrapping around, tastes of hope and something bittersweet.

"I have to tell you something. I should have told you a long time ago and I'm sorry I didn't."

I know where this is going.

"Would you please sit," she says a little impatiently.

I remain standing. Don't say a word.

"Ok," she says, giving up. "You've asked me before about your father. I never gave you a straight answer. You should know—you have a right to know—"

"The General Commander is my father," I finish for her. "I-I already know. I mean, I've known for a while now actually."

Her brows are dangerously close to her hairline, an enormous weight seems to have fallen off her shoulders. "How?"

"Ethan told me."

A flash of anger flits in and out of her eyes.

"Don't be angry with him. I forced him to tell me."

She nods solemnly, a few strands of her auburn hair coming loose from the clip holding them up. "I'm sorry I didn't tell you myself."

"*Why?*" I ask her. It's the one thing I will never understand, the one thing I need an answer for.

Suddenly I'm three years old again. Waking up in a bed, in a room, in a building I don't recognize. Strange faces telling me things like 'It's alright," and "Don't cry," and "We're going to take you somewhere safe."

Lies.

I'm shocked at the lividity of the memory. I could hardly remember a thing about my life before the institutions and now it seems it's all coming back. It never truly left. I'm sick of the bullshit. It's time everyone started telling the truth, even me.

My mom tilts her head to the side, seems confused. That only frustrates me more. "Why *him?* How could you possibly be with someone like him?"

I can't even say his name.

Her eyes betray a sadness even I don't think I have the capacity to comprehend.

"I loved him once." It's hard to miss the way her skin bristles at the memory. "He wasn't always like he is now. We were both so young when we met. And young when we got pregnant with you. I didn't start to see who he really was until just a couple months before you were born."

I can tell she has more to say, but she's hesitating. I sit across from her, my legs suddenly sore from the effort of standing.

"And?" I press gently, clasping my hands together between my knees.

"He was already in the military by then. I knew what his stance was. I thought I could agree with him, with what the NTA was doing. Until...Until about five months into the pregnancy. You were so active, so–so full of life and you weren't even born yet."

Tears well behind my eyelids. I clasp my hands harder together. I don't know if I feel sorry for her. I don't think I can. How can you not recognize a monster when he's right beside you, living under the same roof, sharing the same bed? It's ignorant and it's naïve. I tell myself she didn't know because she didn't want to know. Because she was weak.

"And then," she breathes, her jaw muscles tightening.

"I asked him. I asked him what we'd do if you were born O-Negative." Now she looks me in the eyes. Pain is what I see there, and a plea for me to understand. "Do you want to know what he said to me?"

I want to say no. No, I don't. And yet I'm nodding, yes.

"He told me if you were born O-Negative he would kill you himself. He said he would say you died in childbirth, that he wouldn't have his child made to grow up in an institution, and it would be better to kill you and force them to harvest you immediately. He said you would never see the light of day."

I'm trying to imagine it, but I can't believe someone whose voice sounds as sweet as warm honey can spit words that savor more of acid. This earth, these people on it, they aren't built for love anymore, or any other fanciful ideas, like *family*.

It's the cold-hearted, the clinically insane, and the ruthless who thrive. It's those types of people who get promoted to General Commander. I can see how the system works, encouraging the soldiers of lower rank to be *more* cruel, to be *more* heartless. To breed a new chain of command even more demented than the last.

It's time someone broke the cycle.

It has to end.

"I just don't get it." I'm up and moving now, pacing, it seems to have become a hobby of mine. "You stayed with him for three years after I was born. How could you do that? How—how could," I'm choking on my own words, they keep falling out of my mouth, not waiting to make sense of themselves, just jumping out blindly. My hands are making wild gestures and I can't seem to stop it, can't seem to calm down. I want to crush his windpipe with my bare hands. The ease with which this thought crosses my mind scares me.

"How were you able to see him every day without shooting him in the face? You can't just come back from saying that, you don't–you don't just—"

"Joanna..."

"No, you can't just get over tha—"

"He threatened to kill us both."

I'm frozen. A perfectly still statue, but an earthquake shatters me from the inside. I am a volcano. The plates are shifting; the heat is rising. Eruption is a very real possibility.

"*What?*" My lungs strain to get out this one word. My mind is a minefield. If he at least loved her. If he had at least respected *her* even a little, he may have had one redeemable trait. Having the capacity to love would have made him somewhat human.

"I tried to leave, but he wouldn't let me. One time, I almost did. He—" She swallows back something I'm sure tastes like stomach acid, because it's the same taste on my tongue. "He caught me. I was trying to sneak out with you when he was asleep. I paid for it." Her hand absently goes to her collar bone. There's a scar there I hadn't ever noticed before. A jagged line of white, raised skin. I kick back the urge to vomit.

"He hired a man to guard the house for almost a year after that. He was placated by the false documents I showed him, showing you were A-Positive, but he still didn't trust I wouldn't try to leave him. As far as he was concerned, I, well both of us, belonged to him. I wasn't allowed to leave the house, even for work. He made me go on a long-term leave. He told everyone I was sick. I had to *pretend* for almost two years, just to earn back his trust… We were almost home free. I had everything in place, we were going to Zone One. I was going to change our names, our documentation. But then—"

"But then I fell."

"Yes. You fell. And if I hadn't left, he would have killed me. I was afraid he was going to try to find you. He never did. I'm sure he knew where you were, but it was too late, you were already committed to the institution. It would have looked bad if he didn't follow his own laws and waited until you were eighteen."

It's odd, this quiet rage. It's calming and at the same time liberating. Because I realize what needs to be done now.

Tobin Rivers needs to die.

And it will be me who pulls the trigger.

FOURTY-FIVE

T-MINUS THREE HOURS.

That's all we have left and then we leave behind uneaten dinners and stifled conversations. Trade them in for guns and battle.

It's too soon.

And yet, it's not soon enough.

"You gonna eat that?" Chris asks, mouth watering as he eyes my venison stew. They've been saving the meat for a special occasion and now I can't even eat it. Feels too much like they've prepared it now in case it becomes our last meal.

I push it across the table to him. "How can you eat right now?"

He pokes his fork in my direction, mouth full of half chewed carrot and potato when he says, "What can I say. I'm a meat and taters kinda guy. Can't turn down a good stew."

Ezra sits alone in one corner of the cafeteria. Head bowed into the table, posture rigid. People avoid him as if he's infected. He's been told he needs to decide tonight. Charles and my mom will be coming to meet us at the secondary location sometime in the night to tend to any wounded. If they wait any longer, the baby isn't going to make it. I wish I had the strength to lend him, but I don't. I've used up most of it and what I have left needs to be conserved for tonight.

A warm hand gives my thigh a gentle squeeze, Ethan. "You ok?"

Far from it. "Yeah."

The strain in his eyes, the way they hold me hostage and won't allow me to look away, is the only solid thing keeping me here. My legs twitch, wanting to get up, move.

"You don't have to do this. No one would think any less of you if you decided to stay behind."

Funny, the thought never occurred to me to back out. "No. This was my choice. I'm not going to back out now."

"You know, she's kinda cute when she gets all serious. Are you into sharing?" Chris says chasing his stew down with a few gulps of coffee that I'm sure must've gone cold by now. Waggles his eyebrows at me.

My face goes red. Ethan throws the last of his biscuit at him. "If you want to keep your eyes *inside* your head, I'd watch what you let come out of your mouth."

Over Chris' shoulder I see the girls walk into the cafeteria, both frowning, about to go into tantrum mode. Roman doesn't want them to know. He says they're too young to understand. I've been avoiding them for days.

As soon as they see me they beeline for our table and I

paste on a smile.

"Jo!" They squeal. "Daddy says he's going to a party, are you going too?" Lily asks.

Ethan and I share a look.

They mistake it to mean something else.

"*You're both going?*" Rosie whines.

"We want to go too!" Lily chimes in, crossing her arms over her slight frame. "But Daddy says it's only for grown-ups."

"You *have* to make him let us come."

"We want to see the fireworks too!"

This is so wrong.

"Hunny," Ethan says, pulling Lily onto his lap. "There isn't a single person in this whoooooole place who can make your dad do anything. He's kinda the boss."

Lily pouts so professionally she puts toddlers to shame. Chris tugs on Rosie's braids and she whips around to face him, hands on her tiny hips, "Are *you* going too?" She asks, her little voice accusing.

"Yup."

A groan in response.

"It's not going to be any fun anyway," I find myself saying. "Just a bunch of grown-ups playing cards," I tell them, remembering Ace saying something about never being able to win at poker against Roman.

"We know how to play!"

"Yeah Daddy taught us."

My eyes widen. Roman taught his seven and ten-year-old girls how to play poker. Why am I not surprised?

"It's a different sort of game, you wouldn't like it," I tell them.

It's not far off from the truth. It is a game of sorts. All of this is. Except you don't volunteer to play it, you're forced to.

And if you lose...

You die.

FORTY-SIX

I COULDN'T FIND my mom anywhere, which is saying something since we basically live in a box underground.

"Did you ever think maybe she didn't want to be found?" Doug asks me, but no, I hadn't considered that. Where Chis is lean and wiry, and full of 'piss and vinegar' as Dianna would've said. Doug is big and burly, but not intimidating, more of a friendly bear.

Chris puts yet another knife into a hidden compartment in the side of his boot. He must have somewhere upwards of ten on his person now. Makes me feel underprepared with my one gun and single knife. Then again, I'm the only one wearing a bulletproof vest and they aren't counting on me needing to or being able to use any of the weapons I'm carrying. That's what Ethan is for after all.

"Yeah, Amy's never been much for goodbyes. She thinks they sound too–oh shit, how'd she put that?" Chris takes a second to remember, another second, scratches his head.

"Too final?" I offer.

"Yeah that's it, too final."

Either way, I wish I could have said something to her. We left things on an awkward note last night. Both rushing to go to beds we didn't intend to sleep in. I'm glad Ethan got some rest. I found him face down on my bed when I went into my room, had to use all my body weight to move him over enough so I could lay next to him. He didn't even flinch.

"Don't overthink it, Jo. You'll see her by morning," Liam offers, loading the last of his equipment onto the bus. The way he says it, I almost believe him. The alternative is too depressing and downright terrifying to consider. No one has said it, but I can't be the only one thinking it.

We may not all make it back.

All it would take is a fraction of a second. That's it. Just one wrong move, just one instant of hesitation, and you or someone you care about could be erased from existence. There's no do-over, no way to turn back time. And it's got me thinking about life. How it's so fluid, always moving forward. You fall, and you dust your knees and get back up. Friendships wax and wane. People come and go. No matter how sad you might be right now, how angry, the sun will rise tomorrow and one day you will be happy again. The only thing truly final in life, is death.

Today we run full-tilt towards it. Taunting it. Hoping it doesn't reach out its decaying hands and snatch us up. I've only just begun to see the light of life, of really, truly living. I'm not ready to go back into the dark. So, if death reaches for me tonight, I'll be ready. Finger on the trigger.

Fire in my blood.

FORTY-SEVEN

WE HEARD THE explosion go off twenty minutes ago. We're all in the bus waiting for the radio call from Ethan and Roman to tell us to move. Once they're in range, they'll give us the go-ahead. We'll pick them up on the back road we're taking to avoid the conflict of running into any unwanted company.

I doubt they'd be very friendly towards two buses covered in recycled metal and wood. They even took the time to paint most of the shiny bits in an inky black that'll make us harder to see when night falls. Not exactly inconspicuous if spotted.

Nobody speaks and I'm grateful for the silence. Just breathing has become a labor in itself. I can't think anything has happened to them. It's only been twenty minutes. That's all, and it's a long hike.

I notice the look Chris is giving Liam, see Liam shake his head. My heart skips half a beat, sputters, comes back to life.

"Don't," I breathe, almost inaudible.

The thing is, if we don't hear from them within the next ten minutes, we're supposed to radio Ace to suit up and take Ethan's place. Roman said thirty minutes, no more, and if they're not back then we leave without them. It's August 28th today, the August born O-Negatives will be harvested in three days. We don't have the luxury of being able to reschedule.

I know that look. The look Chris keeps giving Liam, it says *they aren't coming,* without the need for audible vowels and consonants.

Chris' lips part to speak and I wish I had a piece of tape to cover them. "Maybe we should—"

"No. We wait, they'll be—"

The radio crackles.

We all lean into the sound, waiting, Liam holds it high so we can all hear. Something's coming through, but its disjointed and filled with static.

"Turn it up."

He does. Then it comes though, clear as a cloudless summer sky; "MoveMove*Move!*" Roman's voice booms through the speaker.

I'm grinning like an idiot. Chris and Liam are whooping and the sound of Roman's voice has spurred us all into action. The driver, Seth, runs to the front of the bus and fires it up. The engine rumbles the floor. Liam radios Jerimiah, the other driver, and shouts, "Let's make like a tree and get the fuck out of here!"

I have no idea what that means, but I'm laughing at the absolute ridiculousness of that sentence. He notices the way

I'm staring at him like he might be insane, says, "What, you're never seen Back to The Future?"

"What?"

He rolls his eyes at me. "Holy shit, that's just sad. That's the first thing we're doing when we get back."

"Is that, like, from a book or something?"

His eyebrows pull together, "It's a movie. You watch it on a big box, there's a video with moving pictures and sound."

Sounds like the NTA videos we used to watch in school, but they were pictures thrown on a wall through a projector, most didn't have any sort of sound. And they definitely didn't have any curse words in them. I didn't know televisions still worked.

"Ethan hasn't... I mean, you've never–Okay–I'm taking you to see a movie. Damn. That's just sad."

And we're on our way.

FORTY-EIGHT

THE SUN IS FALLING fast behind us. It paints the evening sky in shades of red and purple. Throws rose colored light through the slits in the wood screwed to the outside of the bus. I'm on the edge of my seat, squinting through the long rectangle of uncovered window at the front.

A light flashes a hundred feet in front of us, off to the left side of the road.

It's them, that's the signal.

I'm at the front of the bus in the blink of an eye, nearly tripping over Doug's burly legs sticking out into the walkway.

"There," I say, pointing at the spot.

Seth follows the line of my finger. "I see it."

The bus skids to a stop and they rush from their cover, Roman to the bus behind us, and Ethan around to the door of ours. Seth throws the door open and a thousand pounds of nerves fall off my shoulders, roll down my neck.

Ethan hops on and Seth takes off again, making up for the few seconds we lost.

"Hey, love," he says, his voice light, eyes gleaming. He slides his arms around my waist, lays a soft kiss on my exposed shoulder. I shiver, remembering his hands on my bare skin, our bodies pressed so closely together there wasn't even space for air. A blush climbs up my neck, sets up shop in my cheeks. This is not the time for this, I get that, but his presence does something strange to my body, its like a chemical reaction. I can't control it, and why would anyone want to?

He drops his arms from my body, only to take my hand and lead me to our seat near the back. We sit in the order we've planned to exit, and Ethan and I are to go last.

Liam is the only one close to us, sitting two seats ahead. He's tasked with guarding the bus once the radio signal is successfully jammed and their main power has been destroyed. I find it strange he can do all that or at least most of it with a bunch of contraptions he has set up over the span of two seats. There's still so much to learn. So much they never taught us.

"So, how'd it go? Was it glorious?" Liam asks over the back of his seat as we squish into ours.

"That's one way to put it," Ethan answers, his jaw tightening. I get the feeling he's not in the mood to talk about it.

"Oooookay," Liam says. "I can take a hint, go ahead have your, like, moment, or whatever, just pretend I'm not here."

Ethan rolls his eyes and pulls me close to him so our

hips touch and our legs are flush against each other. I lean into his shoulder, trying not to overthink what we're walking into, try to borrow a little strength for a while.

"THREE MILES TO sniper drop," Roman's voice comes over the radio.

"Roger," Liam replies.

Seth gives a thumbs up from the front to show he heard.

Logan will make his way to the tree Cash and I hid in on foot. I hope I marked it out well enough on the map. It's a big one, a maple, it would be hard to miss once you're close enough.

We won't see Logan again for a while. Once he's played his part and taken out any vehicles that try to follow us, he'll be on his own. He'll have to make his way from safe house to safe house, laying low, travelling only at night, until he gets back. I don't envy him, but that's how it has to be. There's no telling what's going to happen, and we can't afford to be stopping anywhere once we make our getaway. Never mind searching out one guy in the dark. I get it, I do. Doesn't mean I have to be okay with it.

The temperature is dropping fast. It's full dark now, Seth and Jerimiah have turned off the headlights and we move along at a snail's pace, using the moon to light our way. Ethan is rubbing calming circles into the back of my hand, his jaw alternatingly flexed and then relaxed, flexed again. I know how he feels. It's as though I haven't taken a breath in the last two hours. It's a wonder I haven't passed out from the lack of oxygen.

Swallowing back the sand in my throat, I test out my

ability to speak. "Ethan?"

His unfocused eyes struggle to latch onto my voice. "Hmmm," is his reply and I wonder what he was thinking about.

"We're going to be okay," I tell him, just wanting to see him smile even though I may not be able to return the favor.

His face splits into a tentative smile, he kisses the back of my hand. "Are you telling me that? Or yourself."

"You, obviously," I try to joke, but neither of us is laughing.

Our eyes remain locked for what seems an immeasurable amount of time.

The bus stops, starts going again. Logan is on the move.

This is it.

"Five minutes," Roman's voice echoes through the dead air.

Ethan's hand pulls me closer, the sound of weapons being checked, loaded, cocked and checked again begin to fill the silence with their metallic clanking noises. I flinch at each one, try not to show it. The oxygen is dumped from my body and filled instead with something thicker, harder to breathe. My heart is working overtime to pump enough to my brain.

"There's something I need you to do," he says.

I clench my teeth. He lets go of one of my hands and cups my face, his skin is cool against mine. "If anything happens—"

"Please don't say it."

He closes his eyes against the possibility, opens them

with a renewed vigor. "I have to. If anything happens to me, you need to run. Run like hell and don't stop for anything. You get your ass back to this bus and you leave."

"I can't do that."

"Joanna, you have to. I made a promise. If it comes to it, I —"

I kiss him as hard as I dare. At first his lips are stiff against mine. His hands are on my shoulders and I'm afraid he might push me away. But then his arms are hard cushions of protection around me, he's kissing me as if he'd like to inhale my soul. I might just give it to him.

But then he breaks away, too soon.

"You could always just stay in the bus."

"Shut up," I say, though without any mirth. I touch my fingers to his lips, feel his breath coming hard against them.

He tilts my chin up and I'm thinking I could drown in his eyes, just let the tide take me and never resurface again. It would be easy, a beautiful sort of suffocation. "I love you," he whispers.

Three little words. That's all it takes to undo me. I don't realize I'm crying until he thumbs a tear from my cheek and I'm wondering who gave my tear ducts permission to rupture. And I'm wondering why this feeling is something more akin to agony than joy. Because it sounds more like he's saying goodbye. "Ethan, I–I…"

"Don't say it now." He hugs me to him. "Tell me after. Tell me when it's all over."

The lights from The Mill are poking their ugly brightness through the trees now, another few seconds and we'll be in full view.

We're here.

FORTY-NINE

THE CHAIN-LINK FENCE at the rear of The Mill blows apart as our bus crashes through, bits of it soar through the air, crash into unsuspecting soldiers.

We all hold on, hold tight as Seth pushes the pedal as far as it will go. Green Room is just ahead. My breath is coming in gasps so loud I'm almost embarrassed by the sounds. *Why isn't anyone shooting ye—*

A barrage of bullets strikes the bus from both sides, Ethan shoves me into the aisle, pushes my body down.

"Hold on!" Seth shouts.

We hit the greenhouse wall. The bus shakes. Glass falls in sheets and pieces, a lethal rain of shards I'm glad to have cover from. We careen to a dead stand-still. The tires screech, the smell of burnt rubber fills the cabin. It takes less than a second for the gunshots to follow us inside. One finds its way through a crack in the boards, shatters the window to our right.

Ethan moves so he's in front of me. "Stay two steps behind me and watch your six."

I nod, trying to regulate my breathing how Ace taught me.

We move.

My gun is up and ready, safety off, finger just beside the trigger.

Ethan steps off the bus, immediately fires two shots. A yelp tells me at least one made its mark. I step off exactly two steps behind him. My boots crunch bits of broken glass. Six NTA soldiers lay dead or unconscious on the ground. Our men forge forward, me at the very back. Liam is checking to make sure everyone is dead, kicking their weapons away just in case. Waiting for the rest of them to come. He's holding a gun the length of my thigh, twice as wide.

"Joanna, keep moving," he says, noticing me begin to lag behind Ethan. He takes off to make cover from the back of the bus.

Ethan's head is jerking side to side in the dark. And I'm so incredibly happy he has the uncanny ability to be able to see so well in the dark. His body is tense, stone-like, but fluid. He's a snake coiling itself back, getting ready to strike.

A blast to our right makes me snap up my head. Its an explosion suspended in black air. Logan has taken out the transformer.

I'm distracted, I don't notice the soldier come from behind me, snake his arm around my neck. I don't hesitate. I throw an elbow into his gut, wrench his arm down. Spinning on my heel, almost tripping backwards, I take aim. But someone else shoots first. The bullet hits his temple, exits on the other side, sends him flying. Logan.

I find Ethan with his gun pointed at the twitching form on the ground. He jerks his head to the left, scanning the orange grove to determine if any more men are hidden within it. When his eyes meet mine, I notice how his nostrils are flaring, how he looks as though he might throw up. I'm too shocked to say anything.

"Watch. Your. Six."

"Sorry."

ETHAN HAS TAKEN out four more soldiers before we even reach Dunne's office. None of them saw it coming. I sure as hell didn't see *them* coming. I'm realizing just how underprepared for this I am and it scares the life out of me, but the fear is the only thing propelling me to move, so I welcome it.

I skirt around each of their limp forms, pretending they aren't dead, not doing a very good job. They could be someone's brothers, fathers, sons. Bile rises in my throat, but there's nothing in there for my body to expel.

I'm amazed at how my gun is so steady in my hands, the way I can move and duck and dodge when I need to. That's not my training. It's pure adrenaline, it's intoxicating, clearing my mind of fog, polishing my senses into something clean and sharp.

Ethan steps back for me to open the door, I step over the body of the guard he just clocked in the head, but, "It's locked."

"Cover me."

He winds up, kicks the door in. Wood splinters where

the locking mechanism used to be, now the metal piece hangs there like a sad Christmas ornament.

He moves in, points his gun left, then right, says, "Clear," and moves to guard the door.

A riot of gunshots echo from somewhere nearby. I move into the office. Ethan tells me to hurry and slips a fresh clip into his gun.

It doesn't take me long to find the right button on the microphone. I press it. "Attention all O-Orphans," I start, hear my own voice boomerang back to me through the loudspeakers, swallow. "My name is Joanna. Some of you know me a-and some of you don't."

Ethan spares me a second from his diligent watch, gives me an encouraging expression that says *keep going, you got this.*

"You've been lied to. This is NOT a testing facility, it's a slaughterhouse. We are here to help you. We will get you all out of here. I-I know this is hard to hear. I know you probably won't believe it. But please believe me when I tell you that if you stay here, you will die."

The gunshots in the hallway are getting louder, closer. Ethan gives me the 'wrap it up' signal. But there is something else I have to add. "To all the NTA soldiers listening… If you lay down your weapons, we will not shoot, you will not be harmed. But if you stand in our way, if you will stand and fight for this *corrupt* government–The NTA is responsible for the deaths of countless innocent teenagers… How can you justif—"

Breathe in, breath out. "If you stand in our way, we will not hesitate to shoot you down. And," I add, hesitating. "To Commander Tobin Rivers… you know who I am.

Come and find me."

I let go of the button, an incredible, terrifying surge of power runs through me. Because I meant every word.

"You just had to poke the bear," Ethan says, sighs. "Can't say I wouldn't have too. Let's move."

I step away from the desk and that's when I see it. Or rather, her. A perfect black heeled boot illuminated in the feint emergency lighting pokes out from under the desk.

FIFTY

I TRAIN MY GUN on the visible part of her leg. "Get up."

A very small voice says, "Please don't shoot me."

"Get up!"

She does. Climbs out from under the desk awkwardly, trying to keep her hands raised. Her body is a quivering mess, her hair is frazzled, her suit rumpled.

"*Shit*," Ethan curses, pointing his own gun at her too.

Her eyes flit from gun to gun, face to face.

"Don't shoot her," I tell Ethan, he narrows his eyes at me. Ms. Dunne starts to lower her hands, relieved. She shouldn't be. "She comes with us."

It takes everything I've got to keep myself from pulling the trigger, to keep myself from inflicting a little pain on the woman who has overseen the mass slaughter of likely thousands of kids.

Ethan nods his ascent. "You try anything and I shoot

you. You move even a step out of line and she shoots you."

She doesn't say anything. He moves in close to her and she lets out a yelp. He pats her down for weapons, sets his jaw in a firm line, says, "Move."

We move out of the office. The gunshots have stopped. Ethan is in front, Dunne is behind him, and I'm behind her. A morbid parade.

The lights in the atrium flicker. Someone's coming. More than one someone, from the main entrance. We move in tight to the wall, wait. He tells Dunne to shut up, she's been mumbling something unintelligible, something similar to a prayer.

The lights flicker again. They go out. *Don't panic Joanna. Don't panic.*

Closer now. Almost.

Almost.

Two dark figures sprint into the atrium. Ethan doesn't fire, but one of them does, narrowly misses my head. The bullet zips by, snapping into the wall just to my right.

"Chris!" Ethan shouts, stepping in front of me. "Shit man, open your goddamn eyes." He's fuming.

The lights come back to a steady glow. It's Chris, and Doug, who has a sack slung over his shoulder. Filled with respirators I imagine.

Chris' eyes widen. "Man, I am sooo sorry."

Ethan's hands clench and unclench as if he's ready to strangle him, but instead he simply says, "Lets get this shit over with."

"Wait a second, who the hell is that?"

"Hostage." I tell them.

That seems to be good enough.

Chris and Doug are heading towards the North wing, my wing. Ethan is trying to pull me back to the busses. "Wait!"

He glares at me, but he stops.

"We go with them. I made a promise too."

"I'm taking you back to the bus."

I offer him a small smile, shake my head in apology. "I have to do this. Either help me, or don't."

IT'S MASS CHAOS when we enter the wing. Kids running through the halls, yelling, curled up in balls on the ground. Frightened faces peek out from doorways. I'm wondering when I started to think of people my own age as kids, but that's not important. *Focus.*

I'm hunting for one of two faces. Find one of them almost right away. Sophie is peeking out the doorway of our room.

Chris and Doug take over, trying to calm them, handing out respirators. Telling them to leave their things, to follow them, that they'll lead the way.

I run over to Sophie. No presence of mind to wonder where the guard is. The one that's always stationed here in the hallway.

"Joanna, wait!"

But I'm already there, in the doorway, staring down the barrel of a gun. He fires. Ethan is there, faster than humanly possible. The bullet connects with his head, makes it kick back with the force of impact. He crumples to the ground.

I don't think.

I don't hesitate.

My veins are filled with gasoline and someone just lit the match.

I shoot him in the head. Keep shooting until all the bullets are gone. Keep shooting. Ethan is ok. He didn't get shot in the head. Have to kill this guy. Have to make sure he's dead. *Click. Click, click.* Ethan's not dead. No bullets. Need more bullets. I'm shaking so hard I'm afraid I might vibrate myself right through the tile floor.

"Joanna." He's getting up, blood smeared all over the side of his face, down his neck.

He missed. Impossible. Incredible. A flesh wound. *A flesh wound!* I practically tackle him. He grunts, squinting against the pain as I pull away.

"We have to keep moving."

"I'm sorry. I'm so, so sorry. I can't—shouldn't hav—"

"Jo." He's cupping my cheeks in his hands, snapping his fingers in front of my face, "Hey–Hey, look at me. I'm ok. I'm fine."

I nod. Remember what I was doing, turn to Sophie, who's retreated so far into herself there isn't even a real person behind her tear-filled eyes anymore.

"Come on, Sophie." I help her to her feet. Shake her, try to get her eyes to recognize my face, "Sophie!"

"It's you. You're not–You're not dead?"

"Yes, yes it's me. Where's Danny?"

She starts sobbing. I grip her shoulders a little harder. "Sophie, did you see Danny, did she get out? Which way did she go?"

"I'm so s-sorry," She wails. "I-I thought she was crazy. She said–Oh god, she said–She was s-saying horrible things, a-awful things."

My lungs are filled with stones. My arms are full of lead. I'm shaking her again, frantic now and I can't stop myself, can't force myself to be gentler. "Where is she?"

"They took her away," she blurts out so fast I'm not even sure I caught what she said.

But I do register the guilt pouring out of her and I already know. I know they took her. I know where she is. And I know it's my fault. I should never have left her that note. I shouldn't have to told her to be ready, that I'd be back, and not to trust anyone, that she wasn't safe.

"When?"

"I'm sorry."

"WHEN?"

"T-Two days ago."

Only then do I finally look at Ethan. Vaguely aware he's been trying to get my attention. I beg him with my eyes. "She's still alive," I say, my voice breaking. "She has to be. We can't leave her here."

FIFTY-ONE

I HALF EXPECTED for Ethan to drag me back to the bus kicking and screaming. But he didn't. He told Chris and Doug to take Dunne with them back to the bus. They checked their watches in unison. Told us we have exactly eleven minutes to get back to the bus. They didn't ask what we're doing and we didn't tell them.

Ethan is holding my hand, there was only one soldier he had to take care of along the way. Another handed over his weapon, said he didn't want to fight. Smart.

The halls here are eerily quiet, unmanned, almost deserted. It doesn't seem right. I almost tell him maybe we should turn around. *Almost.* But I can't. Yes, I want to keep him safe. I also made a promise to Danny, and I can't let her die like that.

We press ourselves against the wall, just before the turn in the last stretch of hallway. I peek around the corner. See the steel double doors. No guards. Sweat breaks along my hairline, covers my chest in a layer of moisture, quickly freezes. "It's clear," I whisper, begin to move. Ethan stops me.

"What is it?"

He looks like he's fighting to get the words out, opens his mouth, and then closes it again. I lean on my tip-toes and kiss him. I know this isn't the place and definitely not the time. But I need him to understand that nothing I've seen him do tonight has changed the way I feel about him. I can't imagine what must be going on inside his head. He worked with these guys, maybe even befriended some of them. One of them shot him in the face. The others hesitated just long enough, recognition flitting in and out of their eyes, right before he shot or disabled them. Maybe he shouldn't have come at all. Maybe I shouldn't have agreed to this.

"She'll be unconscious," he says when I pull away. "I'll cover you. You get to her, try to wake her. If you can't wake her, you'll have to cover me on the way back. I'll carry her out."

"Ok."

His chest rises and falls. One heartbeat. Two. Checks his watch. "Seven minutes," he says.

Ethan goes first, I follow him inside. A single emergency light throws a bluish haze over the space. No one else is here. No doctors, no nurses, no guards. Only one bed is occupied. Only one monitor is beep beeping through the emptiness. Right at the center of the room, Danny.

This time I don't lower my gun, I don't go charging in. I wait for Ethan to give me a nod, he stays right behind me as I step slowly, carefully over to the bed. My knees buckle as I pass each empty bed. New stock is coming in, they had to make room. I eye the incinerator on the opposite wall, a vicious urge to burn the building to the ground consumes me.

Danny is pale, unconscious. I'm sure I don't look any less lifeless than she does right now. Tubes filled with blood stick out of her body in six different places, and a seventh pumps a clear fluid into her. Something to keep her unconscious? I start to remove the tubes, staunching the flow of blood from the holes in her skin as best as I can.

"You hear that?" Ethan's harsh whisper slices the silence. I stop. Listen. It's footsteps, I hear them too. Coming from both directions if I'm not mistaken. For the first time, I notice a door on the other side of the room. Opposite to the one we came in.

I rip the last tube out. Smack Danny hard in the face. Nothing. Smack her again, "Danny!" I half shout, half whisper in her ear. She isn't waking up. *Damnit!*

"Isn't this cute." The door closes behind them. I fumble to pick up my gun.

"Move another inch and I'll shoot him," Ethan shouts.

Him. Tobin Rivers. Commander General of the NTA. Flanked by three armed men. His blue eyes flash like diamonds. His voice sounds melodic, almost a song. This is what I wanted, I tell myself. Someone has to end him.

The door behind us creaks open. Immediately Ethan is holding a second gun out in that direction too, but I won't dare take my eyes off the four men in front of me.

"Uh, Ethan…"

It's Doug. Three on four now. Our chances are getting better.

Doug walks up beside me. Ethan flanks me on the other side.

We're all thinking it, but I'm the one who blatantly asks. "So, who's going to shoot first?"

"Direct. Straight to the point. I like that, maybe we have resemblances after all."

He knows who I am. Good.

"I am nothing like you!" My hands are shaking, and all I want to do is pull the trigger, but if do, he'd be dead... and so would we.

He's smiling and it makes my skin crawl. No one so evil should be able to smile like that. "Oh, but you are. I should have done away with you a long time ago, but now, I'm at a loss. My daughter the renegade... This is priceless." His black hair shines blue in the lighting. He looks like Hades, I think. Lord of the underworld. Ruler of the dead and damned. A blue devil.

His men spare him a glance, it's apparent they didn't know. I wonder what he'll do to them now that they do.

Hot tears burn at the corners of my eyes. Doug clears his throat. "Look man, we just want our friend. No one has to get hurt."

The Commander smirks, doesn't respond.

"Doug, grab her," I tell him. He never lowers his gun, uses one arm to sling Danny over his shoulder.

"I'm afraid I can't let you do that." His men are taking tentative steps towards us, daring us to open fire.

"If your men fire at us, we might die, but all of our guns are pointing at *you*," Ethan says.

The Commander lazily scratches his jaw, says sarcastically, "And whose guns are protecting your precious little hideout. The Inn, is it called?"

No.

"Oh yes," he says, so candid in his stance, he lowers his gun. "You trusted him, that was your mistake. You see, Cash and I have an understanding. I had to make sure you didn't survive. It was perfect," he purrs. My hands have begun to shake, the realization setting in. This is no bluff. "That waste of skin was on his last strike, and I could offer him the world, and in return, all he had to do was press a little button and lead me to my traitor of a wife and the daughter who never should've been born."

It comes back in waves. The little silver gadget falling out of his pocket when we were in the maple tree, how he was so quick to hide it. How he was trying to figure out what was going on, what the plan was, so he could tell *him.* The way he *forced* Ethan to take him with us in the first place. I'll kill him. I'll kill them both.

"I'm going to kill you," I spit at him.

He has the audacity to laugh. I press my finger against the trigger, grind my teeth. I imagine Rosie and Lily, my mom, Ace, Charles, Erica, all the others. Is the NTA already there? Are they already dead? My heart is racing, pulse pounding in my ears.

"Get Jo back to the bus," Ethan says, aims his gun skyward. Shoots out the only light and plunges us all into darkness.

No.

FIFTY-TWO

PANDEMONIUM.

Someone has left the gates of hell wide open and all the devils are here.

A strong hand circles my wrist, drags me away from the shouts, the explosive sounds of guns being fired back and forth.

"Stay down!" Doug shouts through the chaos.

A red-hot poker of pain punches me in the shoulder, nearly knocks me over. Doug's hand on my wrist is the only thing keeping me on my feet. He shoulders his way through the steel door and drags me with him.

No. *No, no, no.* This can't be happening. Ethan is still inside. The square windows flash with the light of gunfire.

"We can't leave him in there!"

I'm trying to yank my arm away from him. But there are dark spots scurrying in and out of my vision. My legs are filled with something heavy and the whole front of me is covered in something wet and uncomfortable.

Doug stops, glares into my eyes. "That's one of my *best friends* back there! He told me to get you out so that's what I'm gonna do. If anyone can make it out of there, it's him. Now I need you to move."

And we run. It feels wrong, *so wrong* to push on, to leave him behind. I keep turning to look back, waiting for Doug to be right, for Ethan to magically appear behind us. But *Oh god!* He's not there. He's not coming. I've just made the biggest mistake of my life. It's all I'm good for, making stupid mistakes. Getting people hurt, getting them killed.

I can see the doors to green room. We're closing the distance ten feet a second. There's a sound like a whimper. To the left. It's a girl, an O-Negative, huddled in a small ball. Shaking as if she might shatter. Doug sees her too, lets go of me. I take hold of her arms, try to lift her up. She won't budge, her arms and legs lash out at me. She claws at the air. "You have to get up!" I plead.

"There's no time Jo, move!"

My body is weak, tired, every time I try to pull her up a sharp pain throbs in my shoulder. So, I do something I never thought I could do. I leave her in the hallway. Just like I left Ethan.

Numb. I'm so utterly, completely numb. If it weren't for the last dregs of adrenaline coursing through me I'd have collapsed already.

We've made it to the buses. There are upwards of twenty soldiers laying in the pathways, in the dirt. Their blood soaking into the plants their weight is crushing. So much death. So much destruction. But all that's running through my mind is Ethan. *Ethan. Where is Ethan! And* oh god! *The Inn, all those people. Cash wouldn't have done it, he couldn't have. No. Not possible. Bad dream, just a bad dream.*

Roman is there, by the bus. Doug rushes past him, carrying Danny on board.

I can't.

"Where's Knox?" Roman yells over the sound of the engine running.

I'm crying and I have no idea when the tears started pouring out of me, blinding me. "He's coming." My voice is high pitched, broken, bleeding hope and pain.

His jaw clenches. "One minute," he says, trying to corral me onto the bus. "We wait for *one minute*. Alliance Reinforcements are coming. We can't afford to wait."

I'm fighting against him with all I've got left. Pushing his arms away. Rage. It's all consuming. "I will NOT leave him here!"

"Joanna!" He grabs me by the arm and my shoulder screams out in pain. "Get on the bus," he growls.

All I see is red. *One minute*. Is that all his life is worth? No. I won't accept that. I aim my gun at Roman. Hating myself, but so enraged I can't be bothered to care.

"Joanna..." He says tentatively. He doesn't raise his arms. Shaking his head slowly, with pity in his eyes, he says, "You aren't going to shoot me."

But the pain... The *anger*. It hurts–it hurts everywhere and I can't. I can't... I nearly collapse. Drop my gun. Roman catches me. "I-I'm so sorry, I—"

BANG.

Roman's eyes widen. His face goes slack. No, I

didn't–I couldn't have. I dropped my gun.

"Roman!" Liam is shouting, cradling Roman's head, then pressing a wad of shirt to the wound on his chest. Where did he come from? What's happening? What the *hell* is happening right now? There's blood on my hands. Blood soaking the black material of Romans shirt in a wide glistening circle, right over his heart. His eyes never close. But I can tell–I can tell and I wish I couldn't… He's dead.

That's when I see him. Alone. Standing in the doorway of the green room. Not twenty yards away. My father. Holding the smoking gun.

My own gun is somehow back in my hand. I shoot at him wildly. Blindly. Missing him entirely. Liam is shooting at him too.

He retreats.

I start into a full out sprint after him.

Someone grabs me, is pulling me, half carrying me.

I'm vaguely aware I'm screaming. I'm screaming and it's ear-splitting. It is raw, jagged agony embodied in the form of sound. There's a knife in my gut, an ache in my bones and my heart just exploded inside my chest. I've checked out. Whatever sanity I had left just packed its bags and split.

It's too much. It's all just too much.

Something pinches my arm. A needle?

The air gets harder to breath, there isn't enough strength left in my body to scream anymore. My senses are failing. Someone's filled my ears with cotton and my eyes with glue. I'm a piece of taxidermy. I'll be put on a wall and forever be forced to watch the people I love die, watch them and be unable to do anything about it. My eyelids are heavy. The shaking has stopped. And sleep, I think, has never looked so good. Maybe I won't wake up.

That would be nice.

FIFTY-THREE

THE DARKNESS IS my friend. It wraps its arms around me, holds me tight. Nothing can happen to me here. I can see the light behind my eyelids, it scares me. *I don't want to…* I try to say to the dark, but my mouth is filled with broken teeth and something that tastes of metal. Moving is out of the question.

Something jostles my shoulder. The pain it causes is a shockwave jolting me awake.

"She's been shot."

"When is Charles gonna be here?"

"Soon. He better get here soon."

"Wait, she's waking up."

"Joanna? Jo, can you hear me?"

It's Liam's face I see when I finally open my eyes. All my senses come back at once, bombarding me with sights and smells and sounds I'd rather not see or smell or hear.

We're in some kind of warehouse, or maybe it's a

bunker. I'm not sure. The walls are made of cinderblocks and the lights burn my eyes. I've been unceremoniously dumped against a wall, legs splayed out in front of me.

"You're going to be ok." Ace's face appears beside Liam. "We have to stop the bleeding ok–this is gonna–well it's not gonna feel good."

He's got a balled-up piece of fabric in his hand. Liam tears the sleeve off my shirt. I notice I'm not wearing the bulletproof vest anymore.

It all comes back to me. Why I'm seeing Liam's and Ace's faces and not the only one I care to see.

"Ethan?" I ask, but I already know the answer. I double over, clutching at my chest. Eyes stinging like my tears are made of shards of glass. The *air*. It's so heavy, hard to breathe. I'm choking on it, drowning in it. And then, *Roman*. He's dead. And then... His girls. *His girls!* Lily and Rosie... My mom... Ace... All those *people*...

"Jo! Jo, you can't–you can't do this right now. Focus." He's pressed the cloth against my shoulder. I shove him away.

My chest heaves, "The Inn? What hap-happened? Did they make it, did the Commander, did the NTA, did they..."

Liam's face goes instantly red, his eyes welling with tears I never thought his perpetually sarcastic eyes could cry. "Fifteen," he says, his lips quivering.

I start to sit but fall back against the wall, "We have to," I choke, sputter, shake off the dizziness blurring my vision. "We have to leave, now. We have to check. We have to help them."

Ace is made of stone. "Jo, you aren't listening. They're

all dead."

"Fifteen," Liam repeats himself. "Only fifteen people made it out."

I'm about to lose my mind, about to explode, about to completely and utterly allow myself to surrender to insanity, but then…

"What the shit?" Liam says, cursing under his breath.

"Is that the–Is it…"

The utter shock and awe in their voices is enough to break me free of the pain, if only for an instant.

I can feel it. An odd tightening. The muscles in my shoulder squeezing and contracting. There's a hole in my shoulder, ringed in chewed flesh. There's a bullet inside it. I can see it. The little piece of metal and copper. It's moving, slowly, but it *is* moving. My body is pushing it out.

My body is *rejecting it.*

It falls to the cement, rolls a foot away. The hole is stitching itself together. We all watch in a stunned stupor until there's almost nothing. No indication I was even shot.

"What–what did I just watch?" Liam is asking, worried, looking slightly mortified.

Ace stares at me, at the spot where a bullet resided in my shoulder only a few minutes ago.

The pain fades away and I'm smiling. I'm smiling like a goddamn maniac. I'm not afraid anymore. I'm devastated and I've been shaken to my very core, but in the most terrifyingly beautiful way. It's time. This isn't the end. I will *not* back down. I *will* find Ethan. I won't cower in fear of the New Terra Alliance. I will tear them down, rip them apart piece by piece. My father will pay for his sins in blood. And I intend to collect every drop owed.

Because no matter how shattered I am inside right now. This body, *my body*...

It won't break.

TURN THE PAGE FOR

THIS BODY WON'T BREAK

BONUS MATERIALS

LEA MCKEE

ON *THIS BODY WON'T BREAK*

WHERE DID THE IDEA FOR *THIS BODY WON'T BREAK* COME FROM?

About five years ago I was sitting on a city bus, jotting down notes for a novel I was writing at the time (a novel I never completed, but hope to in the future!) when I noticed an advertisement across from me. It said simply, 'Donate Blood. Save a Life." Now, naturally, as a writer, this got me thinking of all kinds of unlikely scenarios where I would go donate blood and something awful would happen. Anyone who knows me will tell you, I *hate* needles. And that got me thinking, as much as I would love to donate blood, the only way I could force myself into that chair, and allow the nurse to stick a piece of sharp metal into my flesh would be if it were mandatory. And that led to the question, *why* would it ever be mandatory? After brainstorming a bit, I had the story 'seed,' from there I simply allowed it to grow until it became what it is today.

WE LOVED WATCHING AS JOANNA DEVELOPED FROM A TIMID GIRL INTO A STRONG HEROINE WHO ARE SOME OF YOUR OTHER FAVORITE LITERARY HEROINES?

That's a tough one! There are just so many... I'd have to

say Katniss Everdeen, of course. But then there's also Arya Stark (total badass!), and most recently Kamzin from Heather Fawcett's *Even the Darkest Stars*.

WHAT WAS YOUR FAVORITE SCENE TO WRITE IN THIS BODY WON'T BREAK? WHICH WAS THE MOST DIFFICULT?

I loved writing Ethan and Joanna's 'first kiss' scene. There was so much going on. Joanna's elation and confusion, and Ethan's guilt and longing. They both wanted it, but neither knew if it was the right thing. Emotionally charged scenes are always fun to write. Scenes written to make the reader *feel* something are always the most fun!

As for the most difficult, I'd have to say the final battle. Killing Roman was not expected, it just... happened. I remember typing it out, then erasing it, only to add it back in again in the end. And then there was Ethan, sacrificing himself to make sure Joanna was safe, to ensure the escape of the others. It gave me physical pain to write Joanna's anguish over his loss. It pains me still.

WE LEARNED ABOUT THE SIDE-EFFECTS FROM SURVIVING TEN. ETHAN'S SUPER SIGHT, LIAM'S ELECTRICALLY CHARGED BODY, AND JOANNA'S ABILITY TO HEAL. IF YOU COULD CHOSE ONE, WHICH WOULD YOU CHOSE AND WHY?

You'd think it'd be the ability to heal myself, but no. I'm quite proud of my battle scars. Being able to charge my laptop when I'm writing in a café and there are *never* any outlets to be found would be nice, but also no. I'd take

Ethan's sight. It's a constant joke among my friends that I'm as blind as bat (even with my glasses on!). And I'm terrified of laser eye surgery. That's some sci-fi sh** that belongs in the pages of books.

CASH'S BETRAYAL CAME AS A SHOCK TO MANY READERS. NOW THAT HE'S GOTTEN WHAT HE WANTED, WILL WE BE SEEING ANY MORE OF HIM IN THE BOOKS TO COME?
I won't give too much away, but yes. Cash's part is far from finished, much to his dismay I'm sure.

IF YOU FOUND YOURSELF INSIDE THE WORLD OF THE O-NEGATIVE SERIES, WHICH TWO CHARACTERS WOULD YOU WANT AT YOUR SIDE?
Ethan, for sure. His knowledge and experience alone would make him a first pick, add on to that the fact that he's loyal to a fault and easy on the eyes, and who wouldn't want him around? My second choice might surprise most people. I would choose Adrien. Remember him? The guy locked up in a cell for the entirely of the novel? Yeah, that guy. Once you've read book two you'll understand why.

JOANNA'S MOTHER IS A BRILLIANT PATHOLOGIST. LIAM IS A GENIUS WITH TECH. AND ACE IS A COMBAT NINJA. ARE THESE TALENTS YOU SHARE WITH YOUR CHARACTERS? IF NOT, HOW DID YOU DO YOUR RESARCH?
Google. I googled crap out of *everything*. In the case of

TEN and the cure, I attempted to keep everything as rooted in science as possible, but it *is* a fictional story, so I took a few small liberties. As for the combat scenes, I had some help with those. My fiancée is skilled in several forms of martial arts and was more than happy to answer all of my questions/give me demonstrations.

WHAT CAN WE EXPECT FROM THE NEXT BOOK IN THE SERIES, THIS FURY WON'T FADE?
Without spoilers? I know what you want to know. If Ethan will live. If he'll find his way back to Joanna or if she'll find her way to him. But I can't tell you that. What I can tell you is Joanna will continue to strengthen as a character, though maybe not in the ways you expect. I can also promise you some more face time with Adrien and Liam. And I can tell you not everyone will survive.

DEFIANT. FURIOUS. UNBREAKABLE

THIS FURY WON'T FADE

THE RIVETING SEQUEL TO *THIS BODY WON'T BREAK* IS ALMOST HERE!

TURN THE PAGE FOR A SNEAK PEEK

PART ONE

"My drops of tears I'll turn to sparks of fire."

-Shakespeare

ONE

SILENCE SUFFOCATES THESE WALLS.

Before TEN, smiles and laughter, maybe the occasional tear were the heartbeat and breath keeping the college alive. Now that soul is gone, replaced with animal droppings and swooping spider webs it seems even the spiders have evacuated, leaving their homes to hang lifeless from corners, strung carelessly across doorways.

We've taken refuge in some sort of emergency bunker built beneath a school. A real one. Not the fake kind I grew up in. They didn't kill you on graduation day here.

Being alone makes it easier. The quiet provides a thin blanket of ease that's just enough to keep me from breaking. I haven't been able to face them yet, the other confiscated youth. My mom, the girls, and Charles should be back soon. I'd like to see them, but what would I say? To the girls, that they're father won't ever come home. That it's my fault he's dead. To Charles, that his son has been taken captive by the Commander General of the NTA himself? That I don't know if he's alright. An aching spreads through my chest, reverberates out to my limbs. Eyes burning, I clutch at a window sill with shaking fingers to try and steady myself.

My shoulder twinges with phantom pain. The bullet wound has completely healed. There isn't even a real mark to prove it was ever there, just a tiny spec of scar tissue, and even that seems to be fading. I wish it hurt, truly hurt. At least it would be a distraction from all the other awful things.

Someone's behind me. I have the presence of mind to tense, hand moving to my gun. But then, I let it fall, recognizing the heavy footfalls. "They're back."

How he has the audacity to sound excited, I'll never understand. "Go away Ace."

He sighs, doesn't move. "It's Dianna. She–they had her at the rebel camp. She was taken prisoner, but when–"

"What?"

A thousand thoughts are racing through my adrenaline addled brain. Dianna was there. She was a prisoner there and we set off a *bomb* at the encampment. No. *No.* I couldn't take it if anyone else died.

I can't lose anyone else.

"Whoa, no, no, no. Shit Jo, come here," he whispers as if facing a rabid dog, inches himself closer to me until he can take my hand, smiles, "She's alright. In the chaos after the explosion, she escaped. She followed the NTA to The Inn. Found your mom and the girls making a run for it. She's downsta—"

I've never moved so fast in my life.

I've flown down all three flights of stairs inside of fifteen seconds, nearly ripping the door off its hinges in my haste once I hit the underground level. Fifty sets of eyes fix their sights on me. They're heat seeking missiles and I'm on fire. I don't care. It doesn't matter what they think of me, the girl who lost her mind in the heat of battle. The one whose nightmare-induced screams keep them up at night. The only pair of eyes I care to see, that I *need* to see, are hers. "Dianna?" My voice is a contorted thing, strangled.

She emerges, Charles in tow behind her. The mix of emotions I feel are mirrored on her soot-streaked face. Hope, pain, sadness, and an ocean of relief.

"Hey Jo." She says, a half smile tugging at the corner of her mouth. I run to her, bury myself in the bones of her shoulder. She rubs soothing circles into my back and lets me cry.

"It isn't your fault." She whispers into my ear. "None of it is your fault."

But it is. All of it.

WHEN I ENTER the little room off the main hallway, I know it's time and my body stiffens, jaw tightening. Now that Roman is gone, the whole idea of a tactical meeting seems wrong. My mom is busy setting up a health unit where she can screen everyone for TEN on entry to the building, and Logan isn't back yet, so it's just Ace, Liam, Chris and Doug, and Dianna and Charles, among a couple others I don't yet know by name.

Eight people to convince. And I *must* convince them.

"I'm going after him." I say in a hushed voice, taking a solid stance across the room from Ace, who sits in a lumpy armchair in the corner.

"No." Ace says.

Dianna stands, leaving Charles to look bereft on the sofa, and lays a hand on my shoulder, "You mean well Jo—I know that—but it's not safe."

"Safe?" I hiss, not at Dianna, but at the very idea of what she's implying. "What is safe? Do you think it's any safer here? Nowhere is safe." Turning my attention back to Ace, I close the distance between us in three steps, "They'll kill him Ace."

"She's right. And you know he'd come for us if the situation were reversed," Liam pipes up, "I'll go with her. I intercepted a transmission last night. I know where they have him."

My heart is a hammer driving nails through my lungs. Liam knows where he is. I could kiss him. I could kill him for telling me sooner.

There are shadows in Ace's eyes, and an exhaustion in the set of his shoulders. I can see the weight of his newly inherited position taking its toll. "You're right, he would have come for any of us. But do you think he'd want us risking our lives to save his? Would you want him to do the same?" He sighs, dragging himself upright, "What we need to do is gather supplies. We have a newborn infant here and not enough formula to last long. We gotta post a watch schedule. Erica is on the roof right now, alone. Jax is on guard, alone. And we need to help Amy get her lab set up. If anyone gets sick right now, she doesn't have the shit she needs to treat them. We were only able to salvage so much. We can't organize a rescue mission right now."

At the mention of my mother's name a fistful of guilt

is crammed down my throat, left to fester in my stomach. I won't soon forget the look on her face when I ran to Dianna, and almost immediately forgot she was right there. Standing off to one side, looking like someone scooped her heart out with a soup ladle.

I was glad to see her, that she was alright, but in that moment I needed my best friend, the only true one I've had for years. But if my mom hadn't made it back, I—well, I don't know what it would've done to me. The idea of losing her, after only just finding her, makes my chest hurt. In that moment, I resolved to make things better between us. She may not understand me, and I may not understand her, or the choices she's made, but things like that don't matter anymore. They can't. I should be grateful for the fact that I still have a mother at all. The child born on the eve of the raid at The Inn will never meet her mother.

"He's right, we need all available hands on deck here right now," Charles says and the lack of emotion on his face as he condemns his son to torture is the spark that lights the gasoline in my veins.

"He's your son!" I shout, backhanding a wooden chair to the floor. It clatters against the concrete and swallows all other sound from the room. "Don't touch me." I tell Dianna as she attempts to comfort me, "He's your son too. Are you just going to leave him there?" My eyes are filling with hot tears and I'm powerless to stop the trembling in my limbs, "They'll torture him, Dianna." And then I allow myself to say aloud the one thing I've managed to stop myself from thinking, "They might have tortured him already."

She has no reply, but I can see the pain I've caused her in the narrowing of her eyes, and the way her chin quivers.

"You're all cowards." I say. It isn't fair, and it isn't entirely true. But right now, I don't care.

"Not all of us can heal a bullet wound in a couple hours, Jo." Ace says.

Charles is immediately on his feet, "Is that true?" he asks me. "Has it accelerated that much?"

When I don't answer, he begins to pace, "We'll have to run tests. I'll need some blood samples. If you could allow—"

"That's hardly a priority right now Charles." Dianna says.

I'm beyond words. Beyond reasoning. And they must know, they *have* to know even without their permission, I will go after him.

Like he came for me.

Liam turns his attention to Ace, "We have Dunne. If I can get within range of their closest two-way signal, we can see if the Commander is willing to trade."

"Ethan for Dunne." I whisper, mostly to myself. *It could work*. My lips spread into the ghost of a smile. The first I've had in days. "Ace?"

Ace nods, pursing his lips together as he considers the approach, "Ok. But I'll be honest, I think Ethan is more valuable to them than Dunne is to us. And even if they did agree, how are we supposed to know they'll make good on their word?"

"Is that a yes, then?" I ask, a little too much fire in my words, and I'm left wondering what happened to our easy conversations, our inside jokes? Will we ever be whole again, or is this what we're left with… clipped voices, and war-hardened faces, with ghosts in our eyes.

"Yes, but I got one condition."

"Name it."

He doesn't speak until he's able to securely latch his eyes onto mine, "If this doesn't work, you have to swear to me you won't go after him."

TWO

THEY ALL LOOK so happy, relieved. And it's strange. Strange because they're all grouped together in clusters of hand-me-down clothes and matted hair. The ~~orphans~~ O-Negatives. They sit in small circles atop their sleeping mats. Pillows and ratty blankets strewn around them. If it weren't for the smiles on many of their faces, and the gleam in their eyes, you would think you'd just walked into a homeless shelter. And in a way, I suppose that's what this is, for now.

Deep breath in. Deep breath out. I've avoided this for too long.

One by one they begin to notice my presence, but there's a specific face I'm searching for.

Danny is acutely aware of the eyes following her trail through bits of bare concrete as she picks her way over to me. But instead of it making her uncomfortable, she radiates a sense of pride. She hugs me lightly and I try not to let the small gesture rattle me. But it does. "Thank you," she says.

"For what?"

"You saved me Jo. You saved all of us."

"We'd be dead right now if it weren't for you and the others," another girl says.

A boy near the back of the room stands, "We want to help."

I open my mouth to speak, but no sound comes out. They stare expectantly. Waiting for me to say something, to give them some kind of assurance, or guidance. But I'm not that person. I'm not a hero. "I didn't save you," I say finally. "You saved yourselves."

"Train us," one of the others says.

My stomach turns at the thought.

I killed someone. I nearly killed others. And some are dead or gone because of me. There are holes in my soul, chasms so deep that I could never fill them again, not in a hundred lifetimes. I wouldn't wish it on anyone.

But I remember how I felt when I first arrived at The Inn. It was the same way they're feeling right now. If Ace hadn't offered to train me, I'd have figured it out on my own. Denying them the same ability isn't fair, no matter what I know now.

"I'll arrange it."

A barrage of whispered excitement breaks out in the crowd, and I'm forgotten for the moment.

"Do you have everything you need?" I ask Danny, eager to find Liam, to see if he's nearly ready to go. The sun sets in a couple of hours, and we've got a long hike to get within range of the NTA's radio signal.

She nods, "Don't worry about us," she tells me, eyes locking on the man stationed outside of a room down the hall behind me, "A couple of us were wondering—what are you going to do with Ms. Dunne?"

Not fifteen meters from the O-Negatives is a makeshift cell where we're keeping her and Adrien, the rebel we had imprisoned at The Inn. Strange thing is, when the NTA attacked The Inn, Charles unlocked Adrien's cell, told him to get out while he could. And instead of fleeing back to his to people, he helped ours escape, and came here with them. When they tossed Dunne in that cell, Adrien put himself in with her.

I don't know what to make of it.

Lowering my voice so the others can't hear, I tell her, "They took one of ours, Ethan. We're going to use her to try to get him back."

Danny shoves her hands into her pockets, kicks at the concrete, "Is he your boyfriend, the one they took?"

"I'm not really sure what to call him. But you know him. He was working undercover at The Mill—er, the Phase Three Institution. He was the one you asked me if I knew." My chest contracts, squeezing the air from my lungs. So many things have happened since then. Good things, and bad things. But Ethan was a part of every one of them.

And now he's a part of me.

A part that was taken.

"They stole Greg from me, *harvested* him. If I can help you get your Ethan back, I'll do it."

BONUS CONTENT

Get access to additional exclusive bonus content including deleted scenes, case files, excerpts from Cash & Ethan's point of view as well as everything you need to know about The O-Negative Series!

Sign-up to receive your extra bonus content using the link below or simply scan the QR code

http://www.leamckee.com/newsletter/

Visit facebook.com/lealately to become a fan!

Thanks for reading!

ABOUT THE AUTHOR

Lea McKee was born and raised in a small town north of Toronto where she spent the majority of her time reading books, jumping off train bridges, and sliding down snow-covered hills in garbage bags.

After working for three bookstores in her teen years, she began to write books of her own. Just after her eighteenth birthday, she left that small town and set off to see the world, armed with a few notebooks, and her favorite pen.

She currently lives abroad, perpetually in-transit, with her fiancée, who should've been born in 9th century Scandinavia, and their five-year-old daughter, who's caught their wanderlust already.

www.leamckee.com